COUNCIL

JENNIFER R. POVEY

PROLOGUE

Skyt existed and did not exist, and was sometimes one and sometimes many.

They existed in this space where their ancestors always had and now might for centuries yet. Skyt was a ghost.

Skyt was more than a ghost. But as they watched Graeme get on the ship they briefly wished they had a body again. Or at least that the code that now made them up could be transferred, could be moved somewhere else like the tyrar AIs, like the human AIs that were almost as well developed.

Alas, they had not been designed for that. They watched as their friend got on the ship accompanied by somebody else and experienced something akin to grief. It wasn't quite regret.

It was a sense of loss, even though they could hope the Ambassador would return.

It was also envy.

They had made the decisions they had made that led them to this point where all they could do was watch.

Well, and give all the advice and data they could to Slyk. Graeme didn't need help navigating his own world.

Slyk did. Slyk was also going to experience levels of cold that might require that odd thing, clothing.

Earth was an ice planet, after all.

Yet they had to go. This had to happen, this thing they were doing. There could be no more genocides, no more conquests, no more attacks on things so fragile they hardly dared to exist.

The intelligences of Glen knew that these species...and the others they would encounter...could not survive if they did not come up with mechanisms to support both unity and separation.

Slyk would be a good representative, chosen by the people of Glen, both alive and dead.

Graeme would be a good liaison to help make sure Slyk did not do anything stupid.

Did they trust the humans' offer to host?

Not entirely.

They rather thought the humans sought to control the location of the new Council. Humans liked to be in control.

The glyn had no interest in hosting this Council.

If it could be created.

Skyt was not sure. But as they watched the ship depart, they knew it had to be tried.

1

SOMETIMES, Dhyanil felt painfully alone. Sometimes less so.

They had a new treatment they could try, one which might finally let him return home. He had learned to appreciate the humans, those willing to approach him. It required a lot of desensitization.

Even their young children were affected to a degree, but they might learn. And a child at least was not dangerous to him. Nor he to them; he would *never* harm a hatchling, any species.

So, he spent a lot of time alone. Right now he stood on the beach, looking up at Earth's night sky. The small island he had chosen, which had once been quite a bit larger and would be again, if all went well, reminded him of home as much as any place on this world did.

But the night sky always reminded him he was *not* home. The looming white disk of Earth's moon, so small to its inhabitants, always seemed to him like something that might fall. It blanked out some of the stars. Just below it was a small white disk, the second planet in the system, Venus. Easily distinguished from a star.

Then there was the pattern, the panoply of heavens, so similar and so utterly different.

The void that touched on all worlds.

He had never been a hugely religious man, but having *crossed* the void he saw what it could be made to mean.

Humans tended more towards worshiping stars. Very diurnal people, humans.

His phone rang. He had learned to speak English (and a smattering of Mandarin and the local language here), as strange as it was.

He answered the phone in that language, which allowed for audio-only communication without any loss of meaning or nuance. An evolutionary advantage, that.

"Hello?"

His face changed immediately.

"Are we sure that's wise?"

"We believe you are safe for other ky'iin to be around now," the voice said. "And you are a ky'iin who is *already here*."

"I am not a diplomat. But I suppose I can handle things while an actual ambassador gets here."

"While they..."

Ky'iin elections could take weeks if not months. Human ones were almost as bad, Dhyanil had noticed, although he did not get to participate. He was not a citizen of Earth and did not want to be.

If he was safe to be around other ky'iin without infecting them with the virus that would render their offspring infertile, then he could go home. He could never father another clutch, but he was old for that anyway.

He could go *home*.

But they wanted him to speak for his world, and he was not sure what his world was any more.

If he had ever been sure in the first place.

DHYANIL COULD NOT TAKE human public transportation. Too much risk of somebody throwing a punch at him. The bright yellow ferry intrigued him, but it was as inaccessible to him as this planet's strange, large, glowing moon.

Instead, he was picked up from the port by a private boat driven by a young human man with dark skin and tightly curled hair. He was one of the neurological minority not driven to a rage by the sight of ky'iin.

They were working on the rest of the population. Dhyanil settled onto, rather than into, the boat, refusing an offer to go below despite the fact that there was rain in the sky.

A boat ride was to be appreciated. Enjoyed. To feel the spray on his face, to feel the salt water over his skin? That too reminded him of home. The ocean here was warm, but the spray brought a pleasant coolness to the air.

He could probably have driven the boat himself, for that matter, but he was just as glad to let the young man, who's name was Terrance, handle that while he enjoyed the feelings of ocean travel.

He might be going home. Home had boats too, but he realized he would miss Earth. It was a messed up world, but still a beautiful one. The ecological remediation had not, could not, solve all of their problems. Yet it had *saved* this world and the same knowledge was saving Tyranis.

From what his people had done to it.

The ky'iin had much to answer for, but so did humans. Dhyanil was pretty sure the only innocents were the verr, and they had surely had inter hive wars in the past. They traded children, which likely indicated that in the past they had *raided* children.

No sapient beings could ever be innocent. Every civilization had its darkness.

Two dolphins swam alongside. He waved to them and they chittered back, but without a translator, he could not understand what they were saying.

They followed the boat all the way to port, where he was hustled into a car and then to the airport.

Then to the spaceport.

The tyrar had cracked space elevators, apparently, so Earth would be building one soon enough, but for now launches had to be done the more expensive way using shuttles.

Kyx would probably build one too.

At one point he would have thought that a bad thing *solely* because it had been invented by tyrar.

He had learned.

But how could one man represent a world?

THE TALKS WOULD TAKE place on Launchpad II, simply because of its size. It allowed space for the small herd the tyrar would no doubt send.

Tyrar did not do anything on their own. A tyrar who had lived as he had would probably go mad, and the only reason it wasn't certainly was because humans, he had noticed, also liked to cuddle.

It had to be a mammal thing.

It was definitely a mammal thing, because humans cuddled their pets too..the mammal ones. The reptiles and birds not so much, mostly because neither appreciated it. Well, most of the time. He had once had the privilege of petting an owl. The feathers were incredibly soft.

Ky'iin didn't fall into any of those Earth categories of life. Closest to birds, the humans had decided, but not *quite* that either.

Humans loved to put everything into categories. To name it and organize it, to set it into trees and patterns. It was how their minds worked. They named their ships. Ky'iin did not.

Launchpad II was at the L5 point, and he felt a slight guilt about the reason it was Launchpad *II*. The ky'iin had blown up the original station during the Contact War, a legitimate military target as it was also Earth's primary shipyard.

A large ship, not as big as a tyrar great ship but still pretty big, was being constructed in the main bay. He wanted to ask what it was going to be...it might be a battle wagon, a small colony ship, or a starliner.

But he didn't because you *didn't*, it wasn't polite to ask about anything which might be a human military secret. Because you didn't know what might happen. He knew there would be plots and sabotage, because there already had been. This was an obvious target.

Everyone had their secrets and their ships. Until they had ships with multi-species crews. Was that even even possible? Not until humans and ky'iin learned not to attack each other on sight, Dhyanil decided.

They docked with another part of the station, away from the skeleton of the ship.

"I am going to take you to your quarters," a young woman with a blue buzz cut said. Human hair did not naturally come in blue, but they were fond of dying it.

He followed her, assuming the pronoun until told otherwise, to a room that was not exactly large, but well appointed and furnished to ky'iin needs.

Which they had learned primarily from him. He had been a hostage-liaison for the last few years, a tradition humans did not share but had rapidly come to understand. Now he had to represent his world.

He hoped they chose a real ambassador soon.

2

BEVERLY WAS HIGHLY annoyed as the *Endeavour* approached Launchpad.

Her and Yoshi's work was important. Perhaps not vital to the future of Tyranis...the more vital work was that being done to fix what had been done to the atmosphere, to slowly wean the planet off the geoengineering so it wouldn't hit a climate cliff. They had had the key idea, but others built on it. But *important.*

So, she was told, was this.

She transferred from the reasonably comfortable chair in her guest quarters to her wheelchair with no assistance from Yoshi, who was flopped on the bed still.

"Yoshi. We're almost there."

The small herd had been split up two and two. And oh, she knew why she was here.

A human who was an official, legal member of a tyrar herd? She was likely the first of many, but right now she was *proof of concept.* And that annoyed her even more.

She had fought her way through college where she had been one of the first women to return to higher education after Austerity. Where she had also been the "proof we take disabled people."

The *last* thing Beverly wanted to be, ever, was a *token*. Unfortunately, it wasn't avoidable.

Proving humans and tyrar could be, essentially, family, would help with the push towards multi-species ships.

Well, at least in part. They still hadn't fully solved the issues that had started the Contact War in the first place. It wasn't anything the ky'iin *did*, but Beverly found them as hard to deal with as any.

She was not looking forward to dealing with any ky'iin representative. Not that she had to do anything but look...not pretty, no, but functional.

Pretty wasn't going to happen right away, she realized.

Her pants were covered in shed tyrar fur. This was a normal state of affairs, but it wasn't the state of affairs she wanted to be on television in. She'd have to get changed before encountering any cameras.

Yoshi stretched languorously, and sat up. She had shed all over the bed too.

The occupational hazard of living with tyrar.

"So..."

"So we are going to go over to Launchpad II."

"What happened to..."

"The ky'iin," Beverly grumbled. True, they hadn't started the war, but she felt it okay to be mad about the damage they did as long as you didn't act on it.

Tyrar knew all about hating ky'iin.

"Well, hopefully this will get a leash on them."

"We all need leashes on us." Yoshi had picked up that human saying from Beverly and become rather fond of it.

"And speak English," Beverly also reminded.

Not that the tyrar didn't still need a frequency transponder to be heard.

"Is it really fair that the human language is lingua franca?"

"It's the only one we can all pronounce, except the glyn, and they use translators anyway."

"Then we buy translators from the glyn," Yoshi said as if it was a decision that had already been made.

"Working on that."

The glyn "spoke" by chiming parts of their body against each other. They could not speak anyone else's language nor anyone else theirs, without some kind of technological assistance.

And within weeks of contact the glyn intelligences had designed a universal translator algorithm.

Beverly wanted a glyn translator badly. She also wanted the algorithms that translated written words.

There were quite a few books written in Chinese she'd never been able to get through with her rather indifferent Mandarin.

For right now, the herd formed up as they walked, or in Beverly's case rolled, onto Launchpad II. Beverly, Yoshi, Pallavi and the newest (and only male) member, Viarin. They had integrated him and they didn't mind.

He didn't mind.

But he was the consensus-chosen representative, the actual diplomat. Integrating him into the herd that contained a human made a statement.

Beverly only hoped people would understand it.

LAUNCHPAD FOUND quarters large enough for the herd. A little cramped, but this *was* a space station, albeit a larger one.

Their luggage followed them inside. The smart suitcases were something Beverly had insisted on. Much easier than carrying everything.

She rolled into the bedroom, which had been set up as a proper nest. She had got used to sleeping in a tyrar-pile.

She was even used to the fur.

Not all humans would manage that. Not everyone could do what she did and that was fine.

But she still hated being drawn away from the science to be paraded.

She had to get her mind on the very important work she *was* doing. But she had also brought all of her notes with her.

She couldn't bring a tyrar AI to analyze them, but perhaps Launchpad's AI could help. She was already mentally dropping the II.

Probably everyone would do that sooner or later.

Their escort was a young EarthForce officer, a light skinned man with neatly trimmed hair and beard. He stopped in the doorway. "Your badges will alert you if you go into a restricted area. That's for your own safety."

Translation: There was equipment they didn't need untrained people around.

"Also, the interim ky'iin representative is in room 203."

That was a warning to Beverly. She had never actually *seen* a ky'iin in the flesh, but she knew, from watching videos, that she wasn't immune. People reacted in different ways, but mostly with violence or a strong desire to flee. It was the Uncanny Valley effect on steroids.

Ky'iin were more like birds than humans.

They were still people.

"I can talk to him," Yoshi said. "I think I can manage not to make any snide anti-colonialist comments."

Viarin wrinkled his nose in silent tyrar laughter. "Talking to the aliens is my job. Well, unless they're human, in which case I might delegate it."

Beverly grinned. "Honestly, the only people I *want* to talk to are the scientists. But..."

But part of her job here was to make sure Viarin didn't make any stupid etiquette mistakes when dealing with humans. There was a very real risk that he would get into some kind of trouble.

"We won't make you deal with the ky'iin."

Beverly shook her head. "We have to learn to deal with them."

Did that mean she did, personally? She did not know. But while humans and ky'iin had walls between them, how could there be a political entity that encompassed and embraced both?

She didn't know that either.

BEVERLY ROLLED out of the room. Unlike the tyrar, she remained comfortable on her own, something the herd had used to advantage before.

Herd.

Family.

The last thing she had expected was to find *family* on an alien world, when she was only there to fix problems.

Major problems. Exacerbated by politics, as much as they had been on Earth. The climate crisis, Austerity, the megastorms.

All in the past now, and she knew where she was going. Somewhere around here, there had to be an observation deck.

Perhaps even one from which she could see her homeworld. Not that she planned on leaving without taking her herdmates down to Earth. There was no reason not to go. The tyrar were not ky'iin; they would be novelties and might need security, but she doubted they would be attacked.

Except for not being able to decide exactly *where* to go. She was torn between the Appalachian hills of her birth, or the Rockies, or the Caribbean. So many possibilities.

Of course, if Viarin became a permanent ambassador or representative then she would not be going back to tyrar anyway.

There were others who could continue her work there. And that would give time for many trips to Earth.

Trips in which she would continue to demonstrate interspecies friendship. Ugh.

But she had not been able to keep herself from falling in love with Yoshi. Phrased that way it sounded like xenophilia, but while they had experimented with recreational sex, it was not a romance, it was what her asexual friends would have called "queerplatonic."

For others, it might be different. Recreational sex between humans and tyrar was quite possible with a bit of creativity.

She blushed slightly at the thought and rolled to the observation deck.

Alas, it did not show Earth. She could, however, see the moon. Stray lights lit its dark side, the lunar colonies were underground, but people came to the surface for recreation, even at night. Cross country skiing was big on the moon.

Luna would have its own representative, likely only one, when things were hashed out. Mars and Venus had already sent theirs.

Beverly had looked them up. Career diplomats, one from Bradbury City and the other from the largest of the Venus settlements, Oshun.

Maybe she could score a trip *there*. The cloud cities fascinated her in concept, but she had never set wheel on one. But the view was enough to tell her she was home. The constellations were not distorted by the short distance and the moon?

The moon was part of what made Earth Earth. None of the other worlds had a large white moon. Kyx had none. Tyrar had three smaller ones. Verr no longer existed. Glen also had no moon, not being a planet at all.

The colors of Earth were not, after all, the important thing.

Beverly leaned back a little and stared at the moon.

3

"DADDY!" Marion squealed as she detached herself from Charles and ran towards Graeme as fast as her short legs could carry her.

Graeme swept his daughter up into a hug. "I want you to see Glen."

When it was safe, which was going to take a while.

"Is that a glyn?" She peered over his shoulder at Slyk, who was looking, to Graeme's now-accustomed eyes, slightly confused by the reunion.

Glyn either had five or six parents or one, depending on how you defined "parent."

They also didn't have husbands. Graeme moved forward with Marion still in his arms and slid an arm around Charles too.

Their daughter who looked like their daughter despite biologically being the offspring of Charles' sister, squeed.

After a moment, Graeme set her down. She ran over to Slyk and studied him. "They look more like beetles than angels."

"Marion!"

Slyk chimed amusement. "It's okay," they said through their translator. "She is a child. Children say things."

Graeme had experienced some comments from glyn children too.

"And you are right, I do look like a very large beetle." Slyk had been reading the files Graeme had given them on Earth, clearly. Then they spread their vestigial wings so the light passed through them.

Marion squee'd again. Glyn wings *were* quite attractive if you didn't experience entomophobia.

If you did, well, you couldn't work with the glyn without doing something about it. And some people had discovered they had entomophobia when you enlarged an insect up to human size. Not that the glyn really were insects. Or angels, for that matter. They were an uplift species, raised to intelligence by ancients who were apparently extinct, but what they had been uplifted *from* fit no Earth category. Exoskeleton meant insect to humans, but they had lungs rather than a diffused oxygen system. They also didn't have a brain focused in their head, it was distributed in nodes through their body. And they didn't have sexes. All glyn were the same biological sex, producing the same type of gametes.

Glyn did not have the *concept* of gender except as something aliens did.

Graeme had found that refreshing, but at the same time? He was a man and rather liked being a man (as well as being with a man). Most humans liked having a gender.

Would those who didn't be more comfortable working with the glyn? They had the wonderful habit of misgendering everyone because they couldn't keep track of even the two human sexes, let alone the four verr castes, two of which came in two different sexes!

Graeme was actually rather looking forward to meeting the verr.

"We need to get Slyk to their quarters."

Marion skipped alongside. Bringing her up to Launchpad was a small risk, but only a small one, and while Graeme missed Glen in some ways, being reunited with his family?

That meant a lot.

He also missed Skyt, though. For that alone he had to go back. And take them so they could meet his friend.

Present tense, even though Skyt was technically dead. In the glyn digital afterlife.

He *missed* Skyt.

LAUNCHPAD WAS STILL BARE BONES, but being built out into something closer to the original. Charles had still managed to find a decent restaurant. Not a great one, not exactly what one wanted for one's first date in months.

It would do. And Slyk, of all people, had agreed to watch Marion. The glyn had raised two children, Graeme trusted them.

"Our daughter is going to grow up in a world where aliens are no big deal," Charles mused, studying the menu.

"And I'm glad of it. The less of a big deal we make them, the less we're going to get stuff like...like..."

"Like the people who tried to fly a great ship into a verr hive."

"Like that."

"The verr intrigue me. Maybe scare me a little. I wouldn't want to be part of a hive mind."

"From what I've read, it's not quite like that. But their idea of democracy is to shoot pheromones at each other until they have a consensus."

Charles laughed. "And ours has been known to involve fisticuffs, so..."

"We can't judge. Everyone's technology, culture, government, is influenced by their biology. I mean, trying to explain the concept of a wedding to the glyn..."

He laughed again. "But I'd imagine..."

"Their big life celebration is graduation."

"They can't all be scientists."

"To some degree, they all are. They aren't all professional scientists, no, but their culture makes reading scientific papers a pastime like Swiss hiking." Graeme mused on that. "Slyk wants to meet as many human scientists as they can...as the talks allow. And once we get Glen's new singularity stabilized, invites are going to be extended."

Charles leaned forward. "Are we going to reciprocate?"

"I would guess so. There are differences between the worlds. That blanket Slyk is wearing isn't normal Glen culture."

"And we need cooling suits on their world. But that won't stop *scientists.*" Charles grinned. "Nothing stops a scientist once they get their hands on a mystery."

"And what about engineers?"

"You *have* to take me to Glen."

Now everyone knew the glyn homeworld was a giant, artificial space station, half of the engineers in the galaxy were going to want to take a peek.

For Charles to be one of them was not a surprise. "Soon," he promised.

"I doubt we can reverse engineer it, but..."

"Honestly, we might. There's nothing there that isn't simply a scale up of, say, a great ship."

"Really?"

"Really. They didn't have technology we don't have. It's an engineering problem, Charles. The thing is...there are enough habitable worlds, and more than enough *usable* worlds, that we may never do it because we don't need to."

"Which makes the question," Charles mused, "Why did they?"

"Nobody knows. The glyn don't even know. Their ancients wiped everything."

"And abandoned them."

"They survived. The ancients, apparently, did not."

LATER, Graeme rescued Slyk from Marion or vice versa...he wasn't entirely sure which. He carried the tired girl to bed. She would grow up with aliens simply being a thing that existed, she would never have to go through the adjustment of not being alone.

Graeme had been excited by the realization. Scared too, of course; the first contact between human and ky'iin had not gone well. But excited.

Others, though, had experienced varying levels of existential crisis. Not everyone was equipped or wired to deal well with the sudden realization that humanity might not be the center of the universe, made in God's image.

Graeme laughed a little at the memory of the Rabbi who's response had been "God is a prism. His image is split into many different colors."

That was one way to resolve it, by saying God had multiple images. In Graeme's experience, Rabbis resolved these crises far easier than, say, Catholic priests. Graeme rather thought "made in God's image" had nothing to do with biology, but was closer to the ky'iin concept of myoran, but then he was slightly indifferent as to the existence of God.

It was hard to believe in a creator in a post climate change world. Some had lost their faith already. Others lost it when the aliens showed up. Others clung to it more than ever, or feared that they had missed the Rapture.

A few weird cults had, of course, started. And some churches, understandably, saw this as an entire bunch of other people to tell about Jesus.

Skyt had chimed very loudly indeed when Graeme explained Jesus to them. On the face ofi it, the entire religion *was* rather ridiculous.

The ky'iin supreme deity was space, which was interesting. And the verr gods were uniformly evil and best left in the past.

God probably came from biology, but as Graeme couldn't *disprove* God, he kept an open mind on the matter.

Tucking Marion in, he thought to head for Slyk's quarters.

Instead, he explored. He had been warned about where the ky'iin interim representative, a liaison who had been living on Earth in a peculiar semi-exile, was housed. Graeme had *not* passed the "Can you look at a ky'iin without trying to punch them" test. He thought he could learn, but if he was going to interact with a ky'iin, he wanted somebody there who could hold him back if needed.

Then he saw a bunch of people heading for the observation deck. He followed.

Looming above Launchpad was a tyrar great ship.

The last representatives were here.

And he understood for a moment why some people might be afraid of the verr.

4

KAYKEK WASN'T EQUIPPED for this. No verr was equipped for this.

As Refuge Hive glided into the inner system, ze checked zir translator, vital given ze had picked up approximately three words of English so far. Ze watched from an observation deck as they glided towards the human station. The human shipyard. It was building something the size of a battleship, although it wasn't necessarily a warship.

Were the humans showing strength? Or was that a starliner that would carry people between human colonies? Ze thought it was the latter. Their own system was well populated, and they needed to rebuild from their war.

There was no docking Refuge with Launchpad even if it had been a good idea. After looming over them for a bit, Alvi pulled back to a safer distance. They were showing the aliens that the verr would not be dismissed or intimidated. Everyone was scared after what had happened.

Could any treaty or agreement prevent genocide?

Yet glyn had sacrificed themselves...and to glyn, dying off planet was a terrible thing...to save the hives. Kaykek seized on that as a means of hope. Zir pups would grow up in a world where aliens were a known quantity.

Ze claimed them as zir pups despite everything. Tayken was inclined to agree.

They were Tayken's pups first, though. Tayken was the one who would name them when they were weaned; while pups dying before weaning was vanishingly rare now, it was still considered unlucky to name them before they had eaten solid food.

Tayken was the one who nursed them, who was with them in the creche even now as Kaykek prepared to represent the verr.

Not equipped for this. But nobody else was *either* and the consensus of the hive was that it had to be zir.

Zir headed for the shuttlebay. Two workers accompanied zir. One was flying the shuttle; Kaykek could have done it zirself, but not as well. The other, Micek, was going to be zir aide. Handle the boring stuff.

If they needed to return to Refuge they could. Scouts in the sagas had stayed outside hives for as long as a month, but they hadn't really studied the impact on zir physiology. And Micek definitely had to be careful; their solitude could trigger puberty.

Which it might or might not be ready for or want. It had agreed to the risk, though.

"You can go back any time, Micek."

Kaykek was safe from further changes and not pheromonally dependent on the breeders to keep zir in the worker phase. Maybe ze should choose a warrior as an aide. That might be perfect. Ze would have to think about it. Micek really wanted to do this.

If it did change, Kaykek would lay bets it would go scout anyway. If zir theory was right and puberty *was* impacted by deeply held desires.

The shuttle docked with the human station and ze took a deep breath. Time to do this.

THE HUMAN STATION SMELLED EMPTY, but Kaykek knew that was because humans did not produce the same kinds of pheromones as verr. They did have a scent to them, subtly mammalian. Humans might be *affected* by verr pheromones, which was why ze could not bring a queen or drone with zir.

There was too much risk that somebody might get...lively. It was hard enough for Kaykek to resist a queen in heat. A human, who didn't know what it was? They weren't *as* affected, but...

Queen pheromones could trigger interesting events, that was all. Warrior pheromones could be intimidating. What did scout pheromones do?

Kaykek shook zir head. One scout could not produce enough of anything to have an impact, surely.

A young human with unnaturally blue hair came to greet zir. "Ambassador, let me show you to your quarters."

Ze accepted the guidance and found the suite acceptable, if a little small after the tyrar-built scale of Refuge Hive.

Negotiate for protection for the verr. Negotiate for ship designs that would allow them to build a defense force. It was a shame they needed one, but they did. It had been made clear.

They needed a defense force that could stop anything up to a battleship. They needed at least one battleship.

Or perhaps there was a way to arm the cities.

Kaykek was not a military person. Ze would have to find people of that persuasion that ze could trust, people who agreed that the verr needed defenses. That everyone needed them.

Refuge could arm up too, as little as Alvi liked the idea. Alvi didn't like fighting. Their daughter, Vyra, was a bit more aggressive, though.

That ship they could probably arm. Or move Vyra to a battleship once they had one, if she wasn't too settled in in that hardware.

Vyra.

Verr-a.

It probably wasn't a coincidence, although the name meant something in tyrar too. Vyra had been "born" after Alvi integrated into verr society.

The two of them were working on designs for AIs that would see themselves as even more verr. That would have a role in hives.

Each hive could then have an AI guardian. If they wanted one.

The verr could never go back to the sagas or even the dark times. They *had* to go forward.

Micek settled in with the terminal in the room. It was going to do all the research.

Kaykek ventured out into the corridors of Launchpad. They smelled of humans. Of human sweat, of mild human pheromones. Also of metal and cleaning fluids. Ze stepped around a cleaning bot and headed for the largest concentration of human scent.

THIS TURNED out to be the main observation deck, where people were still...reacting...to Alvi's little flyby.

One of the humans turned a bit as ze came in, then there were more looks zir way, some of them tense, one slightly disgusted...ze made a mental note to memorize the appearance and scent of that individual and avoid them.

The one who had first turned headed towards zir, showing its...no, his, it was a man...teeth.

Which in humans meant friendliness. Thankfully, Kaykek had already learned that.

"They think you are showoffs," he said as he approached, then bowed slightly in greeting. "Graeme Marlowe, human ambassador to Glen."

Some humans put the personal name first, some last. Ze bowed in return. "Kaykek v'Refuge."

"The verr representative." He showed his teeth again. "Definitely..."

Ze couldn't resist. "*That* was Alvi's idea. The ship AI."

"Aha."

"They wanted to make it clear that..."

"That the verr are a force to be reckoned with, although some won't agree until you have a ship stamped "Made in Verr System.""

"We're working on it."

"And some will probably never agree."

"Well...the point is to..." Ze paused. "Push those people to the side so they can't keep attacking anyone."

"A worthy aim. Your people are more vulnerable."

"Not for much longer. One way or another, we're building defenses."

"Good. You shouldn't have to, but good."

Ze wasn't entirely sure about this human, but thought ze might be able to like him with a bit of time. He certainly didn't seem at all xenophobic, although he hadn't offered zir the other traditional human greeting of an extended hand.

That could say a lot of things, though, and "He didn't want to touch an alien" was only one of them.

"So..."

"I'm acting as a liaison and guide to the Ambassador from Glen."

"Ah. They haven't given us one yet."

"It's in the works. Formal diplomatic relationships are still developing."

Kaykek dipped zir muzzle. "But informal ones..."

"I would like to make some of those, yes, to get to know you a little. I'd also like to introduce you to my daughter."

A female child. "Your daughter?"

He showed teeth again. "She is a young child, it would do her good to meet as many aliens as possible at an age where you aren't a big deal. If you don't mind."

Ze thought of zir pups. "I don't mind, as long as I can give her back if she causes trouble."

At that he produced the raucous sound of human laughter. "Of course."

5

DHYANIL WAS USED to being shunned. At the same time, there was going to be a reception for the representatives. He had to attend. It was an obligation.

It would probably include people who only *thought* they could face a ky'iin. Because of that, he had been assigned two bodyguards. Their job was entirely to block and safely restrain anyone who couldn't handle him.

It was probably for the best he was a male; this was a ly'iin job and that was part of his discomfort with it. However, a smaller individual was likely to be a little less threatening.

The reception would take place on the observation deck, which was being set up for the occasion.

Dhyanil took the quietest route there his bodyguards could find, trusting them to get him to the occasion safely.

Most people simply backed away. They had been warned, but their discomfort was still obvious.

He felt bad about it, but what could he do. He saw three tyrar...the tyrar representative and two herdmates. With them was a human in a wheeled chair.

Two verr, the representative and an aide. Of course, he had no way of knowing which was which. One was decidedly larger than the other, though, which might be a clue. He did not know enough about how verr castes worked. The glyn ambassador was accompanied by a human who did not look comfortable at all.

Dhyanil had to go over there, though. He headed towards the group, noting that Devon, one of his bodyguards, moved between him and the glyn ambassador's friend? Guide? Liaison? The other, Malcolm, was watching for other potential problems.

The verr ambassadors scurried (no other word for it) over. They were smaller than the other sentients, but not by a lot, and they had thinner fur than the tyrar, plus truly splendid whiskers. Of course, they had evolved from burrowers. One was definitely bigger, the difference far more stark now they were closer, and had darker fur.

They could probably navigate this room just fine if the lights went out. Dhyanil might manage. The humans would struggle, though.

Mental note.

If the lights go out and there's a verr around, follow them.

Oddly, the human relaxed as the two verr approached.

The representative's name was Kaykek and that should be the larger individual. Different castes and the...

It didn't work like that, but Dhyanil still had a brain steeped in women on top, men at the bottom and ly'iin making sure everyone got on.

The verr castes were different. Kaykek was more like a ly'iin, though. Not quite, very different, but neither male nor female nonetheless.

"Greetings," he finally managed to say, in English so he wouldn't be gesturing as much and potentially setting off a human.

But the human who was closest (other than his bodyguards, who had been chosen for resistance) seemed... "This isn't so bad."

"I'm small," Dhyanil offered. That was probably helping.

But now there were other humans looking.

And none looked about to attack.

DHYANIL LET OUT a breath after fleeing the room. For a while, it worked. With warning, with space, and with bodyguards he could, possibly, attend an event.

Then, it was like everyone had hit their limit of tolerance and he had had to be escorted out.

He had known it was risky. Humans did not *want* to attack ky'iin, but there was something about ky'iin body language that hit their back brain, in most cases. That made them feel a strong drive to defend themselves. Fear-aggression.

What surprised him was how long it had taken.

"If we keep things to an hour it should work."

"Perhaps," Devon said. "But there was something else. *I* noticed it. Did you notice the verr representative left a bit early."

"Ly was tired from travel, I suppose...or something." Ly's home moved, so travel fatigue should not be a thing.

"I heard that ze," Devon corrected the pronoun gently. "Might have been up early. Something about kids."

Ly'iin had a lot of interest in lin brothers' children. Kaykek might have something similar going on, some related kids they had developed an interest in. "Regardless..."

"Things went bad about three minutes after ze left. That's..."

"The length of time it takes to refresh the air on the observation deck. And verr produce very strong pheromones. I could *smell* them."

"Do they annoy you?"

"A little. Next time I think I will wear a masking scent." It might take a few tries to find the right one.

"Humans don't have as strong a sense of smell. But also...it appears we might be partially affected by verr pheromones. A human who was doing some work on Refuge apparently got into an...embarrassing...situation with a verr breeder."

"As in...oh no."

"A queen was in heat. He was trying to convince her to see if recreational sex works between humans and verr."

Dhyanil laughed. "Recreational sex causes so many problems."

It wasn't something ky'iin really engaged in. When a woman went into heat, she chose a man to father her eggs. Occasionally a woman would be attracted to other women and would get artificial insemination. Occasionally a man pursued another man. But those liaisons seldom ended in actual *copulation*. That was for eggs.

But mammals.

Mammals were weird.

Dhyanil took a moment to be glad he wasn't one.

"Yes, it does." Devon showed his teeth in a human grin. "But...I have to think that the verr's pheromones..."

"But..."

Dhyanil stopped. "That's a *solution*."

"We..."

"If the verr are willing to help. A chemist could analyze zir pheromones." Had he got the pronoun right? "Come up with a drug humans could take when they need to interact with ky'iin, or something we could diffuse into the air."

And in the interim, the verr representative might be willing to sit on stuff. Heck, it might be to zir advantage.

A solution.

"Or even...something a ky'iin who is going into a situation where there are humans could wear as a perfume. A masking scent."

A solution.

Humans and ky'iin might be able to *work together* in the way...

Dhyanil rather thought he had Kaykek's pronoun right after all. And that it might be the pronoun for lin entire species.

"So, your theory..." The human medic wasn't looking at him. Dhyanil spoke English so he wouldn't have to.

"Devon's theory is that verr scout pheromones have some kind of calming affect on humans, that allows you to overcome the psychological impact of, well, us."

"I don't know enough about the verr."

"The verr do." He wasn't thinking of asking for anything... "I doubt sampling pheromones is hugely invasive."

"Well...no. I doubt it is. But I'll need to talk to a verr medic." The young woman furrowed her brow.

"If this works it would solve one of our biggest problems."

"And give a certain level of power to the verr." Perhaps she didn't like that, but then she couldn't be too xenophobic or she wouldn't have been willing to talk to him.

"Not if we can synthesize the chemical that has the effect."

Not that the verr wouldn't push to be the...mediators. As rhe medic pointed out, it would give them power. They were vulnerable, a literal endangered species. Nobody could blame them for wanting power, for wanting to be useful. For wanting to be something people would choose to protect.

Kaykek would no doubt want concessions in exchange for samples of zir pheromones. True, they might just be able to pull them out of the air, but then they would be...they'd need them from the source.

Which might involve...hopefully it wouldn't involve needles. Dhyanil had no idea how verr produced pheromones.

"I will talk to the verr medics if I can."

"And I," Dhyanil said, "Will top up my knowledge about the verr themselves."

He knew what had traveled over the popular science nets. The verr were mammals, like humans and tyrar, and very *not* like ky'iin. True, they were from different evolution, but the human definition of "mammal" covered all three species.

They had evolved from some kind of burrowing creature, were omnivorous, and had survived the destruction of their homeworld in a natural disaster with human help, but only about half a million of them existed.

They were colony or hive animals.

That was what Dhyanil knew and it wasn't enough. He thought he knew enough about tyrar, *knew* he knew enough about humans, but he definitely needed to devote a bit more time to studying both the verr and the glyn.

And thanks to this? He was going to start with the verr.

6

A SINGLE KY'IIN was not a threat. She had her herd. Beverly repeated those things to herself as she rolled into the reception. Made them a mantra. She knew she was probably vulnerable, there was no reason she wouldn't be.

She had her herd. Wrapped around her, even when they weren't physically present. A warm blanket of feeling.

The ky'iin representative was entirely interim, a man who had been exiled to Earth after being exposed to a virus that could not be allowed to get loose on Kyx. He was stuck until they found a cure, or at least something akin to the HIV drugs that had kept people's viral load low before the vaccine and cure had been created. Perhaps they had one now, but they were keeping him here until a permanent representative could be found.

Something to make him safe to be around other ky'iin. The ky'iin were matriarchal to a fault, having many of the same issues humans had had in reverse. In their culture, the third sex, the ly'iin, handled diplomacy. Period.

They were trusting this to a man, for now, because ky'iin elections had much in common with human ones, one key difference being that they took even longer.

Once there was an established council, this wouldn't be a problem unless somebody died suddenly.

There he was. He was about the size of a tall woman or a short man...the females and ly'iin were generally bigger. He was ugly and his movements were nails grating on a chalkboard and...

...but she didn't have any reason to attack him. Part of her wanted to, part of her was itching for a gun to shoot him with, but she was well able to set that part of her aside. It was held behind a sense of calm.

He was, after all, *one* ky'iin. She had three huge tyrar with her. The actual tyrar ambassador was heading over to schmooze with one of the humans, but Yoshi and Pallavi stayed close to her, their scent reassuring.

There was absolutely something to be said for having your family be Bigfoot.

(And yes, conspiracy theorists were now sure that Bigfoot was crew from a crashed tyrar ship. The tyrar said this wasn't possible, but conspiracy theorists being what they are...)

There was something to be said for it. She kept one eye on the ky'iin, and also made note of the verr. This was the first time she had seen them.

There were two. The larger individual would be the representative and the smaller one was...an aide? They rather resembled rats or moles. Definitely a close resemblance with *Rodentia* and she had to remind herself that they came from a totally different evolution.

There was a slightly sweet smell in her nostrils, but she tuned it out rapidly.

Peeling her gaze from the ky'iin, she looked around to see if there were any interesting scientists in the room.

VIARIN CAME BACK to the herd's quarters later. Beverly left after developing a headache.

Then had nightmares about the ky'iin, that told her she might not have dealt as well as she thought she had with the presence of the alien. So she didn't hear him come in, but she did stir when he dropped into the nest. Briefly.

In the morning, she woke to the smell of Pallavi cooking breakfast in the fireless kitchen. It was typical of Pallavi that she had learned how to use it quickly.

Spies needed to be highly adaptable.

She suspected that everyone knew Pallavi was a spy, or suspected it. The humans had plenty. The verr aide was probably one too.

The lone ky'iin? He had nobody to spy for him. And nobody...she really felt for the guy. She lived on tyrar, but she also spent time with the other human scientists there, with any humans who visited. She wasn't isolated out of fear of giving a nasty virus to anyone she met.

She would always be between two worlds, but that wasn't the same as being *exiled*.

Viarin finally stirred. "I got hauled into something," he explained as the herd gathered for breakfast. Yoshi was still yawning.

"Something as in a conversation."

"Oh, you will be interested in this. Did *you* notice that everyone got more tense after the verr left."

The verr representative had ducked out early.

Yoshi grinned. "I heard their...zir...kids kept them up half the night. Or woke them up early. Or..."

"I didn't think the scouts had kids."

"Might be nephews or something. I don't understand how their hives work. Might be more like herd-children."

Every member of a herd was parent to some degree to any children born in the herd. They had no children right now, but Pallavi had made noises.

Right now, it was taboo; you didn't reproduce *within* your herd. Pallavi needed to find a willing man from another herd to father her children.

"So...there's now a rumor circling that verr mind control people subconsciously."

"Pheromones!" Beverly exclaimed.

"What about them?"

"Okay, so pheromones are chemicals that an animal produces that are designed to communicate. It's mostly seen in insects. Bees use them, for ex..." She tailed off. "For example to determine if a bee is part of the colony or a stranger. Larger animals also produce them, but they tend to be more subtle. Tyrar women produce them when they're in heat, for example. Human women don't because our society works better with silent ovulation."

"Right!" Yoshi said. "And presumably ky'iin women also produce them when in rut."

"Nasty ones. I'm told a ky'iin woman can control a man with them at certain points in her cycle...or with artificial assistance." Beverly shuddered. "So. Verr are colony livers. They have hierarchical repro-duction where only some individuals sexually mature. They must produce a lot of pheromones."

"Their representative is..."

"..." Beverly pulled up her terminal. "The verr have four castes, two of which come in two genders. The vast majority are workers, who are prepubescent most or all of their lives. Then there are breeders...the queens who give birth to the young for the hive and the drones who fertilize them. There are warriors, who are also male and female but not fertile. It appears in that case that they go through an arrested puberty that increases size and aggression. Lastly, there are scouts, who are either neither or both depending on how you view it."

"Hermaphrodites."

"Yes and no. Also, that's a slur in English." She didn't chide Yoshi, the topic had never come up between them. "So. Breeders produce the young, warriors protect the hive, workers do everything else. Scouts form a network between hives."

Yoshi looked appropriately chastened.

It was finally hitting her.

"So," Beverly continued, A scout will go into another hive. They trade stories, news, and also genetic material. Scouts can mate with a drone, store the sperm...often from multiple drones...and then..."

"Deposit it in the queens in the other hive." Yoshi's tone had turned amused.

"Which means...if verr have threat recognition pheromones that tell them another verr is not of their hive, although no doubt they can control any instinctive attack..."

Yoshi finished for her. "Scouts have to release pheromones that say 'Scout, don't attack me.'"

"And if humans are at all vulnerable to verr pheromones, then..."

Holy. The verr had *mind whammied* her. But she couldn't find it in her to be mad about it.

BEVERLY WENT on Launchpad's net to check the rumors out for herself. Verr mind control was fairly high on the list.

And technically, if she was right, yes, the verr scout had "whammied" her. But ze had not done it on purpose and it could actually lead to a solution to the unwanted aggression problem. Some kind of pharmaceutical or drug or even perfume.

And in the interim? The human representatives could meet with Dhyanil as long as the scout was in the room. Or in an adjacent room with good air travel between the two. Without Dhyanil needing to hide behind bodyguards.

Some humans could resist the effect. No doubt the two large men accompanying the ky'iin everywhere were resistant. Beverly now knew for sure that she wasn't.

She wanted to thank Kaykek. She also had a morbid curiosity about verr life and what it was like to live in a caste system like that, one biologically determined. Which meant that if scheduling allowed...

She sent a request for a meeting with the verr. She said she was a scientist, that she was curious, but did mention that her field was ecological remediation. Not something the verr needed. Or did they? Ecological remediation led eventually to terraforming.

The verr might well want *that* or other ways to improve any worlds they settled. Either way, she put in the request, then she headed out, alone, into the corridors of the station.

The herd would know where she was, of course. They all had trackers on each other's phones, which Beverly would have found a breach of privacy in any other circumstance. It was her herd, so she didn't mind.

It was interesting to be surrounded by humans again. She could even smell the scent of human, just because she was now so unused to it. She'd only been with half a dozen other humans at a time at most for months on end. She no longer smelled the wet horse scent of tyrar.

"Dr. Marlowe."

She turned the chair, craning her neck to see who had greeted her from behind.

A tall, lean woman of African descent. "I was hoping for a bit of your time." She bowed. "I am Adwoa Olanrewaju."

The interim representative of Venus. "Lunch?" she suggested.

"Lunch would be awesome."

"No aides?"

"I happened to notice you."

Relatively few people preferred wheelchairs over exoskeletons. No doubt, Beverly stood out. "Fair enough."

"I assure you this is not about keeping something off the record. And I want to talk to you as a *scientist*, not a politician."

Beverly grinned. "In that case, I'll answer all of your questions in trade for more information about the sky cities."

"We have a deal."

7

GRAEME HAD to flee the party. Perhaps it had been a bad idea to go. It had overwhelmed him. The ky'iin had gone from being a curiosity to a terrible monster, as if he had...

Charles followed him. They had left Marion in their quarters.

"I was fine until just now."

Charles frowned. "Me too. Maybe we hit our tolerance limits?" At the same time?

"I kept telling myself there was only one of him and it helped...for a while."

"I definitely wouldn't want to talk to an entire pack of them without a solid barrier between us, and I *pride* myself on not being prejudiced!" Charles declared, tapping his own dark brown hand.

He'd certainly faced enough. "It's not our fault. They remind our back brain of cave bears or something."

"I know. But I...I wonder if VR desensitization would help."

"It might. We can give it a try." Graeme did not want to admit that he couldn't work with ky'iin. He wanted to fix the problem.

It was like screening people who wanted to work with the glyn for entomophobia, but with the ky'iin it was most of the population and many of those resistant were on the spectrum. Which didn't necessarily mean disabled, but sometimes it did. The combination of autism and diplomatic skills that had made Suza McRae was not common...most autistic people were better at things like computer code and paleontology. The ky'iin had no written language, either, which meant that if you weren't verbal, switching to writing was not going to work.

How they had gone to space without one, Graeme did not know.

"I'll track down some programs we can use. And I'll see if there's an age appropriate one for Marion."

"Good idea. It'll be easier for the kids."

"Easier all around. To her, the aliens have always been here, she's too young to remember when we didn't know about them."

"Yeah." Graeme leaned against the wall. He rubbed his head. "I feel awful."

Charles was right. It *felt* like an irrational prejudice, and as a mixed race, gay couple they should know better.

Except it wasn't *about* knowing better.

That wasn't how it worked.

Ky'iin were large apex predators. It was like working with a tiger. You might *know* the tiger is friendly, but it might not always keep you from fearing it.

He had to stop feeling bad.

THE NEXT DAY, Graeme and Slyk made their way through Launchpad's slowly growing commercial area. There were three restaurants, a couple of shops. A public exercise suite to help people deal with the slightly lower gravity.

It wasn't a town yet. It was mostly the start of the village that grows up around the castle. The old Launchpad had been almost entirely military.

Things had changed.

The glyn got the usual share of stares and reactions. Graeme did his best to shield them a little. They had to feel lonely and isolated. He had had Toni when he had been in their place. She had stayed on the glyn station to hold the embassy down and talk more to the intelligences.

Slyk had nobody, and didn't seem to mind. Glyn *were* strange. They tended towards a certain equanimity.

One of the restaurants had a selection of juices. To the glyn, fruit juice was like chocolate, and the primary nonalcoholic beverage on their sweltering world.

As cold as the station was to Slyk, who wore their cape, they still wanted juice.

"We need to take you to the Caribbean. Still lots of varieties of juice there, and you can have it with or without added alcohol."

Despite the massive differences in physiology, glyn could still get drunk. Or at least buzzed; Graeme had never seen one actually *drunk*.

Being drunk wouldn't make a lot of logical sense and glyn were, in many ways, all about logic.

Slyk wanted to be seen. Graeme held a door designed for bipeds open for them as they entered the restaurant.

The maitre d'hote raised an eyebrow. "Just two?"

She then led them to a booth. "If we are going to have glyn here regularly...would your office be willing to discuss..."

Slyk chimed laughter as they climbed onto the bench. "This actually works fine, although I think I'm taking up enough space for three of you."

She looked relieved. "Everyone else can sit, but...we want to cater."

"If a lot of glyn start coming through," Graeme said, "Expand your juice menu. And your cocktails and mocktails."

Slyk chimed again. "Graeme accuses us of being addicted to fruit juice."

The waitress laughed. "I'll bring that up with the boss."

Of course, if enough glyn came here, somebody would probably open a glyn style juice bar anyway. Even a human style one might work.

What did verr eat? A lot of seeds, nuts, and insects, from what Graeme knew. The ky'iin where easy.

All you needed to keep *them* happy was a steakhouse.

CHARLES AND MARION were going back to Earth soon. Unfortunately, Launchpad did not have enough children on board to warrant a school. They didn't want to keep the five year old out of kindergarten too long, or she would lose progress.

Virtual school had been proven not to work as well, especially with younger kids. Alas. There was just something about face to face interaction that children *needed*. But Graeme appreciated their company while he had it. Marion was drawing in crayon, as kids had done since crayons had been invented (before that they had drawn in something else).

"It's a glyn," she said.

Graeme looked over. "Ooh, not bad."

"With the wings out. Can they fly?"

Graeme shook his head. "They're too heavy. Their ancestors probably flew, like ours went up trees. And they can in zero G."

"Can I fly in zero G?"

"With enough space and a set of strap-on wings, yes."

Marion grinned. "I want to do that some day. Kind of like swimming, but you can breathe."

"You could learn to scuba dive too."

"I want to live in space," she said, finally.

"Well, we'll see if you are still saying that when you're grown up."

She folded her arms. "I will."

"Maybe. A lot of people change their minds."

"I'm going to live on a spaceship," she said, finally.

Maybe she would. Maybe she would crew a ship, or maybe there would be humans who chose to live on great ships like that one verr hive was doing.

Or maybe she would be an entertainer and live on a starliner.

"Maybe you will. But you need to do well in school."

She mock-pouted. "School."

"Yes, school."

She was a smart kid, but then, so were all three of her biological parents. She had the genetics and they had done their best to raise her right.

"I don't know about school."

"Well, as you get older, you'll have more say in school." They had lots of choices. "You'll work out what you're good at and enjoy."

"And if I want to live in space?"

He considered. "Lots of options, but if you want to crew a spaceship, you'll need maths."

Her eyes lit. "I like numbers."

"See? You'll be just fine."

8

"So, what you're saying," Kaykek said, trying not to laugh. "Is that *I* stop humans from wanting to attack ky'iin."

"Specifically," Micek said. "It appears that the pheromones scouts produce to stop other hives from throwing them out also reduce aggression in humans. They want...uh..."

"Samples."

That was easy enough, probably easier than the humans thought.

"They're hoping to isolate it and produce some kind of drug."

"Or maybe a scent the *ky'iin* can wear."

"I think that was brought up too."

Kaykek considered that. "Or they could..."

"So, what are we going to ask for in exchange?"

Kaykek considered *that* too. "Nothing. We owe them more than we can ever repay."

Starting to even out the verr ledger was important.

"Not to mention..."

"We don't want another human-ky'iin war. Tell them I'll swing by medbay later." Ze smiled at zir aide.

Maybe ze should push for a concession, but it didn't feel right after the humans had saved her species. From disaster. Perhaps they could have managed a few survivors on their own. Not enough to form a hive.

Extinction had been inevitable.

This was repayment, not a gift. Ze would make sure they understood that. And perhaps things between species *should* be like that, should be that kind of reciprocity, taking advantage when one suddenly discovered something useful.

Although there were some things ze wanted for zirself, but ze rather thought those could be negotiated.

"Although, could you let them know that Alvi wants a library card."

Micek chittered. "A library card?"

"You know how they are about books. There's an entire planet full of books down there. They want to read some of them."

Micek chittered again and scurried off. Kaykek felt a little lighter for the conversation.

A little more equipped for this.

The terminal in the room gave zir basic access to the human information networks, although any conversations with Earth experienced a slight time lag. Only just over a second, *just* enough to be noticeable.

But for reading stuff, it didn't make any difference at all and most of what Kaykek was doing was reading and struggling through translations and trying to learn the human alphabets. And symbolic systems.

They hadn't even settled on one or the other! One of their major languages used an alphabet, and the other used a symbolic system. Because humans. Verr had had more languages once, but ze was pretty sure they had never had quite as many as the humans did. Most of them survived only in given names.

Which was when she started resorting to watching human television. Easier to translate and she had *context*. Of course, a lot of their fiction was focused on pair bonding. In a way, ze was pair bonded with Tayken, but it wasn't at *all* the same thing.

Mating pheromones, or "chemistry" as they called it, fighting with practical concerns in a species where men and women (or sometimes other combinations) lived together to raise children.

Ze started looking for shows that didn't go as heavily into it and eventually found zirself watching some kind of weird time travel show that apparently involved the protagonist possessing a variety of people to the snide comments of his best friend.

Human fiction was weird.

But also...

Kaykek realized they might have another trade good.

In all directions.

THE HUMAN MEDICAL bay smelled like...medical bay. It was antimicrobial substances, although it did also mingle with the faint musky scent of "human." Humans only produced light levels of pheromones, but their sweat did smell.

The person in charge was a dark-skinned human with the most interesting hair ze had yet seen. Humans had little fur on their bodies and a lot on the top of their heads.

This one, who was darker skinned, had extraordinarily long hair that faded to an unnatural pink towards the tips, no doubt dyed, and was held together in many small braids.

The effect was truly spectacular and Kaykek could not help but stare.

"What?" the doctor snapped, then softened. "You..."

"I haven't yet seen a human do that with their hair. I'm sorry."

"It's called a weave," she explained. "I'm Dr. Tessa Monterey."

Weave. "It's beautiful. I'm sorry I stared."

Kaykek felt as if ze had hit some kind of invisible mine, but the tension did seem to vanish.

"It should be, it's a lot of work, but worth it."

In some ways it reminded Kaykek of the fur patterns fashionable in Nyulek Hive. So, maybe the tension was because...

Humans didn't have hives, they were a clan and tribe oriented species. So maybe that was where the minefield was. "You wanted to talk to me..."

"We want to test the effect of your pheromones on humans. The theory..."

"Verr pheromones affect humans to some degree," Kaykek said. "We let a human in the creche and he left in an embarrassing condition. He didn't *actually* conduct the experiment as to whether humans and verr are compatible for recreational sex, but..."

The doctor laughed. "Oh dear. But in this case..."

"In this case, my pheromones, which are designed to make *me* not look like a threat to another hive, might be used to develop a substance that could dampen human aggression enough for them to work with the ky'iin without natural resistance or months of desensitization training."

"That's the thought. I'm..."

"Of course I'll help. The humans built the force nets that saved most of my species. We *owe* you."

"I don't think that's meant to be repaid."

"We're verr. It has to be repaid. It might take centuries, mind."

"I think it's not repayable. We may just have to agree to be friends."

Verr laughed. Ze liked this human, despite the awkward moment at the start.

"So, how do we..."

"Oh, that part's easy. We just need a very clean cloth."

KAYKEK STUCK AROUND while the human added the samples to the analyzer. "So, you produce these pheromones..."

"When in a strange hive. My body is recognizing Launchpad as a strange hive. They tell the hive I'm visiting that I'm a scout. I suppose it's a form of biological diplomatic immunity. Before we got smart, we would have attacked any worker or warrior who showed up. Now, we don't do that, but we're still suspicious of people who aren't part of the hive." And it was still considered an excuse for violence, although not for murder.

"Because you have enough intelligence and free will to know when to attack and when not to."

"Also, we didn't have scouts for a while because we got kind of broken, so workers had to act as envoys. So we had to learn." Kaykek considered that. "Now we're getting back to more where we should be, biologically."

"I don't suppose I could sneak access to translations of some of your recent papers."

"I can do better than that for you. We have Livek on board, and he *wrote* several of those papers."

Dr. Monterey showed her teeth in a human expression of pleasure. "Would he be..."

"The difficulty with Livek is getting him to *stop* talking about his work."

"I have met several of that scientist. Some things are universal. So, the other thing I want to do is measure the impact of having you around on...well..."

"Humans."

"Which means brain scans of volunteers while you chat with them."

"I can find time to do that." See what exactly zir pheromones did to the poor humans. "I hope nobody feels..."

"There are rumors of verr mind control. But people on Launchpad are scientifically literate, once we tell them what's actually going on..."

"Tell them if they're nervous, they can talk to Micek instead. It isn't going to, what's the word..."

"Whammy."

"Right. Workers do produce pheromones, but nothing like..."

"I can't imagine what it's like to be..."

"I was happy for years that way. Most are. It's our life, and we don't want to change it, most of us. Not in broad strokes. We *are* doing research now on potentially suppressing or triggering puberty, as well as ovulation suppression. Right now, we can't afford the queens not to breed, but..."

"But once you get your population back up, family planning starts to be a feasible thing for your culture. I don't envy the queens."

Kaykek nodded. "Neither do I. But Tayken is very happy."

"Tayken is..."

"Somebody I'm very close to. In human terms, she would be my girlfriend, but it's far from the same thing."

"I have a girlfriend too. And no children, and no desire for any. But I suppose when..."

"It's been hard for us. We've had to do things to survive," Kaykek said quietly. "We almost had to blow up a ship with 25,000 verr on it to save far more."

"That we won't let happen again."

"That's why we're here."

Marginalize the xenophobes.

And talking to a few humans would help. It was, also, hardly a hardship. Humans were weird. They were also really interesting.

9

Dhyanil wasn't entirely comfortable in the room off the human medbay. It was designed for quarantine, so it had its own independent life support. It smelled odd and he felt somewhat confined. Some of it was the typical medbay smell...disinfecting chemicals and such. Some of it was, no doubt, the air filters.

In the room: Dhyanil, and a woman who worked as a waitress on the promenade. She was currently under restraint.

They were taking scans of how her brain reacted to him as he loomed over her and he hated it. She was a volunteer, but it still felt as if he was torturing her.

"Okay."

The door opened briefly and Kaykek walked in. Dhyanil experienced an odd cognitive inversion. He was used to being short, although he was taller than a lot of human women. Kaykek always made him feel *tall*. And ze was taller than the typical verr worker.

About five minutes later, the woman relaxed.

A bit after that. "That's not..." She glanced between the two aliens. "I hear you're quite the fisherman, Dhyanil."

She mangled his name, but he wasn't surprised. The dhy sound didn't exist in all human languages and he himself mangled a lot of human names for similar reasons. The zh sound they had...that one was a real problem. Ky'iin vocal chords did not go that way.

"I grew up in a fishing settlement," he explained. "In the tropics. On the coast."

"Hurricane country?"

"Oh, yes, but we knew how to handle them."

Hurricanes were a phenomenon found on most living worlds, an inevitable result of atmospheric drag. You built for them, you evacuated if you need to. "Earthquakes, those are more of a problem."

"Tsunamis?" she asked.

That was not a word he was going to attempt to pronounce. "We call them dhyen," he said. "But I do know what you're talking about."

"If the ocean leaves, run, because when it comes back..."

"You grew up in an earthquake zone."

She nodded.

Kaykek finally cut in. "I'll remember that when I visit Earth."

"You want to?" Dhyanil asked. "I can give some tips."

Kaykek laughed. "I'll take those. I just want to explore a little bit. It's a beautiful world."

The woman said wistfully, "It was and will be."

"Is," Kaykek insisted.

Dhyanil nodded. "This planet has issues, but it's lovely."

"I hope no people...none..." Kaykel's ears flicked back. "...ever again know what it means to lose a world."

Dhyanil had lost his world, but the difference was? He could get it back.

EXCUSED FROM THE EXPERIMENTATION, Dhyanil made his way back to his quarters with his bodyguards. This felt hopeful. It felt as if he could actually be with the humans some day, not just kind of among them. Not just next to them.

It felt as if the two species might actually find a way to get on.

Well, they were trying. People on both sides were determined to somehow make it work. At the same time, though? Biology got in the way as it always had, as it had when ly'iin had had to stand between men and women.

It was that which had built civilization and now the verr might be standing between humans and ky'iin and somehow that made sense.

And what if scout calming pheromones impacted everyone? No, that wasn't the case, sadly. They didn't seem to affect him, they certainly didn't affect the glyn. Just the mammal types.

Somebody could weaponize that. Increase the effect, use it to attack humans or tyrar. Make them not want to fight back.

Dhyanil misliked that idea, but no advance could ever be stopped. All advances had their good and bad sides, all could be used for right and for wrong, for good and for evil.

There was no getting away from it. People knew now and they would use that.

He had, too, to trust the verr. How much did they understand of how their pheromones worked? What about the pheromones of their warriors?

Would those, in fact, rile people up?

Likely only when a hive was threatened, or the presence of warriors...but then, supposedly, warriors had vanished. Or been mistaken for breeders with disorders of sexual development and locked safely in the creche. What was going on there, Dhyanil was not sure of. But it was possible that a hive without warriors would be more peaceable.

Or less, given they subconsciously knew what defenses they lacked. It was not something he could understand. Warriors were coming back, though, and that was likely a good thing. The plague would have stripped the ky'iin of the ly'iin, and that would be disaster even without its other effects. The verr needed their scouts and warriors just as much.

He let them take him back to his quarters, let them leave him there. He could not leave just yet. The verr pheromones promised him a freedom he had not had in the years he had spent on Earth.

But human science also promised him the chance to go home. He would not turn that down. If home was within reach, then he was absolutely, one hundred percent, going home.

Once there was a proper, ly'iin, representative to take his place.

IN THE MEANTIME, he settled down to study the preliminary material provided to him.

Written language was not a ky'iin thing. He was learning its utility. Unfortunately, ky'iin brains were not really wired to deal with it. He could manage a few words, but it was a struggle. Children might deal with it better, their brains still developing.

Instead, he watched hours of videos, curled up in his quarters with a mug of Earth tea, a beverage he had learned to appreciate. It had a mildly stimulating effect on both species, helping him focus.

There was a lot that had to be decided if the council of the world was going to become a council of worlds. But all of the species except the glyn understood the concept, had some beginnings of it.

The glyn were a monoculture, but quite willing to learn. To understand how others did things. To work with them.

It *could* work, Dhyanil decided. Whether it *would* work depended on people's willingness to try. He was willing to try. He knew others who were. Yet, he also knew those who would sabotage everything they tried, who would stand against it with word, with deed, with their very lives.

Whether it worked, he supposed, depended on how stubborn *everyone* involved was. Which side had the most will. He was fairly confident he knew, but they were dealing with people willing to commit genocide.

So...who knew what they would do? There were ky'iin and human warships acting as escorts for Launchpad, which had its own point defenses. He was pretty sure that the half-constructed ship had weapons already installed too, just in case.

He felt as safe here as on the planet. Nobody had started dropping rocks yet, but after the incident in Verr system, he was pretty sure that at some point somebody was *going* to start dropping rocks. It felt sadly inevitable.

It was hard to defend against that, although Earth and Mars both had good defenses. Venus, he was less sure on.

Easier to deflect the natural, which *generally* didn't come straight out of the primary at you. Avian predators would come out of the sun on their prey. So would fighter pilots.

So, ultimately, would any attack on a world.

10

ADWOA OLANREWALU WAS ELEGANT. Refined. Her braided hair was drawn back to reveal sharp features, with purple woven into it, falling further than those who work in zero G would likely keep it, the end of the weaves touching her butt.

It was clear that she naturally moved in the kind of circles Beverly herself had had to learn to handle.

She felt a little inadequate.

"So, the tyrar are also victims of bad geoengineering."

Beverly nodded. "They fell into a temptation we managed to avoid by the skin of our teeth." There had been some rogue attempts, but thankfully none had succeeded well enough to disastrously fail. They had only been *expensive* failures, not *catastrophic* ones.

"Unfortunate." She opened her mouth to say something else when an alarm echoed through the station.

"That's the breach alarm," Beverly said, managing to stay calm. After all, the air was not rushing out through a hole where they were."

"Indeed it is." Adwoa glanced around. "Nearest shelter is fifty feet that way."

Abandoning the rest of her lunch, but tucking her drink onto her lap, Beverly rolled towards the shelter. Adwoa followed after her with many of the mannerisms of a crane. The bird, that is. She was tall, and she moved with that kind of delicacy.

Beverly still hadn't found out much about the sky cities, the new colonies on Venus that were vulnerable and beautiful and an *incredible* feat of engineering. Maybe she could visit one some day. They weren't really tourist attractions yet.

They would be. They and others made it into the shelter area, but the hatched areas remained open. Wherever the breach was, it wasn't affecting the small commercial area of the station.

Yet.

Despite that, Beverly stayed in the shelter, waiting for the all clear. "I hope this doesn't happen often."

Adwoa pursed her lips. "At least acid isn't coming *in*."

Beverly shuddered. Venus was not hospitable, and the surface was the province only of specially-hardened robots.

The cities, at Earth atmospheric pressure, held up by their atmosphere, were another matter. "I suppose..."

"We all get used to the threats we grow up with," Adwoa mused.

"We do. And then they change." Earth had changed, with climate change and then again with the mitigations, the carbon drawdown. They couldn't ever restore what was before, but they had a stable, livable planet now. One on which humans could still thrive.

That had once been a question.

And had she been born a decade sooner, Beverly would not have been a scientist.

The all clear sounded, but Beverly was determined to find out what had just happened. And why.

―――――――

"Isolationists," Parvati said, flatly, having managed to get information out of human security. "Human ones. Religious fanatics who, apparently, think we're all made by an evil god or...something."

Beverly facepalmed. "I *know* the people you are talking about. Only humans are made in the image of God, so all other sentients must be evil. How did they..."

"Get hold of a spaceship? Bought one, apparently. A ky'iin *yacht* of all things. We're lucky they tried to use its asteroid defense weapons instead of just flying it into Launchpad." Parvati reached for her mug of tea, wrapping huge tyrar fingers around it.

"Which is what you would have done."

Parvati shrugged. "Think like the opposition. It has a singularity drive."

Implosion. Beverly shuddered. "So, what if the next batch are more competent? Launchpad isn't a great venue."

"Nowhere is. On planet, just open to hoards of protesters. And, almost as bad, fans."

Beverly laughed. "I don't have..."

"Oh yes you do." Parvati grinned. "You should get yourself a PR expert because there are unauthorized action figures and you probably want in on that."

"I do *not* have..."

Parvati showed her a picture.

She shuddered. "Oh man, that doesn't even look like me." It didn't. She was not that good looking and did not want to be, with a perfect hourglass figure she hadn't had in years. "But you're right, I need a PR expert."

Scientists getting action figures didn't happen very often. Once or twice during the plague years that immediately preceded Austerity, certainly not *during* that tough time. Dolls, sometimes. Action figures?

She *did* need a PR expert. "What are they..."

"You are, apparently, *entirely* key to why the scary Bigfoot people aren't attacking humans."

"Seems like more people need to meet the *cuddly* Bigfoot people." She grinned and ran a hand through Parvati's fur, a herdmate liberty.

"I am not cuddling them."

"No, but you *are* cuddly." Tyrar liked to cuddle, groom each other, sleep in piles...

Parvati wrinkled her nose in tyrar laughter. "They have one of me too. It's even worse."

"Bigfoot people."

"What *is* Bigfoot, anyway?"

"A legendary hairy biped that supposedly lived in parts of the United States and hid in the woods. Likely a folk memory of giant ground sloths." A pause. "You look a *bit* like Bigfoot. It's not an unreasonable parallel. And Bigfoot is also supposed to be a vegetarian, but shy, not cuddly."

Parvati was, of course, a herbivore, not a vegetarian. She was not above sampling small amounts of meat. "We are not shy."

"Maybe if you were endangered on a planet dominated by others, you would be, but the existence of Bigfoot was thoroughly debunked decades ago."

"Alas. I would like to meet one."

Beverly reached for the phone and pulled up several supposed Bigfoot images right as Yoshi came in to their laughter.

THE DAMAGE to the station had been minor, cracking the doors of one of the shuttle bays. The yacht was still being pursued.

Beverly hoped they wouldn't think of what Parvati had thought of. Even crashing a singularity-equipped ship into a planet...wasn't something people wanted to think about, although the singularity would dissipate before...

Put it this way it wouldn't destroy the planet, but if it hit a city it could destroy it. It had never happened. Hopefully it never would. Even a tame black hole was a nasty beast indeed. Some people made the reasonable argument that singularity-equipped ships should stay well away from planets, and the effect of coming out of FTL in a planetary atmosphere gave them more ammunition. It was not something you did unless you needed a significant distraction, in the form of a massive electrical storm.

The reception thus went off as planned, in part because nobody wanted to bow to terrorists.

"So," the young medic was asking. "What did you think of the ky'iin?"

"Ugly by human standards, they probably feel the same way about us. Why?"

"We're running some tests, but it appears that verr scout pheromones dampen the human desire to attack ky'iin."

"Oh...that's..." It was awesome, but also. "I don't know that I like the idea of the verr messing with my head."

"I can see thinking that way, but think of it this way. Your biology making you hate somebody?"

"Excuse used by racists for centuries," Beverly quipped, grinning at the young man, who's skin was dark enough to know what racism felt like.

"True, but in this case it's real. We're working on a perfume that ky'iin who visit Earth could wear to keep them from being attacked."

"That would be better than..."

"You can't have, say, all of Paris take something just because a group of ky'iin tourists want to climb the Eiffel Tower."

Beverly grinned a bit. "No, we can't."

She still wasn't comfortable with it, but she knew how it would feel; she had already experienced it once, and she hadn't felt controlled.

She hadn't noticed. That was, perhaps, even scarier. "How do the verr feel about this?"

"The verr ambassador is helping us with samples. They like the idea of keeping people from shooting each other."

Beverly didn't understand the verr yet. The tyrar lived in herds, but she got that. They lived in chosen families, and that concept had been part of a number of human cultures.

The verr lived in *hives* and it was biological and...it was strange, and no doubt they found others equally strange.

She could only think of one solution to this.

She had to talk to the verr.

11

GRAEME WAS VERY glad that Marion and his husband left for Earth before the alarm. He did not want them to be unsafe, or to dent Marion's wide-eyed enthusiasm about space.

At some point it would need to be dented by realism; but not yet. She was a child, after all. The real dangers could wait until she was old enough to fully understand them. A terrorist attack. It could have been worse.

Charles could be receiving a "We deeply regret" message right now. Yet, he still wanted to take them both to Glen now it was somewhat stable and while it still existed. There was still the risk that the planet would have to be evacuated.

They had hope, which is sometimes all you can manage, all you can expect.

The terrorists had fired from a ky'iin yacht, but one which had recently been bought by a human shell company. Charles could do more digging back on Earth where the internet was faster. Could and would. He was an engineer, but he couldn't have survived being married to Graeme for this long without picking up the basics of spycraft.

If they could find out who was behind this then they could do something about it. In the meantime, a system-wide search was on for the yacht.

Charles would bet it had gone out into the Oort Cloud. Or out of the system altogether; although small, the yacht did have FTL capability.

Of course that meant hiring a qualified pilot. Another thread they could trace. Another way to find out who these people were.

Unless, of course, they went old school terrorist and claimed responsibility. Not that that couldn't be muddy too; history had a number of examples of an organization claiming responsibility for something they did not, in fact, do.

He stared at his terminal. The internet here was a little slower, inevitably, but the days when the infrastructure had not existed were long gone. But he was more trying to think of other leads than actually researching anything. It was starting to give him a headache.

He knew that he could leave it to others, especially those looking for that yacht, but he was not constitutionally suited to delegation. Something he knew he needed to work on.

He was just glad Marion was safe in Glasgow with her other father and her mother-aunt. Very glad. It had felt so hopeful, too, especially with a potential solution to the ky'iin problem. It wasn't the ky'iin's *fault*, but they were still a problem.

He turned the verr over in his mind. Hive defense pheromones, and a countermeasure. They were sentient, but they were still bound by their biology.

Just as he was.

"MR. MARLOWE, would you please join us in command and control?" The young officer favored him with a smile that clearly said that this was not about anything he had done.

They had worked out he was qualified intelligence, perhaps? "Of course."

He followed them...from the hair, he couldn't tell what gender they were...through the corridors of Launchpad. Nobody paid them any mind, not really, although he did pass a conference room where the Martian representative, Kai Bowie, recognizable by their pink and purple hair, was in some argument with the Earth representative, Chan Chih-Cheng, recognizable by his boring grey suit.

That was probably unfair. Chan was probably interesting in *some* way. Graeme had yet to really talk to him, although he had introduced Slyk to both of them before backing away and letting them talk.

Slyk and Kai Bowie had promptly got into a discussion about gender which left Chan uncomfortable.

Graeme still found that quite amusing.

He walked further, though, leaving the wrangling behind, and through a door marked "Crew only." Into the secret places, he thought.

The officer led him into a room off command and control. The station's commander, Galyna Movchan, stood at one end of a table. "Thank you for joining us, Mr. Marlowe. You can go, Mr. Leigh."

The young officer nodded and made themselves scarce. Graeme recognized the other person in the room as Liu Syaoran, an aide to Kai Bowie.

A Martian spook, in other words. Graeme wasn't stupid. The three sat down.

"So..."

"I have a contact on Earth running some searches," Graeme said. "Trying to establish who bought that yacht and where they might have hired a pilot."

If they did. Of course, they might try to run FTL with somebody who wasn't webbed and who's primary experience was in a Piper Cub. FTL pilots still started their training in small atmosphere planes, it being better prep than anything in space normal.

They might. Especially if they didn't care where they landed other than "Away". It was surprisingly hard to FTL right into a star; space was pretty empty. So...it was possible they didn't have a qualified FTL pilot.

Galyna grinned at him. "And I don't even need to..."

Graeme shrugged. "I know who Mr. Liu is."

The Martian also shrugged. "Did you peg me?"

"It was either you or that little Desi woman."

"Nah, she's a secretary."

Graeme laughed at that. "I believe you."

He didn't, of course. "So, what thoughts do you have?"

"The yacht was purchased by an Earth company with no open ties to Mars," Syaoran said, keeping his voice quiet. "That doesn't mean it didn't have *covert* ties to Mars, we're still poking at that."

Graeme nodded. "I think we're probably dealing with xenophobes." And some xenophobes thought even Mars shouldn't have been colonized.

"Most likely, but we can't discount a political motivation."

"We never can."

He glanced at the Commander. She was pursing her lips and not looking nearly as lost as he thought. Then she spoke, "Or somebody who feels that their freedoms are threatened."

"That could mean the last vestiges of Great America." They had risen before Austerity, gained a lot of power during it, but were pretty much scattered remnants now. "Those types feel that their freedom is threatened by other people breathing."

Syaoran laughed. "It could be. Definitely on the list."

"But some people," the Commander said, "Might truly feel that contact with offworlders threatens them."

Graeme had placed her name and accent. He nodded. "They are not Russian, Commander."

She laughed sharply. "No, I don't believe they are."

THE COMMANDER'S words stayed with Graeme.

People who think their freedom is going to be curtailed. There *were* numerous candidates there. Assorted religious groups. People who had been victims of colonialism and were afraid of it happening again.

In truth, Graeme suspected an unholy alliance was building. Each world had people afraid of alien influence.

No, that was not true. The glyn had people afraid of change and the verr had people who had become so rigid in their attempts to survive that their society had fractured. But any verr xenophobes were hiding in their hives somewhere, not causing trouble.

Humans, ky'iin, tyrar. He mused for a bit on what those species had in common, but wasn't quite able to nudge it out. He did not make it back to his quarters, where he had planned on talking to Charles, or at least trading emails with him. He got about halfway there when the new comlink the commander had given him went off. He managed not to sigh openly as he pulled it out.

"Head's up. There was a claim of responsibility. Be ready for that to break."

And place your bets now, Graeme thought with amusement. He was placing his on Great America, but there were so many other candidates.

And, again, unholy alliances. Had the ky'iin who sold the yacht known *exactly* who was buying it? It wasn't impossible.

He should talk to Dhyanil, see if he could work that side of it too. The man...Graeme was getting used to thinking of him that way...had history, after all. For right now, he quickened his pace. He wanted to be off the streets if the announcement caused any reactions.

Not that people on Launchpad weren't, by definition, well disciplined.

Making it there, though, he left the door open a crack, just in case anyone needed him, just in case he heard something. Launchpad had a decent amount of space, his assigned quarters were smaller than those given to the tyrar, but hardly a closet, and right next to Slik's.

Slik.

He should ask *their* opinion on this. But before he could move next door to see if the glyn was there the broadcast hit the news feeds.

He sat there and watched it, and his frown deepened further with each sentence.

12

KAYKEK'S COMMAND of the two primary human languages (let alone the hundreds of others) was still limited to a word here and there.

Thankfully, Alvi's translation algorithms allowed zir to understand the broadcast anyway.

Well. Not thankfully. Ze would much rather have remained blissfully ignorant.

"That was a warning shot. We are now moving into position to destroy a major city on Earth. Unless the aliens leave the system within sixty days and the treaty with them is voided. We will not tell you which city."

Which meant they would have to evacuate all of them. Destroy a city from space. Kaykek knew how easy that was. All you really had to do was throw a rock at it. The right size rock at the right speed and angle. Orbital bombardment. It felt as if there should be a treaty to ban it, but that would not stop these people.

Aliens meant zir. To zir, they were the aliens, but such delightful aliens. Such a beautiful planet, such wonderful art work. Tayken had bought volumes of human poetry, in digital form. She had also bought language tutoring material for English, Chinese, and German, so she could read them in the original.

That was such a Tayken thing to do. Thinking about zir preferred mate did help some. But it was also bittersweet.

Kaykek had watched zir world break up, fly apart into pieces, become something useful only to miners. Ze could not face the idea of even the destruction of a city. A major city.

No saying which one. Making it harder to stop. There were somewhere between five and six billion people on Earth, down from a much higher peak. A viable population on Mars, mind, and other colonies being formed. Humans were not an endangered species, would not become one even if their homeworld was destroyed.

Plus, these people could be bluffing. Kaykek could not read human body language. Could be.

All of these reassurances did nothing to quell the chill that ran through zir. The gods came from above, after all. The gods...who were all dead and gone and perhaps there was a tragedy in that.

How did they stop this. Perhaps Alvi's sensors could be useful? Ze could ask them to keep them peeled, it wouldn't even be a hardship for the ship mind.

But ze did not...

Ze had the ability to calm humans down, but whether ze wanted to intentionally *use* it was another matter. It felt in many ways as if it was a wrong thing to do. Rude, without a good reason. And these people would not listen to zir.

They would only listen to humans and perhaps not even to humans who worked with aliens.

Ze needed to talk to a human.

Alvi's voice through zir comlink, coincidental in that moment. "One of the humans wants to talk to you."

Just as ze had come to that conclusion. "I would very much like that. We can...trade."

ONE OF THE small number of businesses on Launchpad was what humans called a coffee shop. There, humans indulged in mild stimulants and conversation.

The medics had *not* recommended Kaykek try the stimulant; it was mild for humans but might, in their terms, "Have you trying to dig through metal."

Instead, zie had ordered a herbal beverage that *was* safe for verr, sitting in the corner opposite the human queen...woman.

A woman who used a wheeled chair to get around. Kaykek was not going to ask; you didn't ask a disabled person about their disability, you only asked if they needed anything.

Which this Beverly clearly did not.

She was one of the human scientists who had gone to Tyranis, and had now come back as a member of Ambassador Viary's *herd*. Could a human become part of a hive?

Alvi had.

"Thanks for meeting with me," Beverly said.

"I was honestly about to ask Alvi to find me a human willing to talk." Zir whiskers curled. "I want to understand you better..."

"Especially with what's going on. And I think that you...your people...are going to be very important to our shared future."

The human had an interesting smell, Kaykek noticed. Floral. "Just a question. Are you wearing scent?"

Beverly blinked. "No, but I recently showered. I hope it's not unpleasant. Our sense of smell isn't nearlly as good as yours because we don't live underground."

"No, it's just not the same as you smelled last time." So, humans wore body scents, which verr would not do because...because humans didn't rely on pheromones.

"We have much better color vision, though," Beverly mused. "Each species has what they need."

"And we have what we need to avoid the gods...but also apparently to help others get on."

"I always thought that would be humans, because we form pack bonds with other species so easily." Beverly considered that. "I should have known our tribalism..."

Kaykek lifted a hand. "If that word means what I think it means, we have plenty of it too. Truth is there are people who get on with other species and people who don't, and I don't think species has much to do with it. We just have to let the people who can handle it do it and the people who can't can go live in a small hive somewhere."

Beverly laughed. "If only they would."

Human laughter was an interesting sound. Kaykek recognized it from videos she had watched. They were arboreal animals who had then become plains animals, not burrowers at all, and they relied on both vision and hearing over their poor sense of smell. "We just need to convince them of that. And with pups who grow up seeing aliens."

"The kids will help, yes." A wistful tone in Beverly's voice. "I sometimes wish..."

"Is it too late?" Kaykek asked.

"Older human females face more risks in pregnancy and I face higher risks yet. Biologically, it wouldn't be a good idea, but I could adopt." A pause. "And I may have herd-children, which is close enough." If she, though...if she adopted a human child that would grow up as herd-child with Pallavi's children?

"Most verr never have kids."

"We're not verr," Beverly said. "Which isn't a value judgment. Humans have a strong desire to have their own biological children. I just had desires that were even stronger."

"Science," Kaykek said. "I know people who are obsessed with science. Plenty of verr are that way."

"Whilst you..."

Kaykek chittered laughter. "I *was* a life support tech."

The human found that funny too.

"Do you think they're bluffing?" Kaykek asked Beverly, finally.

"I don't know. A long time ago there used to be an organization called the Irish Republican Army. They were displeased about part of their country being occupied by another." A pause. "We tribalize by land area."

Kaykek nodded. "I think I get it. Hives claim territory too."

"One of their favorite tricks was to plant *one* bomb in the other country's capital city. Not a very large one. Just big enough to cause a few casualties. Then they would tell the police they had planted four bombs. One of which was real. They did this when everyone was trying to get to work. Their goal was to cause disruption. They only had to plant one bomb..."

"...to paralyze the city because you didn't know where the real bomb was." Kaykek shuddered. "We have terrorists too. I can see how that would work."

Beverly nodded. "I'm reminded of that little historical detail...ask Graeme about it, he'd know more...by the fact that they didn't name a target."

"If they had, you could evacuate it."

"Mostly. Some people would refuse to go. But yes. We'd have a chance."

"So do you think..."

"I think they are not bluffing. I think they are hoping they won't be called on it. But I'm not a terrorist. Graeme really is the one you want to talk to."

Kaykek's ears twitched. "He knows more about this?"

"From what I've seen."

"He's a spy," Kaykek said, finally, as if it was expected. "Alvi warned me there would be some. I'm not too bothered."

"Of course, what does your hive have to hide?"

"We're working on a lot of technologies, but..." Kaykek's ears drooped. "We don't want to be dependent."

"Oh, you won't be. Not for long." Beverly grinned. "I've seen some of the papers your hive's scientists traded. You aren't stupid, you were just trapped in survival mode."

"Still." Kaykek studied her. "You study planetary ecology and reclamation?"

"I do. Which also ties into the possibility of terraforming, but it would take a *long* time and most people aren't going to be that patient."

"Not unless they can't find a suitable planet any other way," Kaykek agreed. "We got lucky with Kyverr."

"You did. Although..." Beverly studied her. "You prefer the ship?"

"I intend to die on Refuge." Kaykek knew it was true, and from the human's face? She was surprised but she, perhaps, understood.

13

A GENUINE, actual threat of planetary bombardment. Dhyanil was angry.

Not afraid. Angry. He was not going down to the planet any time soon. But he had become somewhat attached to Earth, at least to certain parts of it. The fishing was good, after all.

And humans? They might not be easy to understand, but he had come to recognize that they really were just people at their core. Different from him, but those differences were biological not...ethical or spiritual. Of *course* the relationships between the sexes were different for live bearers, for starters.

And of course a species who's young still went through an arboreal phase would have a semi-worship of trees. The human fascination with forests made a hundred percent sense.

Plus they cooked well. They had myoran, he could not deny that. So did the verr, so did...he began to understand that there was no distinction. *All* sapient beings had it, because it was, at its core, the basic social sense that allowed them to evolve. That allowed them to build these complex societies. He even suspected that, in addition to dolphins, the crows had it.

They were people. So, yes, he was angry. Angry that one of their ships was being used this way. A yacht could, yes, easily move an asteroid into position. This might be five or six people attempting to hold a world to ransom.

Just that. Or it might be part of a much larger organization. He knew they existed. In fact, he had had to set a hacker on some of them who had started sending him some rather nasty messages through the human global network. "Go back to Kyx" was the mildest of them.

The worst part was that they did it to each other too, because of course they did. Humans. Worse than ky'iin for going after those who were different. Well, maybe not worse, perhaps it was more about how they did it.

Either way, his anger was palpable. He wanted to find these people and sharpen his claws on them. A primitive urge, that.

An urge which had to be dealt with, which was why he and his escort had made their way to the gym. It was a quiet time, not many humans in there to disturb. He kept his claws retracted while he took his anger out on a human punching bag. Had he extended them, he would have destroyed the equipment. He had enough control left not to do that.

"I'm glad you're on our side," one of the bodyguards said afterwards.

"Normally we only do that to things we intend to eat. Not fellow sentients." He turned away. "But..."

"You ain't too fond of people shooting at you?"

"I'm *not* fond of it, no. I'm also not fond of..." A pause. "People like I used to be." That was a part of it. He had moved on. He was better now. Why couldn't they achieve the same thing? He didn't know.

A NOTE FROM THE HUMAN, Graeme Marlowe, was waiting on his terminal. A request to get a search run on the ky'iin ship registry database to identify who had sold the yacht.

He sighed. He should have thought of this without needing prompting, which said something about exactly how angry he was and had been.

Angry enough to make mistakes, angry enough not to think of the obvious. Maybe he should go hang out with the verr scout for a bit and see if zir pheromones calmed him down. He doubted ze would mind overly much as long as he told zir more about what Kyx was like. They hadn't seemed to affect him before, though, so it seemed like a slim chance.

A very curious person, Kaykek. Which was, of course, not a bad thing. He liked curious people. People who were curious were less likely to be...well, lack of curiosity had been his *own* failing for far too long. Had been...well. He wasn't that person any more.

He sent a message back to Graeme, first saying he was on it, and then suggesting they meet. "I know how people like this think."

He might not know how *humans* thought. But he understood the urge. No, he would never have threatened to drop an asteroid on a city. But he had killed people for the cause in the past, for a cause he now knew to be folly.

He could be of help and channel the anger into that. He added, "Should we call the verr?"

Kaykek would help them work together and ze was very smart, ze might have insights too.

The response. "How about the three of us, conference room four. I'll call zir."

The verr were useful people to have around, which was a horrible way to think, but it might be a very good thing that the humans had saved them without any concern for the consequences.

So far, there had been no *bad* consequences of saving them.

There were some unpleasant verr, he was sure of that. Kaykek was not one of them. A few messages later and they had agreed to meet for lunch.

Two omnivores and a carnivore could eat together without anyone being too upset. And it wasn't that Dhyanil couldn't eat vegetables, he could and did, he just needed meat more than they did.

Lunch in a private room, of course, a conference room rather than the canteen. And his bodyguards to protect him from any humans who were still struggling. They did say it got easier.

And at some point he would try the "perfume" the biologists were coming up with based off of Kaykek's pheromones.

For now, borrowing the verr ambassador worked. And ze *was* another perfectly good brain to put on the matter.

HUMAN-STYLE FOOD SHOWED THEIR ADAPTABILITY. The tough climate of this world had bred people who could eat anything.

Dhyanil had, for example, been warned that a popular treat that was all but addictive to humans might make him dangerously sick. Lunch was safe, though. Sandwiches with processed meat.

He skipped the cheese. There was something about eating the solidified excretions of another being that bothered him. Kaykek, he noted, did not. But the verr had almost certainly known hunger, which Dhyanil never had.

Graeme, of course, piled his sandwich with everything available. This was his native cuisine, or at least...

It might not be, it might be a completely different part of the planet. Dhyanil did not ask. Even after his time on Earth, he couldn't always identify human regional accents, an unfortunate thing given how many of those there were.

Two dominant languages, hundreds of others, *thousands* of accents and dialects. Ky'iin language had tended to converge into the two or three remaining. Humans considered language so integral to culture that they would preserve languages with only a couple of hundred speakers and treat them as if they were special and magical. Valuable. Even the humans who couldn't hear had their own languages, which led to a peculiar culture thing, a pride in their disability that he was both mystified by and, oddly, understood.

Ky'iin valued precise communication and split culture other ways. Verr had a language per hive, but with only four hives having survived the disaster, they only had four languages and those had drifted close together. Tyrar had hundreds too.

And glyn had one, but AIs that could make incredible translation algorithms.

Everyone ate for a bit in silence, then Graeme finally spoke. "Thank you both. Dhyanil, I was hoping..."

"I can absolutely send a query and find out who sold them that ship. It's older, highly likely they just bought it from a broker, though." Dhyanil wasn't expecting it to be a lead.

Graeme nodded. "Would a broker sell to humans?"

"I can't see any reason why they wouldn't if they had the credits." Dhyanil considered. "But it would flag somewhere."

Kaykek finished zir sandwich and cleaned off zir whiskers, which had a bit of cheese on them.

"I would think there would be export duty. If there wasn't..."

"I have a feeling evading taxes is a universal."

Kaykek chittered. "We don't have taxes."

"What, you really do naturally just work for the good of the hive?" Graeme asked, amused.

Dhyanil recollected that that chittering sound was a verr laugh. "Bear in mind that they have been doing that to survive for generations. They may well not need taxes."

Kaykek chittered again. "Our good *is* the good of the hive. We don't separate those things."

Dhyanil considered that. "Maybe a lesson we could all learn."

"Not humans. We have tried that kind of system. It doesn't work with our biology," Graeme mused. "Communism turned into terrible tyranny every time it was tried. So, back to our ship?"

Back on focus, but Dhyanil had a little more insight into the verr.

14

Viary was tense. Beverly waved a grooming brush at her when she noticed the fact. It was hard to groom certain parts of oneself, after all.

One good reason to live in a herd. Beverly never wanted to live alone again and with luck she would never have to.

Viary nodded and wrinkled her nose, and Beverly rolled over and went to work on the tyrar's slightly messy back fur. "So..."

"So...we're making progress, but we already know what the major sticking point is."

"Location."

"The humans, ky'iin, and us all want Council located in our territory. The verr don't care and the glyn..."

"The glyn don't want to invite anyone to their homeworld until they've finished repairing it," Beverly quipped. "Nobody wants guests in a messy house."

"Nobody does. And I am arguing for us, but..."

"Nobody gets it. And everyone gets it," Beverly said, finally. "On Earth, in the days before fast transportation, kings went on procession. They moved their court around so that petitioners would have access. We *move* Council."

Viary considered that. "Not a terrible idea, but I'm under instructions."

Beverly grinned, running the brush through the dark brown fur. "I'm not."

And she was a respected scientist. With an action figure.

"Oh man. I still need to hire a PR person."

"What for?"

"Apparently I'm a STEM icon on Earth now."

Viary's face wasn't visible, but there was a faint rumble. "You?"

"Me. There's an unlicensed action figure. So I need a PR person. And a lawyer."

She didn't want to have to sue them.

"To get them to stop?"

"Viary, it's awful. It doesn't look like me at all. If I'm going to have an action figure I want it to vaguely resemble me!"

If she had to have an action figure.

Viary was still laughing, which was a lot better than tense.

"So, what are we stuck on other than location?"

"Somebody in the human crowd wants everyone to choose their delegates by closed ballot election. The verr don't like that."

"Democracy, the worst system of government except for all the others."

"Right. But humans are set on *their* kind of democracy. The verr are going to take caste into account when choosing delegates. The glyn are going to make it just another job you apply for. I'm arguing that the treaty should place absolutely no rules on the choice of delegates. Each world does their own."

Beverly considered. "Require that each world have a way to remove a delegate. Otherwise we're going to have somebody bring back hereditary monarchy."

Viary shuddered. "You're right. We are. At least we need to make sure that if it's hereditary they pick the most competent relative, not the oldest daughter of the herd."

"Exactly. A delegate could also be expelled, and then their world would have to choose somebody else."

"The ky'iin expel delegates from their council all the time. In the bad old days I think it involved claws."

It was Beverly's turn to laugh. "Or windows."

"Windows?"

"It's...a long Earth story."

"For once," Viary responded, "I have time."

BEVERLY DIDN'T HAVE much time after that to think about her idea, but she did tuck it away in the back of her head.

They had the more urgent concern of how to deal with the terrorists. They could do what they were threatening. Whether they *would* was, of course, an open question. It could be a bluff.

But she didn't think so. She wanted to talk to Graeme about it; while he wasn't old enough to remember the Troubles, he was still from the culture they had happened to. There was something generational there.

Something dark in the background, but her own Irish heritage was enough generations back that it was academic to her. Her Irish ancestors had fled during the potato famine. Which was the fault of the English, of course, like so many other things.

Graeme was Scottish, so it wasn't his fault.

A bluff. But if it was not? They needed to find that ship, which was not a thing she had any qualifications to help with. She was a scientist.

Really, she wasn't much use here except as Viary's herdmate and a symbol of inter-species cooperation.

A symbol. If she was going to be a symbol with an action figure maybe, as much as she hated, she had to *be* that symbol.

She picked up a tablet and started to look up PR firms. She rapidly realized she had no idea where to start, what fair rates were, or anything. She was a scientist, not a...personality.

So, did she know anyone who might know who would be good to call? Who might have recommendations.

Various exes flitted through her brain. Chloe had even reached out to her, but she had dumped Chloe for reasons. Chloe would know, but

Chloe would also think any contact was preliminary to getting back together. Now Beverly was famous, she was worth Chloe's time again.

Chloe wasn't worth hers. Who else was there? Darren? He might know of somebody.

Graeme? He was a spy, he wouldn't know about PR people, but he also knew a lot of people. She sent him a message and then contemplated the list again.

What was a fair rate? She didn't even know where to start.

Oh!

She was an idiot. She glanced around the herd's quarters for a moment, because even with the slight time lag, this needed to be a video call. There was no unreasonable amount of shed fur in the shot. It was very hard to avoid shed fur when you lived with tyrar.

"So...you need a PR person."

Beverly nodded. "Yes, Uncle Clarence."

He was old. He liked video calls. The lag was enough to be annoying, but far from enough to hinder their conversation. "I'm jealous of you up there in space."

She grinned. "You know you could..."

"I could go to one of the hotels, but I'm jealous of you getting to be on a *working* station."

Could and had, albeit for a short trip. "I need a PR person. Does Nancy maybe know of somebody?"

"Hrm. What kind of PR?"

"Look me up on the net."

She waited while he did.

"Oh my...that is *awful*. You need a lawyer."

"One of those too," she admitted. "The hair. The *hair* is so wrong. I would never..."

"You have taste." Clarence grinned. "I'll ask Nancy. And as for a lawyer, why don't you call Paul? He has a partner who does IP stuff."

"I will!" She hadn't thought of Paul, but she also hadn't known they'd brought on an IP lawyer. She definitely needed one.

The action figure thing had to be dealt with, but it looked like they were selling well. If it wasn't so awful...

...but she wanted it shut down, not to get a cut, at least for now. She could get a cut of a *good* action figure, one she'd helped work on the design for.

But...she wanted to do more than that.

"Thank you." Then she called Yoshi and Parvati. Viary was in a meeting.

She had shown them the action figure. "So...I am thinking. Half of why I'm here, the other half being that we love Viary, is to be a symbol of interspecies cooperation. We have people threatening to destroy cities. We had people on Tyranis willing to destroy *their own homeworld*. Maybe it's time to be that symbol."

Yoshi considered. "I don't want to be famous."

"Neither do I, but it's too late. I'm engaging a human PR expert and also a lawyer to get the awful action figure shut down."

"And then..."

"Then I am going to hire somebody to make good ones. But I think it needs to come with a tyrar too."

"Use me," Parvati said, running a hand through her own fur. "I'm the pretty one."

Beverly didn't disagree, but that started a mock fight between the two tyrar. Really, they were both pretty.

"You girls are....impossible," she ended up saying, shaking her head at them. "Impossible."

Then she chased them with a brush, wheeling across the room and nearly slamming right into Yoshi. They fell into a laughing pile.

15

THE VERR DID INDEED HAVE some insights. And helped him face the ky'iin, not without fear, but with little enough fear that he could *pretend* he wasn't afraid.

He still was. Part of it was academic; the man was an apex predator in a way humans really weren't, like a large feline. The fact that he had refused the cheese said it all. But it was kept down to a shiver that ran through him whether he wanted it to or not.

He didn't know if ky'iin could handle lactose; not being mammals they didn't have a mechanism to turn them off it at weaning time, but not being mammals they also had no evolutionary pressure to digest it in the first place.

Maybe he couldn't. The verr certainly could. He'd even asked, and yes, verr were lactose tolerant and had once had livestock they had milked. At least cheese, anyway, if not milk.

The verr might well...their livestock were extinct. Would they buy cows? Maybe. Graeme set that aside for something to bring up in trade talks. The ky'iin, though. He didn't think they'd find anything by tracing the sale of the yacht, although they had indeed established that export duties would have been owed.

Unfortunately, that made it all the more likely that the sale had taken place under the table, without said duty being paid. Ky'iin were as keen to avoid taxes as humans were, apparently. But they could, at least, trace where it was made. Maybe get the specs, too, which might make it easier for the ships combing the solar system to find it. It might have left the system.

It wasn't hiding in the gas giants. *That* trick didn't work as well as it once did, because people looked there first these days. The asteroid belt was not dense enough. Somebody was checking the Jovian trojans, which *did* make a fine hiding place.

Maybe they had just jumped. He would have. Come back in a few days, see if.

No.

Wait.

If they were actually planning on dropping a rock, they *had* to be spending this time getting it into position. If they weren't, then they were bluffing. He wasn't a ballistics expert and could safely leave the where to them...although with no listed target, there was still a huge amount of space to search.

Charles sent a message. "I traced your shell company. You were right, it traces to Texas."

Texas. The most problematic part of a problematic country, and a part that still kept up a lot of Austerity. "I called it," he said grimly, then sent that to Charles. He then pored over the evidence his husband had sent him.

It was not enough, but it started to give a picture of what was going on. Not sophisticated.

But they did have a starship, albeit a small one. That was not good news.

"You were right," the Commander said. "They were bluffing. No sign of any ship in *any* place that could nudge a rock to land anywhere in less than, oh, six months."

"They left the system." Graeme leaned against the wall. "But what will they do when we call their bluff?"

"Rant and rave? It sounds like they're that type of fanatic, not people who would actually achieve anything."

"They did make a small hole in the station," Graeme mused. "And if they get desperate..."

"...they could just crash their ship."

"They could get out and autopilot it down, but Earth's planetary defenses would take it out *easily* if they tried that."

Rocks were harder, because they didn't give off any energy. Harder to see. Angle them right and they might not show up until they hit the atmosphere. A ship?

They were ready for that.

"What do we do when it shows up?" Graeme added.

"Blow it up? No, I suppose not." She took a deep breath and sighed slightly. "You were right *and* I was right."

It was about xenophobia and freedom.

"There's one other thing this could be." Graeme's tone turned a little grim. "A distraction."

"That is scarily possible, but a distraction from what?"

"Some more sophisticated attack. The talks themselves? Economics on Earth?" Graeme considered. "Texas is in drought again. They might have just decided to blame the offworlders."

Galyna laughed. "Isn't it always the offworlders, or whatever that generation's equivalent is. The difference is that *our* celestial influences can be talked to. Reasoned with."

"Have you met the verr ambassador yet? Ze's interesting."

"I haven't. They must have a completely different worldview."

"They do. They don't have *taxes*."

"They...what?"

"They don't have taxes," he repeated amused. "Which leaves only one inevitable thing in their lives."

"The ky'iin and tyrar..."

"They have taxes. Glyn have them, albeit a bit different, they're more paid in labor or work than money, like an old-fashioned cuvee, but they exist. Verr don't see them as necessary because their good and the good of the hive is one."

"They're..."

"Natural communists. For them it works because it works with their biology and their hierarchies." Graeme quirked his lips a little. "It may help them in trade."

"Apparently they have forged an alliance with the tyrar to build great ships," Galyna mused. "They provide the raw materials and the labor, the tyrar are handing over the plans."

"A large group of people who are coordinating through pheromones can build a starship faster than any of the rest of us." Graeme considered that. "But they're still individuals."

"I have to wonder how it feels. But I think my ancestors might know that."

Graeme rather thought she was right.

EARTH's planetary defenses were varied. The primary line of defense was to spot anything a good way out when a small nudge from an impactor could convince it to change orbit.

But there were secondary defenses too, some of them intended to protect against attacks.

The terrorists had not been bluffing. No, it was worse than that. They had *already thrown the rock*. It came at an angle, and killer satellites turned to face it. Graeme watched helplessly from Launchpad as they tried to deflect it.

It helped. Much of it was thrown into an orbit where it could be caught, but a small part remained on course, streaking towards Charlotte, North Carolina. It blew up in the air, blowing out windows and blowing down some clapboard homes. It could have been worse.

"Who would blow up Charlotte?"

"I don't know," Graeme said to Charles, the delay in their conversation reminding him that his family were safe and not. "Maybe their ex lived there."

Charles laughed. "I've had exes..."

"They're going to come back and try something worse. This was...not a warning shot."

"It was proof they aren't bluffing. Nobody was killed, at least."

"This time." Graeme sighed. "Not sure where..."

"It's about to be school vacation. Marion has been asking if she can go to the Outer Hebrides."

"Nobody's going to throw any rocks there," Graeme agreed. "I'm jealous. I'll *try* to join you if I can, but..." A pause. "I need to check on Slyk."

The glyn ambassador had barely needed his services as liaison, but that didn't mean he could completely neglect them, no matter how understandable the reasons.

Slyk did understand. He headed for the glyn's quarters. They were uncomfortably warm. Graeme was used to it, but still stripped down. He thought of taking off his shirt; not that the glyn would care, they didn't wear clothing anyway.

"Slyk?" he asked.

"Come in!" the glyn chimed.

Graeme came in and then *did* take off his shirt, with nobody to see but the glyn. Their homeworld was so warm they called Earth an ice planet, and not without reason. The heat was normal to them, and Slyk had to wear a blanket when out in human-rated temperatures.

The blanket was resting nearby. The glyn was reading something on a tablet, station issue.

"What are you reading?"

"The plans for the space elevator."

The tyrar had built one. And cheerfully sold Earth the materials science needed to finally create their own.

Of course it would be the tyrar. Only one known species was better at huge structures.

The glyn's forgotten ancestors.

16

THEY HAD ACTUALLY DONE IT.

A small rock, a small city. A demonstration that they would do it. And Kaykek had hardly missed the fact that they couldn't have stopped it when they sent the initial message. It had been a warning shot, of sorts, but also the opposite of a bluff. They would not stop.

They needed to be stopped.

Ze was not sure how to stop them, but they needed to be stopped.

So ze asked Alvi. Ze did not return to Refuge to do so, but simply used the comms to do so, trusting that they were reasonably secure.

"I am looking for them," the AI said in their oddly rich voice. "I am talking to the ships in system. We will find them."

"Thank you." Kaykek had had a nightmare that night, one ze had regularly. Ze dreamed about Verr breaking up.

Ze knew it was a sign of trauma, and ze had talked to people, but that shared trauma was never going to leave zir people. It would always be there in the back of everything they did, passed on to pups in the milk of queens.

Ze wondered if that was part of why ze had no desire to live on a planet.

Part, but not all. Some of it was that ze just wanted to keep moving, as a scout was supposed to. When the *hive* moved, ze got the best of both worlds. But some verr would never set foot on planets, some would choose to move in the void between the stars.

Ze took a deep breath. "I don't know what to do, Alvi. They're fighting over all kinds of things, and the next rock will be bigger and aimed at somewhere more important."

"Maybe the aliens should leave," Alvi said. "Fake leaving has worked before."

"We..." A pause. "Yes, we could. They'd have no way of knowing the council was still meeting. I'll bring it up as an interim measure. While the warrior types hunt these people down."

Whether ze would be listened to was another matter. "I just don't want..."

"None of us want that."

Alvi didn't have nightmares, as far as Kaykek could tell. Or dreams. Maybe that made them better off. Maybe it meant they were missing out. It wasn't fair in some direction or perhaps both, but then?

You could never enter into the consciousness of another. Telepathy did not exist, even if pheromones could make you feel a oneness with others.

Kaykek did not know what it was like to be the verr next to zir, let alone Alvi, let alone a human.

That was probably for the best. These varieties of viewpoints were like the workers in a hive. You listened to all of them and found consensus.

But there were a lot of arguments on the way.

THE ONLY THING Kaykek wanted to do after the talk with Alvi was go to the creche and snuggle with Tayken and the pups.

The only other thing ze wanted to do was get drunk on human booze. Some varieties of which were quite tasty.

The first option was out of reach right now; ze didn't really have the time. The second option was a wholly bad idea. For, mostly, the same reason. Ze had a meeting with the Martian representative (whom ze liked and who was teaching zir about human gender expression and identity) in...

...about long enough to get food.

Food. *That* was what ze really needed. Ze needed Tayken too, but food was a lot more accessible. Ze headed to the main canteen. The humans were starting to ignore zir, which ze considered a good thing. It meant they were used to zir alien presence and less likely to be uncomfortable about it.

Ze had the advantage of being able to eat human food pretty much as it was, as long as ze avoided chocolate, coffee, and a couple of berries that contained compounds toxic to verr.

But the canteen had plenty of options. It was ordinary human food, so nothing special, but it worked. Ze claimed a club sandwich, and found a table on zir own. Sometimes somebody would join zir. More often not.

Ze was not sure if it was because ze was an alien or because ze was an ambassador and thus a slight bit intimidating. Just a bit. Probably both.

But this time, company showed up. In the form of an aide to the representative from Venus, a young man who sat down, but had little to say. Ze glanced around and realized there were not that many open seats.

He just wanted to eat quietly, and ze was happy enough to let him. As it became clear conversation was not going to happen, ze pulled out zir tablet and started to look a few things up.

Tayken's poetry was attracting human readers and more interest. That was a good thing, Kaykek thought. Good for Tayken, who was appreciating it. But also good to show people that aliens could make art that would touch them, would be appreciated by them. Would be...

Art was one of the things that could bridge gaps between hives. It could bridge gaps between species too. With that in mind, ze opened zir ambassadorial account and purchased a number of classic human books. Alvi could translate them for zir.

Ze could gain even more understanding of humans. A lot of their stories seemed to revolve around mates and mating, understandable in their society. But there were definitely others too.

Ze was not sure when zir would have time to read them, but ze would find it. Somehow.

AFTER ZIR MEETING with Kai Bowie, who was wonderful as ever, Kaykek made zir way to the observation lounge. Ze could see stars, planets, *Refuge*. It was a beautiful view, even if part of her did not think ze should be there after the breach.

The terrorists had not shown back up. Perhaps they realized they were being hunted.

Perhaps they were...

Kaykek's whiskers drooped. There was something ze could not quite put zir finger on. Something ze was not thinking of.

One little yacht. One little rock. How big a rock could the yacht nudge?

The further away, the bigger the rock, but the longer it would take.

They probably couldn't do that big a rock. But if they could...

They would have to... Ze shuddered, because ze knew how they were doing it.

She called Alvi, right there, through her tablet. "Alvi."

"What?"

"What if they are *parking* rocks in suitable spots?"

"I thought of that, I'm looking. Part of the issue is that how would we know? How would we distinguish *their* rocks."

Kaykek deflated. "Unless they tag them somehow so *they* remember where they are, we wouldn't."

"Don't feel bad. It was a good idea."

"I guess I just want to do something."

"You are doing something. Your job. And talk to Tayken."

"I want to..."

"Just *talk* to her. Do a video call. You *can* come over, but tide yourself over until you have time."

Kaykek knew they were right. "How do you understand?"

"I don't. But I observe. Sometimes that has to be enough."

They were not organic. They did not fall in love. They did not have mates. Just friends. But friends were something...

"I think I'm making a human friend."

"That's good."

"Well, I..."

"You'll find ways to stay in touch, and if they make you the long-term representative..."

Was it a conflict of interest to be *friends* with Kai Bowie? Kaykek didn't think so, but the friendship might be damaged when they had to take opposing viewpoints.

But ze was not sure ze could *not* make friends with them. No, Ze could decide not to be friends with Kai. Ze would just regret it if ze did.

More than ze would regret *being* friends with them? Ze wasn't sure yet, and not making a decision was almost the same thing as being friends. Not making a decision moved them further down that path.

Ze could not worry about it.

Alvi finally spoke again. "There's another broadcast."

"Can you...no. Let me get to my quarters."

Ze did not think it wise to watch it in public.

Ze did not think that was wise at all.

17

"You have now seen that we are serious. No aliens should be in the sol system."

That was not something anyone could police, Dhyanil thought wryly, especially if they wanted to claim all the way out to the uncertain boundary of the heliopause.

Space was big. Even a single solar system was big. Or they would have found these people by now, for sure. They would have found them and hunted them down and maybe killed them.

Dhyanil was not sure about killing them. It might create a martyr; a thing with humans as much as with ky'iin. Both species would rally around the dead under the right circumstances, which was likely strange to others.

Of course, to the glyn, "dead" didn't even mean the same thing. But the verr did not rally around the dead, neither did the tyrar. Just the predators. There was a pattern there that might help them learn about others, for others *were* out there. It was mathematically impossible for them not to be.

"If they all leave, there will be no further attacks. If even one remains...on Earth or off it..."

Dhyanil knew they meant him, the only alien to have lived *on* Earth for an extended period of time. He might well not be the last. The ironic thing was that the treaty *did* give them ownership of their own solar system. Legally, they could ask everyone to leave, *if* they represented their planet. They didn't.

Practically, it was just unenforceable. The rules were aimed at protecting and ensuring the ownership of *planets*, not random empty space between them. He wondered if the military signals intelligence people were having any luck tracing it.

It was video this time. The speaker was an older human male with heavy facial hair. Most human males removed that particular secondary sexual characteristic, but some chose not to. It probably meant something. It certainly did to *some* humans. Not all of them, but some. He was going on at some length now about how aliens were not made in the image of God.

Well, obviously not, species either made God in their own image or chose a God that worked for them, depending on whether one believed God was real.

Dhyanil didn't, but respected those who still held that the void of night was more than empty space, that it contained a consciousness and awareness that was part of the primordial awareness of the universe.

It wasn't scientific, but it wasn't harmful either. Human religion, though, seemed to too often be a source of harm. Made in the image of God. An excuse to explain their own dominance. The ky'iin did not need that. The verr hadn't even *been* dominant, just better at surviving than the other sentient species on their planet.

Dhyanil turned the broadcast off. He had heard all he needed to hear and saw no reason to inflict more of this on himself. Ky'iin isolationists feared cultural influence. So did most human ones; he'd read what they had to say. These people were religious fanatics.

This was not something he knew how do deal with. It was not a ky'iin thing.

It never had been.

THEY HAD TRACED THE BROADCAST, but the yacht was gone by the time anyone got there. Which told Dhyanil for sure that they had gone FTL.

And had a competent enough pilot to be sure of getting back again. That probably told the spies something, even gave them another lead.

Dhyanil wasn't technically a spy. But at the same time?

He *did* know how people like this thought. So, where had they gone?

He frowned, touched the intercom. He spoke English, which he still struggled with pronunciation on...a ky'iin maw was not made to generate human linguistic sounds...but which was easier for intercoms. "Mr. Marlowe?"

"Yes."

"It's Dhyanil. I have a theory."

"Which is..."

"That they have not left the solar system."

"A micro jump." Dhyanil could see Graeme's face crinkle into a human frown in his mind's eye.

"They think," Dhyanil said, "of the solar system as humanity's exclusive territory. And from what little I know about their religion, it includes the concept of a place of punishment from which demons come. Which they define as outer space, I suspect."

"That's..." A pause. "The solar system is still a big place."

"It is. I wish I could be more helpful. But I wanted to run it past somebody."

"Of course, they're also using a ky'iin ship. Which would also be evil."

"There aren't any human starships of that size available for purchase. I suspect it's a case of..."

"Using the Devil's tools because they are the only tools available. Or they're lying."

"And aren't religious fanatics at all. In which case they could be anywhere."

It hadn't been worth it.

"But it does make me think of some things. Thank you, Dhyanil."

He hung up, and Dhyanil picked up his tablet again.

He had read up quite a bit on human religion, especially as some of them *did* think the ky'iin were, rather obviously, servants of an evil deity. It wasn't an unreasonable conclusion to come to. After all, some ky'iin had used the Void as an excuse for their treatment of tyrar. They were prey, thus the Void had put them there to be exploited.

Stupid attitude, and just an excuse.

So.

What if they *weren't* religious fanatics after all? He wanted to get a look at what was going on in that yacht.

There had been a video, so there were...

...and now his mind was getting even more suspicious, and probably going down rabbit holes. That was a sign it was time to stop and get something to drink. A mildly alcoholic beverage was just what he needed to relax and get his brain to stop churning. It was beer, which he had developed a taste for.

Humans were *excellent* at alcoholic beverages.

THE NEXT DAY, the talks lasted for hours and achieved nothing. This was not unusual. They were wrangling details.

Lots and lots of details.

Details that even went into, on a couple of occasions, the treatment of non-sapient animals. Also, one of the human delegates wanted to discuss reproductive rights.

These had to be internal matters...because the glyn immediately pointed out that "We all have different reproductive strategies. Let's keep that off the table so we aren't morally judging other people's biology."

Dhyanil found it hard not to morally judge the glyn over what they did with surplus eggs, but he also understood the biological forces behind it. You could not raise two or three hundred offspring at a time.

"I agree with the glyn. This has to be an internal manner."

The human delegate said, "And what about reproductive coercion."

"Any civilized species..."

"Not all humans. And I am sure..."

Dhyanil thought of an attempted rape he had witnessed not long before his involuntary exile. "Rape is a crime," he said simply. "We can agree on that, I think. But it may not be defined the same way."

Kaykek finally spoke up quietly, "It is not. As civilized people I think we can agree that sexual assault and reproductive coercion are wrong. But I am verr. Queens have a *job*. And we are changing. We don't need another species to tell us..."

They finally agreed to table it. Then the tyrar delegate, Viary, brought up something else. "Solar system territory. In the original base treaty. What if there are two systems so close together that the heliopauses overlap and they are claimed by different species."

It was a great question to get everyone back on topic, but by lunchtime Dhyanil still had that vague headache that came from working harder than he wanted to, and there were hours yet to go.

He wanted to use the spycraft as an excuse to leave. But he couldn't. Not right now.

This was the job he was really here for, until they got somebody better trained and then he could go back to hunting terrorists.

Kaykek, of all people, gave him what he recognized as an encouraging look before they plunged into arguments about overlapping heliopauses. At least there was no emotion on this one. It hadn't come up. It was an academic argument.

True, the heliopauses were close between Sol and Proxima Centauri, but that system lacked great real estate and the humans would probably just use it for mining anyway. Nobody else wanted it. But in the future? Who knew what would happen.

Not him, that was for sure.

18

VIARY CAME BACK to the herd's quarters that evening with a headache. Beverly and Yoshi had spent the day running numbers they had been sent by ansible from tyrar. The mushrooms were doing a good job, as far as they could tell from here.

They might be in another solar system. Science still had to happen. But when Viary dragged himself in, they stopped and Yoshi gave him a big hug. "Bad session?"

"Just more stupid arguments. I got them back on track, but inter-species diplomacy is harder than I thought it would be," he admitted.

Beverly rolled into the kitchenette to get him some tea, which he clearly needed. While she was at it, she poured mugs for herself and Yoshi too, although she brought Viary's first.

He need it more. He took it, wrapping slate-furred hands around it while she retrieved Yoshi's and then her own.

She sipped at it. "I think Parvati is the only one without a tired brain."

Which practically summoned her. Or, more likely. "I smell tea." She went to get some for herself, then joined them.

"Not fair," Viary said, "You..."

"I have not been chilling. I have been talking to Graeme, as Slyk didn't need him today. I was lending my security expertise. But you guys definitely look more tired than I feel."

They kind of drifted together. "Viary had to do with arguments about..."

"Whether we need to put something in the constitution about reproductive coercion, which hit the rock of the verr."

"They can't afford not to have their queens breeding right now," Beverly mused. "But..."

"Kaykek feels the same way, but putting it in the constitution would be a strong protection. And then there's the glyn. Rock of biology, I suppose. You?"

"Sulphur wind-down levels and that lake near Omora that's been causing the locals problem," Beverly said. "It's a nightmare and if we ever get back to Tyranis we might want to go over and chat with them."

"So...there's one cure for everyone having tired brains," Yoshi said, then grinned slightly, and activated the big screen. "Human or tyrar."

"Oh, I have a good one," Beverly said. "It's so bad you won't be able to stop laughing. Late twentieth century monster swarm movie."

"Tell me it has awful special effects," Viary quipped.

"Oh, the worst."

"Queue it up!" Parvati said. "I'll get the popcorn."

One human thing that the tyrar seemed to universally like was popcorn. It seemed to fit with their herbivorous diet.

And Beverly was decidedly fond of popcorn herself, so it worked.

About an hour into the truly awful movie, the alarms went off.

THEIR QUARTERS WERE in a shelter area, but Beverly paused the movie. They sat, listening. Then the entire station shook.

"That was a hit," Parvati said in the oddly matter-of-fact style she tended to use when under fire. She reached for her prosthetic foot, which she had removed for comfort, and resecured it quickly.

Once on, it wasn't really visible. They were working on designs that the wearer would not even notice, for tyrar. They already had them for humans.

It was one of the trade goods, that. But at the same time, Parvati was not sure she wanted one. She saw her injury as a badge of honor, after all.

Beverly glanced at the others. Exhausted as they all were. "I doubt we're needed."

"Unless they have to evacuate the station," Parvati said with that same calm. "We have emergency suits in the locker." Yoshi nodded.

She moved to get them while Parvati finished messing with her foot and stood up. Then the herd was in motion, helping Beverly into her suit before donning their own. It didn't take long. They had practiced this, drilled it, but they still stayed in the suite.

For now.

It was a shelter area, it was a safe place, but Beverly badly wanted to know what was going on.

The station shook a second time, and then the artificial gravity went out. She floated upwards a little, but there was no violence to it. Except that wheelchairs don't work in zero G at all. Nothing with wheels works well without friction.

Yoshi and Parvati had her, stabilizing her. She could probably leave the chair, but she didn't want to risk abandoning it. A good chair was not something you left behind, ever. It was something that you kept as a part of you.

Besides. Gravity would likely come back at any moment, and then she would need it.

Then the intercom sounded. "Are you all okay?"

"We're fine," Beverly said, as the one with the best English. "No gravity, but we're fine."

"Keep moving. The air vents are out too."

Beverly ditched the chair at that point. If they didn't move, then the carbon dioxide of their own breath would gather around their heads and suffocate them. That was also part of the drill, part of what you had to think about when you spent time in space. "What happened?"

"What *happened* is that one of our own ships went rogue."

That...was a bad scenario. "And?"

"*Refuge* beat them up some, that AI can shoot very straight, and they fled."

But a rogue... "An *EarthForce* ship went rogue?"

"The EFS *Columbia*."

They had to be stopped.

And that probably meant that they had to be destroyed.

THERE WAS the faint distant clanging of repairs. None of them felt like turning the movie back on. Instead, they raided Beverly's stash of vodka then just slept in a pile in the middle of their quarters, one human and three tyrar breathing in surprising synchrony.

The next day, Viary headed towards the council as normal, but Parvati went with him. Not to be a bodyguard but because he was tense enough that even a few hours alone could cause herdsickness to set in.

That left Beverly unable to leave Yoshi for the same reason. Neither of them felt up to science. Neither of them felt up to anything except the worst possible thing to do, going over and over in their minds, talking about what had happened. They knew they shouldn't, but Beverly wasn't able to break that cycle.

Launchpad could have been destroyed. And an EarthForce ship was rogue. In some ways this was worse than all that had happened on Tyranis, because it was more...personal, somehow.

No, that was unfair. It was her world having these issues now and that *did* make them more intimate and real, but the stakes weren't nearly as high.

Nobody was poisoning Earth's atmosphere. Earth was not going to split at the seams like the verr homeworld.

"So, why does this feel worse?" she said out loud. "Than Tyranis, than Verr..."

"Because," Yoshi murmured, "We're a bit too aware of how thin the hull is right now."

"You definitely have a point there. So. We can't sit around and mope all day."

"No, but doing anything else would involve moving." Yoshi was draped across the couch like a sapient fur rug. Shedding on it, of course.

"It would," Beverly mused. "But it would be good for us. Come on. Let's go to the cafe."

Such as it was.

"Whatever we do for a permanent council location has to have better food and beverage options."

Beverly grinned weakly. "It will." She couldn't promise that. "Any humans or glyn involved will make sure of that."

"I think I heard Slyk talking about juice bars."

"Glyn get mildly high off of sugar the way kids are supposed to but really don't. They are fond of mixed fruit juices and of juices and berries of all kinds, I hear."

"I wouldn't mind a juice bar too."

"I think that with reasonable precautions that would work for all species."

"Alcohol works for everyone, so far," Yoshi mused. "Even glyn."

"Ah, but the rest of you are missing out on..."

...and when Beverly got to the cafe she ordered hot chocolate. Which was unfair on the tyrar, but after last night she needed it.

She needed it badly.

19

GRAEME WAS SEEING red in a way he almost never did. He prided himself on his equilibrium, but this...this felt personal. He ran the sensor log again, holographically projected into a 3D map in the Commander's conference room. She wasn't exactly amused either.

The EFS *Columbia* had attacked Launchpad and then fled. It had done quite a bit of damage, slicing through point defense systems that had automatically recognized it as friendly in the IFF systems.

The *Columbia* was listed as being under the command of Nicholas Aw, a native of Singapore. Not Great America, then, unless they had spread their recruiting.

Or unless Aw had been the victim of a mutiny. Looking at the crew, that seemed somewhat unlikely. The entire crew?

Who knew what had been said to them. If you weren't on the bridge you didn't know what was going on on the bridge. And pretty much anything could be faked unless you looked outside. Which you typically didn't.

Taking over a starship wasn't easy, but it was *possible* that only a few people on board the *Columbia* had rebelled.

It did not matter. They would try not to destroy the ship...but they might have no choice. Its next step might be to attack another world's facilities to start a war. No.

If that was the plan, they would have done that first, *before* attacking Launchpad. They would have led with that and watched the diplomatic confusion. No.

The goal had been to destroy Launchpad and perhaps to start a war *that* way, through the deaths of the delegates, but they had shown...

...less competence.

Could the *Columbia* have been *stolen*? If so, nobody had heard from Aw or anyone else, if they had been put ashore somewhere. Of course, there were automated outposts where you could maroon somebody. Or more likely just kill them.

Nicholas Aw.

He turned off the holo and pulled up the man's face. A mixture of Han and Malay. Slightly long hair, touching his collar. In his forties. A solid commander. The *Columbia* was FTL capable but had been built primarily for system defense.

They were building more of it. In fact, they were building another of the class right now at the smaller construction bay. Graeme frowned. Pulled up the ship's status.

Not close to spaceworthy, but the hull was in place, the basic layout set. He could get an impression of what the *Columbia* was like.

He'd need an EVA suit.

But he'd done far worse. This wouldn't be dangerous, just annoying. If he could get permission.

If he could explain to the construction workers *why* he wanted to do this.

That would be hard, as he could not even explain it to himself.

THE HALF-FINISHED STARSHIP, not yet named, was empty. It was not silent, no, or rather Graeme's suit was not silent. There was the faint, slight hum of its backpack life support system, vibrating through the suit. More felt than heard in the silence of space.

It was a framework of a ship, but there was security at every possible entrance point and even somebody in what would be engineering.

No singularity yet, of course. That came *after* launch, in case the singularity breeding process went wrong. He nodded to the suited worker.

"So, what are you looking for, Graeme?"

"I am assessing how easy it would be to take this layout and how many people you might need for it," he said, finally. "So far, I'm thinking a small team could do it."

"The crew..."

"The crew were well trained, yes. They should have been able to prevent a hijacking. A mutiny, obviously, would be tougher."

"Or Aw is a traitor."

"Or that. It doesn't seem to fit, though. Two wives in Singapore, three children, no gambling debts. I can't see any motivation."

"Somebody should talk to the wives. They might see one we missed."

Graeme felt sorry for the women even if they had each other. He didn't understand polyamory, but it appeared the relationship was a true triad, not a "greedy guy having more than one wife."

Still wasn't legal everywhere, that, although things were slowly changing. "Somebody should."

That wasn't his job, though. His *job* was supposed to be making sure Slyk navigated everything okay, and he needed to get back to that job before the glyn left the meeting.

Slyk was enjoying themselves. They *liked* arguing and discussing, which was part of why they were the glyn representative.

It was the opposite of the normal theory of the last person you wanted in charge being the one who wanted to be there. But...Slyk didn't want power. They wanted to negotiate. They didn't even mind that much when they lost.

Graeme headed back to the airlock. A team of six could take the ship. Three if it was empty at the time, but it hadn't been. But they would have needed some advantage on the crew. He thought of asking Dhyanil, but the former freedom fighter had never been involved in anything like that.

Who had?

A thought hit him, but he had to retrieve SLyk first and make sure the glyn ate something. They had a habit of forgetting. But he did know somebody who knew somebody.

KAYKEK WAS IN ZIR QUARTERS. Ze looked quite surprised to see Graeme, but let him in.

The furniture was rearranged for verr, but there was a seat he could use nonetheless, a little low, but it would work.

"So, you need something?"

"Your people captured a ky'iin frigate."

"We did."

"I would like to ask the people who did it how they did it."

"You think that your rogue ship got hijacked." Zir's whiskers curled. "Is that real or are people..."

"*Can* verr go rogue?"

"Of course. We're individuals, even if we do have a drive for the good of the hive. But typically when a verr goes rogue like that, they think it *is* for the good of the hive."

"Well, these people might think that too."

"They might. But I can get your questions to them. I can also ask Alvi. They can run simulations."

"Would they be willing?"

"They had to fire on it, and they're not happy about that. Also, you can get Alvi to do almost anything for a human detective novel they haven't read."

Graeme laughed. "Your AI is addicted to Sherlock Holmes?"

"And Miss Marple, and Poirot, and...yes, they are."

"A tyrar AI working for the verr who likes human mysteries. That's...the future I want to live in," Graeme admitted. "Do verr have detective novels?"

"Yes, but humans seem to have mastered the art, at least according to Alvi. They think verr are better at comedy."

"Verr comedy. You'll have to recommend me some."

Of course, that was the opinion of one being that might or might not have taste close to Graeme's...or more accurately Charles'. He might like some Verr comedy.

"So, I can ask them."

"Do *you* have an opinion?"

Kaykek hesitated, then produced a bag of nuts from somewhere, popped a couple in zir mouth and then offered Graeme the bag.

He was about to ask if they were safe when he realized they were, in fact, walnuts. He took a couple, ate them while he waited for zir to respond.

"I think it's more likely an inside job. That's the phrase, right?"

"It is. We don't think the commander is a likely suspect."

"But mutiny seems more likely than hijacking."

"I agree. I suppose I'm living in hope that EarthForce people didn't do this. That they're loyal."

"They're still," the verr pointed out, reaching for another nut. "People."

Ze popped it into zir mouth.

20

KAYKEK SENT a message to the survivors from the raid on the frigate. Then ze turned over in zir mind what Graeme had said.

He didn't think it was the commander. He didn't think it was the commander because the man had *two* preferred mates (very common for verr, but unusual amongst the normally monogamous humans), several offspring and no history of anything that would make him vulnerable to blackmail.

Ze had to admit that Tayken was a strong motivation...unless. Unless this Aw thought he was helping or protecting his mates and children. Unless that. Humans would do a lot for their kids, just like ze would.

The fact that the majority of humans were fertile didn't change that. Well, it might make them less likely to protect other people's kids, but that didn't seem to be the case. All children were valuable. They might disagree on *how* to protect them or what from, but humans were strongly protective of those not considered old enough to make all of their own decisions yet.

As were verr. As were glyn. As were...it was a universal desire, if one which might vary in the details.

So.

Ze put the nuts ze had bought from a human away. They were delicious, and a potential trade good. Walnuts. Ze was going to remember walnuts. The seeds of the trees might be too, if they would grow in Refuge's parks or on Kyverr.

Ze was going to let Tayken try them and see what she had to say on the matter. Still. Then the alarm went off again.

Ze was tired of this. Ze retrieved zir suit, which ze had brought from *Refuge*. Ze hoped not to need it, but ze was not going to risk *not* having it if there was a breach.

The station shook again. No doubt the rogue ship was back.

This couldn't continue.

Ze had some ideas for how to stop it. But for right now, ze couldn't act on them.

Ze put on the suit. It was not as unpleasantly heavy as the surface suits they had used to protect themselves from the wind on Verr; it was a much more sophisticated design.

Ze still hated it. It felt like it pressed down on zir fur uncomfortably.

But it was a reasonable precaution. Then Alvi's voice, "Are you alright?"

"I'm in my quarters."

"Stay there. There's a breach near you."

Ze had not noticed any loss of atmosphere, but "stay there" seemed more than reasonable. So, ze did.

"I THINK we should move this to the planet," the Earth representative was saying.

"And have a rock dropped on us?" That was Kai Bowie, the Martian, and there was something snide; a memory of the Martian War of Independence, perhaps.

Kaykek closed zir eyes for a moment. Ze preferred to stay quiet and save speaking for when verr interests most needed it. But...

"I have a better idea," ze chittered softly. "Accept *our* hospitality."

"And..."

"Refuge *moves*. And while our jump wake is substantial, Alvi has some expertise at avoiding pursuit. If things get too hot, you will be in a place which can, at least to a point, *dodge*."

"He has a point," the Earth representative said.

"Ze," Bowie corrected before Kaykek could say anything, glaring at their rival.

Kaykek's ears flattened. Bowie was more offended on zir behalf than ze was.

"Apologies," Chan said and gave Kaykek a slight bow.

It was not the first time Chan had accused zir of being a drone. Ze was pretty sure it was an accident, solely because he had not used the wrong pronouns to refer to Bowie.

Or perhaps Bowie had drilled him on them before this even started and made many, many points about which pronouns to use.

Slyk chimed, the translation a moment later, "I think I agree with the delegate of Verr. *Refuge* would be a good venue. They certainly have the space."

Chan templed his hands. It was clear he didn't like it. "The point..."

"We are on a *human* station now. Not a neutral location," Kaykek pointed out. "Furthermore, by removing to Refuge, we can make it look to the terrorists as if we left, without ever actually breaking off negotiations. I am *not* trying to get an advantage here."

"Ze's right," Viary said, thoughtfully. "While Refuge isn't a neutral location, it's a mobile one. Honestly, I tried to say we should do this on a large ship."

"And were thought paranoid." Chan finally subsided. "How long will it take to set things up there? Some people here..." He glanced at Bowie and Viary. "Might have issues with verr furniture."

Chan himself was short for a human male, but...

"Not long. Workers will set up furniture in a suitable room and we can move people to make quarters."

"I know that that is a translation of a biological term," the representative from Venus said, "But I am..." A pause. "I am uncomfortable with your caste system, which I know I should get over, but..."

"I understand. Perhaps when we are on Refuge, I can introduce you to some people."

Kaykek knew the history...that there had been a period when light skinned humans had enslaved dark skinned humans and that there were still quite a few people who bizarrely thought the light skinned ones superior.

Verr hives tended to run to a specific fur shade, but even that was only a tendency, especially right now with people moving around.

"I...would appreciate that."

"So, it's decided then?" Bowie asked. "Let's get moving on this."

They were often the quiet leader of the group.

Chan, on the other hand, seemed to *think* he was in charge.

KAYKEK TOOK it on zirself to talk to Olanwerulu.

"Call me Adwoa," the tall woman said.

"Did I mangle it that badly?"

Adwoa laughed. "No, you did better than most, I thought you might appreciate fewer syllables."

"I do."

"So..."

"Refuge is a tyrar greatship refitted to house a small verr hive. Our initial purpose was to secure a viable population and find a colony world. More recently, we have been transporting significant numbers from Verr system to Kyverr."

"But you are a hive?"

"A smaller one, but yes. We have queens and drones, we have children...including my own preferred mate's children."

"So, you are..."

"I am a scout. I am not their father, but I am in a sense a third parent. Biologically. And their biological father is not in this hive."

"So you *are* their father." Adwoa smiled. "How many?"

"Three."

"And they will be workers."

"Everyone is a worker unless they change." Kaykek waved a paw at a couple of techs.

"Which..."

"Which is arriving in your head as a subcaste, isn't it."

"Sub...yes. Yes, it is."

Kaykek shook zir head. "The vast majority of us are workers. The most experienced in their jobs. We value elders, and it is the old who lead us, assuming competence."

"Gerontocracy."

That was an odd word, but Kaykek thought ze got the gist of it. "Queens and drones, the breeders, are expected to devote most of their energy to raising and teaching the children, but that doesn't mean they don't do other stuff. Now we aren't in desperate survival mode, we're...giving them more freedoms."

"So it's the *breeders* who are curtailed. And...purdahed."

"They spend most of their time in the creche. It's the safest place on the ship, safer than the bridge."

"Because it's also where you keep the kids."

"The breeders are valuable. The kids...are also valuable. Of course we want them to be safe. But Tayken, my preferred mate, is also..."

"Wait. Tayken. The poet is your girlfriend?"

Not exactly, but Kaykek didn't want to correct her. "You..."

"I have seen...I would...you would owe me if I could meet her. Perhaps get her to...read?"

An idea came into Kaykek's head. "I will talk to her about it. I need permission to take you into the creche, but you certainly don't seem like a threat."

But Kaykek had a better idea. A bit of entertainment for the delegates. Kaykek added, "The queens and drones initially chosen for Refuge were chosen because they had other skills too. A number of them are scientists."

"So, not reproductive slavery then...but your reaction."

"Our customs are biological. Only a small number of us can breed. But one of the things we are studying is suppressing and inducing puberty."

"Giving people the choice. And then..."

"There are scouts, like me, who are neither male nor female. Then there are the warriors, who look like queens and drones, but don't breed."

"They protect the hive."

"In survival mode, we weren't producing scouts...and the warriors were coming out a bit off, so we thought..."

"You thought they were infertile breeders." A pause. "You are not what I thought. You are slaves, yes, but to your biology."

"Aren't we all?"

21

DHYANIL HAD NEVER EXPECTED to leave Kyx. Never expected to see Earth.

Never expected to be walking along a corridor in a tyrar greatship. Of course, it had been refitted by the verr. It smelled.

Not an unpleasant smell. Not even that *strong* a smell. A little bit wet fur, a little bit petrichor, a little bit musk.

Pheromones, some of it, and some of it just the simple smell of verr. Cleaning or filtering the air would affect the hive's communication. The bond that kept the verr together.

Dhyanil knew he would get used to it with time, probably not even that much time. His brain would tune it out as background scent.

But right now it was a reminder that this was no longer a tyrar ship. It was still built to tyrar specifications, though. That is to say, huge. The smallest adult tyrar was about the size of a large woman.

Tyrar were big. Verr were small. It gave it less of a warren feel and more one of things not being quite in place. No doubt when the verr built their own colony ships they would make the corridors a bit more reasonable and comfortable tor their size.

For now, the two verr that scurried past wearing tool belts and chittering at each other looked like children, or the legendary halflings...which had existed only on an island but had somehow found their way all the way across human mythology. Little people.

Rats in the walls.

Having seen a rat, Dhyanil understood the comparison. He did not understand why a human or two had used it as an insult.

The rats he had seen and handled had been friendly, clean, affectionate pets.

But apparently wild rats carried some pretty nasty diseases, so no doubt that was the root of it.

That and the syllable verr was the same as the first syllable, in a primary human language, of the word for a worthless pest.

Ironic given the verr were how he could talk to Graeme without Graeme trying to strangle him and him possibly hurting the human defending himself.

They were going to have him and Graeme...who was on board as liaison and company to the glyn...test the pheromone perfume they were developing. In medbay, in an isolation room so they could be sure it was not stray pheromones from *Refuge*'s two scouts.

Of course, if only being on the hive ship worked then...now that was an idea, but it would give a lot to the verr.

A lot to them, but in some ways, they deserved it.

IF *REFUGE* WAS MOVING, Dhyanil did not feel it. Not like a smaller ship where there was always faint vibration under one's feet.

Refuge was a small world, not a ship, but it was perfectly capable of traveling through hyperspace. Not *quickly*, no, not at this size. But it could. He knew that they did plan on moving some, away from Launchpad and the vulnerable construction work. Nobody wanted to have to build a Launchpad III any time soon.

And away from the orbiting resorts and hotels, which had been broached as a site, but turned down for security reasons. Not so much safety as keeping paparazzi and citizen journalists out. The delegates would have been unable to move for them. Launchpad had more controlled access.

Now there was no access, but it was necessary. Unfortunate. A few press people were being allowed to tag along to ensure that humans had the information they craved. Humans believed in free information.

Necessary.

Refuge, as Verr had mentioned, could *dodge*. They had taken on large amounts of supplies. The verr, after all, could eat most of anything that was left, and they could always send the chocolate back.

Apparently they were all missing out on chocolate. It was the food of the gods or something. How could humans eat so much toxic stuff? The verr weren't far behind. Dhyanil envied them a little.

On the other hand, Earth offered some fantastic fish, even now after the environmental disasters and remediation. Delicious, delicious fresh fish. That was the...

But this ship was huge.

Maybe they could actually farm fish on it, if they found the right ones. The verr no doubt hadn't thought of it; their world had lost its oceans generations ago. He would have to find somebody to suggest it to. It could only do the verr good to add to their diet, after all; like most omnivores they needed variety.

As fresh fish was utterly out of reach and would be for a while, he headed to the canteen set up for the delegates. It still didn't feel as if he was on a ship. The canteen didn't, of course, have fresh fish, and the meat was vat grown. Vat grown meat would keep him healthy, but it had always had a faint aftertaste he was assured was all in his head.

It didn't matter whether it was or not. It was real to him. But it was needed, he'd rather the vat meat than pills. He did take some other stuff, glanced around. No humans present. But the glyn ambassador was sitting in a corner sucking up juice through their mandibles. Glyn were a little disturbing in appearance.

He hadn't managed to catch them alone. This might be a good opportunity.

SLYK LOOKED up as Dhyanil came over. "Hello," the glyn chimed.

They vocalized by rubbing bits of exoskeleton against each other like some insects, and it sounded musical before their translator took over.

"Are you settling in?" There was no sign of the human liaison right now.

"Well enough. The verr are being generous, but no doubt will get advantage from it."

"Given where they start from..."

Slyk's wings were folded into their carapace, but Dhyanil was still sure they drooped. "We are not doing much better."

"Your problem is fixable?"

"And being fixed. The verr...none of the ones I have talked to ever want to live on a planet again. Some of them..."

Dhyanil shuddered. "They saved most of the population, but traumatized them in the process. If being afraid of planets is the only impact, they're lucky."

"Truth." The glyn considered. "We have more to do than stabilize Glen."

"I feel as if my species are the most fortunate. Well, until the next ice age, anyway."

"Which you have handled before and will handle again. You *are* fortunate...although I don't envy that." Slyk pointed with a forelimb at the vat meat.

Dhyanil sighed a bit and tucked in. "I was just thinking that diet-wise it would be nice to be a human."

"Or maybe a verr."

"Human. They have the most insane toxin tolerance. Have you tried some of the things they eat for *pleasure*?"

"You mean...the little red fruits."

"I do mean the little red fruits."

Slyk chimed laughter. "I don't have taste receptors for whatever that is."

"Well, I do, and it hurts."

"I think that's actually why they do it. It is like exercising to the limit."

"Or chasing a tricky prey. I think I can get that, but they can keep the little red fruits. Or yellow. Or green. Or whatever color they are."

They seemed to come in all of them.

"In any case, I don't notice it, which makes eating them pointless. There are sweet ones, though."

"I tried those. Those are not bad at all. Where did you get that juice?"

There was a slight vibration.

Now, Dhyanil was sure that *Refuge* was moving. He did not know where.

He did not need to know. When the entire world moves, what is location? He wasn't sure. But he did know that this felt safer than a static station with only low powered orbit adjustment thrusters.

Much safer.

It could dodge.

22

REFUGE WAS in many ways more comfortable than Launchpad. They might have displaced some verr into less comfortable quarters, which Beverly felt somewhat bad about. But the ship was built to tyrar scale, which she had become used to on Tyranis. It felt better.

She had really gone native. She brushed out her hair and felt the slight vibration that, no doubt, indicated that the ship was moving. Very slight.

Not like the smaller courier that had brought them from tyrar. Everyone had more ships than Earth, but Earth was catching up.

Now she was on a tyrar great ship converted to a verr hive. It was an interesting situation. She would get to see how they lived, which did interest her, although no doubt they wouldn't let her or anyone else near the precious creche.

She had a new tablet that accessed the ship's systems, most especially the *map*. It would be so easy to get lost on this ship. So easy to get very, very lost. She also had access to the ship's mind. AI wasn't the word she wanted to use; AI had been so watered down. Alvi was definitely an AGI or artificial sentient. They had welcomed her on board in a voice that sounded tyrar, but spoke fluent English. The pronoun they used was one used by tyrar non-binary people.

AIs could be any gender they wanted, she supposed. It wasn't like they had a biological sex to worry about.

(Sex androids? They'd been considered, but there were too many ethical concerns to make one, although she supposed an AI could choose to have a fully functional body).

She spoke now, "Alvi?"

"Yes, Beverly."

"Am I disturbing you?"

"I have enough processing power right now."

She thought she heard a smile in that voice. "Did we displace people?"

"No, those are transient quarters."

"Oh, thank goodness, I was feeling bad."

"We are actually interested in what humans need so that if necessary..."

"I can talk to people about that." And get accessibility built in. She had yet to see a disabled verr, but she had no doubt they existed.

"Thank you, Dr. Marlowe."

"Beverly," she corrected. "I don't see any need to be formal."

"So, what did you need? Just that?"

"I think so for now. Thank you."

She turned towards the door. "I'm going to check out the dining area."

She got a couple of grunts, one from Yoshi, the other from Parvati. Both had their snouts buried in work. Outside in the corridor, she followed the map on her tablet, balancing it on her lap as she made her way. A verr worker chitter-squeaked something at her.

"Hello," she responded. They didn't have translation turned on. Probably simply forgot they had the option.

But they didn't need a common language to exchange greetings.

THE DINING AREA was a mixed crowd. There were indeed verr, one of whom had grey fur and a limp and was accompanied by a younger worker. That had to be very strange. To reach old age without ever having gone through puberty. But then, it wasn't strange to them. Graeme was sitting at a table with the Venusian representative. She elected not to disturb them for now, but headed for the counter.

The food was labeled by which species it was suitable for in several languages and Beverly smiled. That was a nice touch. She was able to fill a plate without worrying about whether she would be spending a long time in the bathroom that night. Most of it was probably synthetic or vat grown, certainly the meat was. Dhyanil was sitting in a corner. She hadn't even noticed him.

Probably the verr pheromones. That solved a lot of problems. What if?

The ship vibrated a little bit again. She found a table on her own and sampled the food, cautiously. It wasn't terrible. Some of it *was* fresh, taken on on Earth. But even what clearly wasn't, wasn't bad. The verr ate well. But then, this wasn't a station where people worked. It was a ship where people lived. It was a *town*.

One of the verr came over to her, chittered. Then messed with their tablet. "Sorry. Hello."

"Hello."

The verr hesitated. "Can I join you?"

"Of course."

She hadn't been avoiding company so much as not wanting to sit with the ky'iin, just in case the proximity set her off. "What's your name?"

"Pirkek."

"Beverly," she introduced.

"You are an aide to Viary?"

"More like...a family member who got dragged along. What do you do?"

"I'm a cook."

"Well, thank you. The food is good."

"It's..."

"I know it's institutional food. It's good."

She swore the verr's whiskers curled upwards. No, wait, they did, or rather the base of them lifted inwards.

That was a smile. "Thank you," it said.

"Thank you for even having us on board."

"We want to make sure that you can do your job. Get frameworks so it's easier..."

"I'm sure you want more than one planet."

"Those of us who still like planets."

Beverly envisioned an entire flotilla of verr ships, just moving from place to place, never putting down roots.

People, at least human people, had always had a conflict between the nomads and the settled.

Even if the nomads were...

Perhaps especially if the nomads were...

She thought of the decades and centuries of antisemitism and antiziganism and knew the verr had to be protected if that was the life many of them chose.

Especially from humans.

23

THE SHIP WAS FANTASTIC.

Graeme, of course, had seen building on a much greater scale, but this was so much more human and feasible that he was, in some ways, more impressed.

People could build this. People had built Glen. But that level of technology was so far from what he knew that it felt like magic. Like Arthur C. Clarke's old saying.

They were still *people*, but he couldn't relate to them. Couldn't understand them. He could get his mind around the tyrar easily. Just cross a horse with Bigfoot and give them human level intelligence, and you got a tyrar.

As for the verr, they were science fiction ratkin with a hive mind. He'd played a few games of *D&D* as a kid, and liked ratkin. They also seemed so...

Nice wasn't the word he was looking for.

Open.

He knew one of their hives had gone full blown fascist. And he was pretty sure that *Refuge* was self-selected for the least xenophobic verr. But as he explored the ship, he learned more about them. He found a dining area and shared a meal with Adwoa that was not even all about business. He also saw Dr. Marlowe there.

He understood her in the most general sense, a dedicated scientist. After that, he continued to explore. He paid attention to any place the verr clearly did not want him to go.

This area of the ship appeared to be the part set aside for transients and passengers, in any case. The verr he saw seemed to work here, not live here, and likely commuted to and from quarters elsewhere. They were cooks, stewards, that kind of thing. Clearly here to make sure that the delegates and those with them could focus on their jobs, not their needs.

Which made sense. That would be how a hive would work. Everyone doing the work they were...how *did* a verr hive assign jobs?

He wondered.

"Alvi," he said, having been told he could ask the AI. "Where is Kaykek and is zie busy?"

"Zie is in the creche."

"Oh..."

Zie had gone to visit zir girlfriend and kids. He had no right to interfere with *that*.

"What do you need?"

"I have some curiosity about verr society."

"You could ask me."

He found a place to lean against the wall. "If you have the attention to spare." Graeme had talked to artificial sentients before. He knew that Alvi might be having three or four different conversations at the same time.

"I do."

"How do the hives decide who does what job?"

"Pups are given aptitude tests at various ages and allowed to try several things before being put in an apprenticeship."

"Ah, so it's not..."

"It's not dictated from above, but aptitude is part of it. As is caste. Traditionally, in the old days, all diplomats were scouts. Whether that will continue is, of course, uncertain. And warriors are warriors."

Graeme nodded. "But that's something that happens later in life. Kaykek told me zie was in life support maintenance."

"Ze was a climate control technician."

"So, a solid hands-on job. But it doesn't sound that different from how humans do it."

"Or tyrar."

You went to school, found out what you were good at.

Not different at all.

OBSERVING the verr taught Graeme much. He had been impressed with the classless Glyn society. Eliminating class and gender did help people reach for meritocracy, although it was not an option available to other species. Biologically.

He'd read some dystopias that tried to do this with humans. Their failure was, of course, inevitable. People liked having genders...they just wanted the freedom to tweak and adjust and be things outside the binary.

The verr were, in many ways...the opposite. Their society had more than two genders, but they were so *strongly* gendered. Well, in some ways, queens and drones were the same gender: breeder. Worker, breeder, warrior, scout. He was reminded of the fact that in Uralic languages, the genders were "person" and "not person" not "male" and "female."

Your caste, your gender, they determined everything. Most jobs were closed to queens. Some were closed to workers. But everyone started out as a worker, learning their skills, becoming and growing. They didn't seem to feel it as a restraint.

They didn't seem to feel as if they had less freedom than he did. He thought of the backlashes against gay people during Austerity, and was glad to have the freedom he did.

True freedom to be exactly who and what he was, to live, to love, to have a husband and a daughter. That was it. That was what made him uncomfortable.

The three verr who were working on something technical as he walked past? They didn't have the freedom to love. In theory, they didn't miss it.

In theory.

Kaykek did love, if not in the same way as a human. It was very clear to him that zir relationship with Tayken, encompassed in the word sve, "preferred mate," was not anything like human marriage, and not just because they needed the help of a drone to produce their next litter.

Understanding it as that, or even as boyfriend-girlfriend or partners was a pitfall. But how could they not miss it?

How much of love and being in love was biological? Asexual people could have deeply loving relationships. Did verr workers have anything akin to queerplatonic relationships, anything more than what was typically called a friendship?

He didn't know, and he didn't know how to ask. But they must have love, or they were robots.

Just not lust. At least they claimed not.

Maybe Kaykek was the wrong person to ask. But seeing these people stunted in sexual development? He had to get over it.

There was one way to understand them. He headed back to his quarters, pulled out his tablet. Hesitated.

"Alvi, can you recommend some good verr fiction?"

"I'll send you a list."

"Thank you."

The best way to truly understand people was through their art.

THE COMMOTION DISTURBED Graeme from his reading. He was reading a verr historical novel that involved a tyrant...a warrior taking over a hive...and the fight against her. He didn't understand all of the nuances, but it reminded him of similar human sagas.

Until he heard the chittering of angry verr and set his tablet down and poked his head out. That verr was easily half again as large as any he had seen and was pinning down a human figure.

Did they have a *stowaway*? Or had the verr captured another kind of troublemaker?

"What's going on?" Graeme said as he approached, watching the two warily. He could see that the large verr wasn't *hurting* the person.

They knew how to restrain safely.

"This one is not on the manifest."

They *did* have a stowaway.

"Let them up."

The verr did. They turned out to be masculine presenting, scruffy looking, not much more than a kid. Exactly the kind of person who would sneak on a ship for the fun of it.

Graeme did not let his guard down a nanometer. He was absolutely not going to budge from considering the stowaway a threat.

"Let me guess, you got curious, wanted to see the verr ship, sneaked on board and then they left with you."

The kid nodded.

Graeme glanced at the...this was a warrior, he realized, a female, but not fertile, not a breeder. Hence the larger size. Larger than the workers and a bit larger than Kaykek.

Verr queens were the largest of the species, on average. "Don't trust him."

The kid swallowed. "I..."

"Tell me the truth. That's a verr warrior, kid. It's her job to protect the hive and she isn't likely to care how much she hurts you if she thinks you're a threat."

He sent an almost apologetic look to the warrior. He was using her as a bad cop without consent, which was a little rude in human terms. He had no idea how it came over in verr terms.

He really didn't understand them. The warrior loomed.

Good. That was the reaction he wanted.

"I was paid to get on board."

"And what were you paid to leave on board?"

The kid shook his head. "Just..."

"You were paid to get on board by people who didn't care if you got back off. Think about that for a moment. Then make the right decision."

The kid swallowed. "Okay, I'll show you."

Graeme knew what they were going to find. The real question was whether it would turn out to have been put in the right place or not.

24

A BOMB IN LIFE SUPPORT. Now Kaykek, Graeme, and one of the warriors assigned to security for the delegates sat in a conference room with a young human male.

Graeme had said he wasn't much more than a child, and Kaykek believed him. He also looked terrified.

"This," Graeme said. "Was designed to make you some real problems if you were still a life support tech."

"Is that a bomb?" Kaykek asked.

"Yes," the warrior, Pivrin, commented. "Made me sweat while he disarmed it too."

The kid swallowed. "I didn't..."

Graeme cut in. "We know. You didn't know. Your family needed the money badly. It's okay. We know."

He relaxed.

"Doesn't mean you aren't going to face consequences and *Refuge* is verr jurisdiction."

He swallowed again, looking between Kaykek and the warrior.

Kaykek decided to let *him* sweat for a while. "So..."

"He was told exactly where to put it. At a junction that would have knocked power out to this entire section. Hopefully it wouldn't have killed anyone, but it would *certainly* have caused significant problems."

"Who paid him?" Kaykek asked.

"I don't know," the kid said, quietly. "It was all anonymous."

"You got the device from a dead drop."

"Sophisticated, then," Pivrin said finally. "Connected to your stolen ship?"

"Possibly. I don't know for sure." Graeme was keeping one eye on the kid.

Kaykek could smell that he was still a little tense. Zie supposed that disarming a bomb did that to you.

He added, "But I plan on finding out. Pivrin..."

"I am more than happy to work with you. This one goes to the council?"

The kid swallowed yet again. It was clearly a nervous tic.

Graeme nodded. "Yes. We could argue that the part of *Refuge* we are using is international territory, but to be honest, shipping him back to Earth would be expensive."

He swallowed some more.

"I'll take him," Pivrin said. "He won't go anywhere."

The kid had apparently already been sat on by the warrior once. He followed her out, docile.

"What will the Hive Council do to him?"

"Oh, they'll find some use for him." Kaykek's whiskers twitched. "As we can't ship him back to his hive with our compliments *just* yet." A pause. "If he was a verr spy from another hive he'd be digging burrows until we sent him back. As he's human and we're on a ship..."

"The *human* tradition involves disposal of bodily waste."

Zir whiskers curled. "You mean...you make them..." Zie could envision various possibilities.

"Scrub the toilets. Good military discipline."

"I'll suggest that to the council." Kaykek was amused by the idea and if it also fulfilled human justice.

In the very old days, of course, a hive infiltrator would have been killed. But they were more civilized than that.

And of course had the kid been part of the hive, he would be doing punishment duty for a while.

Scrubbing toilets.

Zie found zie could live with that as a consequence of the young man's actions until they sent him back to Earth in disgrace.

Also, it meant he was around to question further.

Once Graeme had left, Kaykek made some notes. Interspecies justice hadn't been something they had discussed yet.

Also international and council jurisdiction, as Graeme had mentioned. While the council was using part of *Refuge* did it fall under their law? The logic was yes, to a degree. Their law for things which did not affect the workings, not to mention the safety, of the ship itself. The latter would still fall, zie thought, under Refuge Hive law.

Which meant the kid would be scrubbing toilets for a while. Zie believed that he had not known it was a bomb, that he was a patsy and was intended to get caught. Maybe the people who sent him had hoped he would get killed. But this was an opportunity. To show the kid and other humans what hive justice was like, and how civilized the verr could be.

Of course, had the kid actually been caught planting the bomb, Pivrin would have been well within her legal rights...as would any other verr...to kill him to stop him. That was probably something that should be made clear. If you threatened a hive then you might end up dead. Most civilized verr would try not to kill you, especially if they didn't know who sent you.

But you *might* end up dead.

"Alvi?"

"I am here."

"Could you do me a small favor and pull together a package of well written, easily translatable information about hive justice systems and how they work and send it to the delegates, with a note saying that I would appreciate reciprocation."

"A good idea."

"That poor kid, I think he thought we were going to airlock him."

"He would have to do a lot worse than that. But..."

"I know you would have no hesitation about cutting off life support if you had seen him."

"I should have," Alvi said.

"You can't...even you can't pay attention to every inch. I don't always notice if something's crawling on me, after all."

"I have set up subprocesses to alert me if it happens again. He might not be the only one. And dispatched workers to look for any other devices."

All of which struck zir as excellent ideas. "I have one more. Make sure we scan all the food for contaminants."

"Also a good idea. Poison would..."

"Poison would be a good way to target just the delegates. We can't assume all threats are external to the hive."

"You're thinking like a warrior."

Kaykek's ears drooped. "Sorry."

"No, it was a good thought."

"I just want everyone to be safe and I want us to achieve what we set out to do."

Which was going to be hard. Very hard indeed.

But zie knew it could be done.

"TAKE HOLD." Alvi's voice.

Then Refuge jumped. Kaykek was not jump sensitive, ze felt the vibrations through the great ship, but was not disturbed by them.

"Alvi?" ze asked.

"The rogue Earth ship showed up again. I decided it was best we be somewhere else."

Kaykek headed for the council room. It was zir job to explain this to the delegates, on the way, "What somewhere else?"

"A waypoint between Earth and Kyverr, I have all of my senses open."

Kaykek lifted zir whiskers at them, or rather at empty space, but hopefully their sensors would understand the gesture.

Ze walked into the conference room.

"Did we jump?" the Venus ambassador said, mildly.

"Our friend the *Columbia* came back. Alvi decided it was best to be somewhere else. They'll do another soon so they can't just follow our wake."

"Understandable."

Kaykek dropped into zir seat. "You all seem to be okay. If you have any questions..."

"What are you doing to the young human?" Viary asked.

Kaykek glanced at Graeme. "Punishment duty until there's a ship to take him back to Earth. In our culture, we would send the person back to the hive they came from in disgrace. Failed spies tend not to have careers after that. Of course, that's assuming they don't get killed by hive defenders."

"And if he was from your hive?"

"There are many boring jobs to be done in a hive to repay your debt, as it were. Unless it turned out to be for treatable reasons, such as mental health, burnout, hating one's job and really needing a different one...something which can be fixed. Or some combination of both."

"Ah. On Venus, we cannot afford to waste the time of offenders. So, our approach is similar. But humans have a long history of locking people up."

"Why?" Kaykek asked, glancing at Graeme. "It seems wasteful."

"It was seen as a more humane alternative to just killing them, or as a way to keep the rest of society safe. But it degenerated into a form of slavery, and now we try to do it a lot less."

Slyk spoke up at that point. "We do lock people up if they will not stop being...anti-social...but generally we have them repay the victim directly in some way."

"That's a better approach," Graeme agreed. "I suppose in the hive..."

"We were talking about a case where the hive was the victim," Kaykek pointed out. "In attacks on individuals, then obviously reparations to the victim are important."

"Is that so obvious?" That was Kai Bowie. "On Mars we also can't afford jails. But human history has shown that it is *not* obvious."

"Maybe it is," Graeme mused. "Much of our justice system is based off the concept of wergild."

Kaykek's whiskers curled up. Their minds were working on something important.

Dhyanil finally spoke, "We were once highly barbaric about this as, I know, were humans. And a lot depends on the nature of the crime. What do we do with cold-blooded murderers?"

Kaykek knew that every single species in this room would once have answered with kill them. Including zir own.

25

IT WAS as if the change of venue had made everything more productive.

Or maybe they were all being affected by verr pheromones. They should test that by separating life support, Dhyanil thought. Not that he would turn down anything which made things less contentious.

They had agreed that the death penalty would be verboten under the charter, as would torture, but that otherwise punishment was down to individual species, who held jurisdiction. Extradition was on the table, and of course agreements might happen case by case to, for example, send a criminal home.

The verr were inclined towards that anyway. You sent them back in disgrace, that was apparently the way it was done. Dhyanil suspected a darker origin to that as there was almost certainly a darker origin to child trading.

He did not want to know what it might be.

In the observation lounge, he looked out at space. The great ship had jumped a second time, hopefully to a location not so easy to find. A blue-white gas giant, pale on one side, glowed outside the ship. A beautiful little system with no good real estate, but quite a few resources. To be negotiated over. Not fought over.

They had achieved, at the very least, a significantly reduced likelihood of another war in space. That was, had to be, the primary goal. And perhaps they could... They had to do something about every world's isolationists, and then the ship began to turn away from the gas giant, gliding slowly. Perhaps Alvi, the ship's mind, was giving them a variety of views.

A tyrar AI that had become part of a verr hive and was addicted to human mystery novels. That was the future, Dhyanil thought. The future he had once feared, but now found himself embracing and even working towards, found himself part of in a way he had never imagined. In a way that sometimes made him feel like a traitor even though he knew better. He wasn't one. He had changed his mind because he had seen what clinging to the past could do.

And that there was a better way to preserve ky'iin traditions. By helping the offworlders understand them so they would appreciate them. They had never tried to understand or appreciate the tyrar, just exploit them. Now, though?

Now he sat at table with one as an equal, and had even gotten used to the faint smell all mammals seemed to give off.

Refuge glided through space but it felt more like he was still on a station than a ship. A full-sized small town of verr, and *their* smell was the one that dominated, particularly musky.

Those pheromones again.

His tablet activated with an incoming message.

Alvi wanted all of the delegates in the council chamber.

They claimed it was an emergency.

THE VOICE of the great ship's AI had a deep resonance to it that made Dhyanil want to gender them female, or perhaps ly'iin.

He knew, though, that this particular AI had elected not to choose a gender at all. Or perhaps AI *was* their gender.

In Ky'iin terms, se would be the best pronoun to use, but that would infantilize them. The English them was better suited in many ways.

But he could not help but think of Alvi as ly'iin at some level, as rude as he knew that to be.

"They have found us again."

"How, when they can't track our wake? We're big, but..."

But they had spent enough time in realspace. Graeme lifted a hand. "They..."

"...put a tracer on us."

That was in stereo between Graeme and Dhyanil, resulting in awkward human and ky'iin laughter.

"Of course they did. The hive workers and my robots are looking for it, but..."

But they were only going to be followed and despite its size, Refuge wasn't a warship.

In other words...

"Jump to Kyx?" Dhyanil suggested. "We probably have the strongest system defenses."

"It is worth a try, but I suspect they are smart enough not to follow us there."

Alas, the AI had a point. Certainly, Dhyanil would not do that...he would wait for them to jump again.

Or attempt to leverage other assets.

Kaykek spoke up, softly, "We could pop into *that* system. The one with the black hole. We know, they don't."

"If the..."

"It wasn't moving *that* quickly, Alvi. It should still be there."

A trap involving a natural singularity? A system...with a black hole. No wonder Kaykek was trembling slightly as ze spoke of it.

Verr would not appreciate black holes, although none of them seemed to be afraid of the *tame* singularity *Refuge* carried around. It was a friendly one, it was artificial, they trusted it. Mostly.

"It might be worth a try. I doubt they will be that stupid. But..."

The great ship began to turn, ready to jump. Before it could do so, there was the faint vibration of, perhaps, something hitting the hull. Dhyanil braced himself, and *Refuge* jumped, shaking its way through hyperspace.

It did not move nearly as much as a smaller ship, though. More vibration than turbulence, the swirling currents of hyperspace not able to toss this amount of mass around as much. He felt it nonetheless, felt it through him. Trusted Alvi.

Then the ship dropped out into real space and *immediately* turned. Or stopped. Or perhaps twisted. Faster than even a webbed pilot could react. Dhyanil did not want to know what was going on out there, but at the same time?

He had to.

He *had* to know.

SILENCE. Dhyanil waited, then he ventured the question. "What happened?"

"All is well," Alvi reassured. "However, there was more debris in the system than I expected. It appears the black hole..."

"Captured the system or vice versa?"

"Indeed. But we can hide amongst it, even a ship this size."

Dhyanil felt himself relaxing. He hated to hope that the *Columbia* would have worse problems; alas, as a smaller ship, it could dodge better. But he could still hope it. He didn't really want them to blow up, he was more civilized than...

More than that, he knew it was possible to come back from the road they had gone down, to stop, to look around, to realize where you were and trudge back, one step at a time. For him, it had taken the death of a young girl to start that realization, though, and tragedy was never good, no matter what good it might work or appear to work.

Not that it would have been better for him to be the way he was, but he did wish he'd seen things sooner, because if he had, she might still be alive.

Maybe.Or maybe somebody else would have been involved in the plans which killed her.

There was supposed to be a push for progress and a pull for tradition, but these things were supposed to balance. To say "Why" and "Not yet" was a good thing.

To say "No" and "Never" was not.

With the ship quiet, he headed for the canteen. Poured himself a mug of peppermint tea, which he had developed a taste for while on Earth. Sloshed bits of it into his maw as he thought. No. Never.

Change was the only inevitable force in the universe, and this place had changed by the forces of nature. The same forces of nature that had destroyed Verr and set *those* people onto the path of which this ship was a part.

And that tragedy was immeasurable even if they had saved most of the verr with a technological feat unimaginable before. One which said that working together, perhaps, they could one day build an artificial planet like Glen, or even the mythical dyson sphere, capturing the entire energy of a sun for its inhabitants.

That scared him. He was still at heart a man who said "Why" and "Not yet." It also excited him, but there were... Apart from anything else, there was whoever had bred and then abandoned the glyn, as they now admitted more freely. They were learning not to be embarrassed by their past.

It was nothing to be embarrassed about.

But was that civilization still out there? Or worse, was what they had hid that world from...still out there?

He finished his peppermint tea and took his dark thoughts back to his quarters where there was no temptation to share them with others.

26

It was hard not to be angry. Beverly did not want to take it out on the herd, as alien a concept as that was to tyrar (amongst whom it was perfectly acceptable to yell at the herd as long as you cuddled afterwards).

She was still human, and you didn't snap at the people you loved over things they didn't do. Ideally, you limited how much you snapped at them over things they *did* do, but that was often a challenge for her and for everyone else she knew.

She rolled around their part of the ship and almost thought...the verr seemed so welcoming that she did wonder if she could get a tour of something else.

Not the creche, she would not presume so far. Maybe their parks? There were green, open spaces on the ship, part of life support both physical (for the oxygen) and psychological. Well, yellow-green, Verr vegetation tending towards that color, but it was still open spaces with plants.

Not a terrible idea. Humans needed open spaces with plants too, and the plants being alien didn't make them not plants, it just made them *different* plants.

Not directly involved in the negotiations, although she was no doubt giving Viary an advantage by helping him understand how humans would view something, Beverly was honestly left with little to do.

So, she explored. The verr gave off a very faint musky scent that wasn't at all unpleasant and was already starting to fade as scents do when they change little. Her human nose was not good enough to consciously detect the variations that were their pheromonic communication.

Of course, she wasn't entirely sure that the verr themselves *consciously* detected it. She wasn't sure that it wasn't as subconscious as the social influences on humans that meant nobody was entirely free nor could be. It probably was.

They seemed happy, though, but was that her imagination? Was it that they were *busy*, which made them look happy.

Or. She was only seeing verr on shift, doing their jobs and, furthermore, supporting people they wanted to keep happy. The more she thought about it, the more she thought that she was only seeing what they wanted her to see.

"Alvi?" she asked the air. It took a moment for the AI to respond. "Any way I could get a tour of some other parts of Refuge?"

"Of course, but you will absolutely need a guide."

She smiled. "I did say a tour. I'm not stupid, but also not smart enough to be able to navigate this ship without help. I don't want anyone to have to rescue me."

Not that she would be in any danger, but getting lost was a very real possibility.

"What do you want to see?"

"I suppose, as best as possible, what people are like when they aren't in service industry mode."

Alvi rumbled tyrar laughter at her. "I suppose..."

"It's a universal thing, I think. Unless you let robots do all of those jobs, and..."

And that had been tried during austerity. Robots did do *some* of those jobs, but it turned out people needed and wanted human service.

Or verr service. It probably amounted to the same thing.

"I will find you a guide."

"Thank you."

HER GUIDE WAS a young worker named Lorkek. It, which was what the translator insisted on making its pronouns, had darker fur than some of the other verr she had seen.

She did not ask, but Lorkek volunteered the information as they went through a door. "I'm from Vrycek Hive."

"You're from the one that..."

It chittered, "Yes. And I'm not going back."

"I don't blame you."

"Some are going back, to fix things, but I like it here. I can't help it."

Beverly laughed. "I'd imagine, too, quite a few verr don't feel comfortable on planets. Ships can dodge."

"They can indeed." It considered. "So...I can't show you everything in one go."

"And I'm not asking to see the bridge, engineering, or the creche."

"The creche might be possible. Maybe even a good idea," it mused. "I'd need clearance from the breeders, but...would be good for the pups to see offworlders."

"Actually, how about we make arrangements for the pups to come meet *us*?"

"I can run that past the drones."

"They don't spend all their time locked in after a certain age, surely?"

"Oh, of course not. And it would be educational."

School groups. Viary would "kill" her. But...the verr pups should get this chance to see aliens, to talk to them.

"So, what..."

"Actually, I would like to see a garden."

Its whiskers turned upwards. "I have an idea." It changed course and she followed.

The verr here still seemed fairly busy. "How long are your work shifts?"

"Ten of our hours, which equates to I think about six of yours. Not sure."

"I can ask Alvi for something more precise. What do you...and I mean you personally...do when not working?"

"I paint a little," it admitted. "I'm not fantastic, but I can make something reasonably worth looking at."

She grinned. "I bet you're better than you think."

"What do *you* do when not being a scientist?"

"I read a lot. I'm a bit of a..."

"You're a scientist. Scientists always work more, because they wouldn't do all that school if they didn't love it."

Beverly laughed again. "A universal. What's your actual job?"

"General maintenance. Fixing doors, replacing lights, that kind of thing."

"Very needed. So, what do you think of offworlders?"

"If I said I didn't like you I'd be in trouble."

She laughed again, liking this young...her brain wanted to gender it male and she told her brain to stop. This young person. "And the fact that you said that..."

"We owe you. It's going to be difficult to have a relationship other than owing until we can pay that back. The hives *owe* you. But for me? I hope we can go back to Earth and I can tour an art gallery."

"When we get back to Earth, I'll take you to the National Gallery of Art," she offered. "Fair return for *this* tour."

THE PARK DID HAVE a yellow tinge to it that reminded Beverly of pictures she had seen from the days when street lamps cast a yellow hue. That was long before her time, but she'd seen pictures and videos. But it was still a park and she felt something unknot in her stomach. "We need to get all of the delegates here."

"I'll talk to the hive council about that."

This kid wasn't just a general maintenance worker. Beverly didn't show any sign that she knew, though. *Obviously* it was verr intelligence, who else would they send? It was one of those things that you expected. That anyone working with you would be reporting in.

"Thanks." She looked around. "Is anyone listening to us here?"

"Only Alvi."

"If we can't trust Alvi...how many verr don't like us?"

"Most of the verr who don't like offworlders stayed in the Verr system."

Which meant they were in the city stations. "Good. People who don't like offworlders should stay away from them."

"But you're fishing for security risks."

"I'm not intelligence, but it seems like a decent opportunity. And if anywhere..."

"Alvi can hear us. And we can trust Alvi. We have to."

Alvi could turn off life support.

"So, who can't we trust?"

"A couple of the drones who are...I believe embarrassed by our dependence. Most people don't want the kind of...we don't have isolationists, we have people who want to show the verr aren't orphaned pups looking for a queen to suckle."

Beverly laughed. "Some of whom might do something stupid or reckless to prove themselves, but they aren't likely to attack us."

"There are a few people who simply aren't comfortable around you. They're assigned to work shifts that limit interaction."

"Sensible, but they should probably have *some* interaction or they won't become comfortable."

She examined a purple flower. "You..."

"We saved seeds on Verr. Even of things we couldn't grow anymore. We kept them out of hope."

Of course the verr had seed banks. "We have seed banks too. For emergencies. Because of the climate crisis, but they predate that. You never know when a plant might become useful."

"You do?" A pause. "I was actually planning on introducing you to somebody, and there it is."

The worker who approached them wasn't young at all. In fact, it walked with a cane. It's fur was speckled with gray.

"Who is this?"

"This is Mrylek. It is our head gardener."

An important title, and no doubt this verr was not just a gardener, but a highly trained botanist.

And...

Beverly inclined her head.

"Mrylek, this is the human Beverly Marlowe. The ecological remediation scientist."

Beverly laughed. "Who is always happy to talk shop with a fellow scientist."

"You know that I don't just dig holes, then."

"I'd imagine you have people and robots for that."

She had to think that this was planned. And if so, she knew exactly who had planned it.

It was, obviously, that meddling AI.

27

GRAEME KNEW A FEW THINGS.

One of them was that a society which appears harmonious isn't. That's not to say he didn't trust the verr. He did. For the most part, they seemed to be nice people. At the very least, they had done a good job of making the not nice people disappear. Sometimes that was all you could ask for. The troublemakers could work on the far side of the ship.

But it was a factor he had to keep in mind. Slyk was doing their job and needed little help from Graeme. So he was analyzing their situation. Right now, they were hiding in a system that looked like it had been dragged through a hedge backwards. Not good, really.

The *Columbia* had followed them, hit something, and jumped out to somewhere safer. That was better. Part of him wished the ship had been destroyed.

It would, in old terms, have saved the paperwork. Nobody could have been blamed for it other than the people on board. Whoever they were.

An ansible message from Earth told him that Captain Aw had been found in a fleshpot in Bangkok. He had apparently been drugged and left there, no doubt to add further humiliation.

It made sense that he wasn't the traitor, and it appeared the XO was the problem...and Aw had seen some people with him that weren't part of the crew. Muscle. The crew might even think they were still acting under orders. They might have been told Aw was sick, or dead.

But at the same time, it would still be *easier* if *Columbia* was destroyed. Even if there were innocent people on board. They were EarthForce, they had signed on to the risks.

Refuge should leave the system, but that wasn't Graeme's decision. It was the AI and the captains...there were three captains, which made sense on a ship this size and for a species that was fond of communal decision making.

Verr and tyrar committees were actually efficient, unlike human ones. Or, he had heard, ky'iin. And, to the surprise of those who had completely misunderstood the verr, all three captains were workers. Had Graeme also completely misunderstood the verr?

"We will jump in ten minutes. Please get to a good takehold point."

Alvi and the captains had made their decision. They weren't saying where they were jumping to.

Which meant.

They thought that...

...they had thought a tracer on the hull, but the other possibility was somebody with a portable ansible. Such things existed, but they were incredibly expensive, surely beyond the reach of terrorists.

But not beyond the reach of...

Oh...

...crap.

Not beyond the reach of some organizations at all.

THERE WERE two entities on *Refuge* Graeme felt comfortable fully trusting.

One was Slyk, whom he did not want to bother with this.

The other...

"Alvi," he said quietly in his quarters. "Is there a place or a way we can talk where I can be sure only you will hear."

He trusted Alvi more out of the situation than anything else. Bluntly, if Alvi could not be trusted, they were all dead anyway.

"Yes. Follow the green lights."

A visual wayfinding system. "That must have been put in for the tyrar. I haven't seen the verr use it."

"The verr are burrowers. They can navigate in complete darkness."

"Have you used that against boarders?" Graeme mused.

"Unfortunately, the last time, they were ky'iin, who are almost as good in the dark. But it would work on humans and tyrar, and probably glyn."

"And would be worth trying on anyone else we meet."

He followed the lights, and they led him out of the area normally used by the delegates. This resulted in verr heads turning in his direction, curious. They didn't try to stop him, though.

"Do you have people who..."

"We have people who aren't comfortable with offworlders. They have been assigned to the far side of the ship."

Graeme nodded with a grin. His prediction had been right. "I don't feel unsafe, but was finding it hard to believe..."

"Anyone who really has problems with aliens isn't on Refuge anyway. The hive self-selects for the openminded by its nature."

"You have a point." Graeme finally turned a corner and entered...an open space with plants.

A park.

In the center of it, it would be impossible for anyone to sneak up. He pulled out his bug detector. "I hope you won't be insulted..."

"The only sensors here should be mine, but by all means check."

He worked for a few minutes, cross checking with Alvi, and established there were no bugs that were not *supposed* to be there.

"So...I note you didn't tell anyone where we went."

"We are in a system claimed by the tyrar with a small colony. And a military outpost. Just in case."

"You think somebody on this ship is..."

"My robots and the hive's workers have found no trace of a tracking device. So yes, I do think we have a leak."

"The question is whether it's a mole." Graeme stopped. The verr did look a bit like anthropomorphic moles. So, that probably wasn't the best phrase.

"I don't *think* so, except in the general human language slang sense. I think it's somebody with the delegates."

"So do I. A human somebody. I think we can eliminate Dr. Marlowe."

"She would have to be a really good deep cover agent to be involved in this, yes," Alvi agreed. "Also, I have been monitoring most of her communications so I can read the scientific papers."

Graeme laughed. "Does she know that?"

"Yes. She is helping me obtain human science for my library, and Refuge's scientists are very happy. But I think we can eliminate her from suspicion."

"I also think we can probably eliminate the actual Martian and Venusian representatives. People like the ones who stole the *Columbia* don't like people like them."

"Which I fail to understand."

"She is the wrong ethnicity and they are the wrong gender."

"Ah. There have been issues on Tyranis with ethnicity. Just ask Parvati."

"Perhaps I will, or not. My husband and I face those issues."

"Because he is the wrong ethnicity and gender to be an acceptable mate."

Graeme laughed. "Precisely. Precisely that. But both brought aides. As did Chan."

"Chan is also..."

"Chan is a possible suspect. Which is one reason why I wanted this quiet. He is always trying to take over the council."

"Of course he is. Earth is powerful and populous."

"But I don't *think* it is him."

"It couldn't be the dolphin?"

Graeme laughed. "All she cares about is which colony worlds have nice oceans on them."

"I noticed that. She wants living space for her people, no more, no less."

AIDES WERE ALMOST ALWAYS SPIES. The glyn did not really spy, not having ever had nations on their planet. No doubt their ancestor-creators had had them, but the glyn world was artificial in all ways.

But everyone else? Graeme assumed every single aide on Refuge was a spy. Hopefully most of them were spies for the person they were officially working for, but that wasn't something that could be guaranteed. Not at all.

He needed somebody to go through them with, and he couldn't ask Charles for help this time. True, he could access the ansible.

But the bandwidth was too low for the kind of conversations they needed to have.

Alvi could do it, Alvi could spin off a subprocess, but he needed...

He needed to be physically in the room with the person. He needed somebody who understood how humans work. He needed somebody he knew for sure wasn't the mole.

That last was the sticking point. How could he know for sure? He couldn't, that was the issue. He could eliminate people with an over 90% certainty. He couldn't eliminate anyone with a 100% certainty.

Slyk couldn't do it for the same reason Alvi couldn't.

So.

He had to take a risk and trust the person least likely to be the mole, even if they had no intelligence experience. But plenty of intelligence of the other kind. He sent a message to Viary's quarters saying he needed to borrow Beverly.

Got back a response that she was talking to verr. Of course she was. The scientist wanted to understand the ecology and culture she was currently temporarily living in. And the ship was absolutely an ecology.

"Who is she talking to?"

"She was last seen disappearing into the office of Refuge Hive's head gardener."

"Well, if she ever surfaces, please tell her I'd like to meet with her?"

"Yoshi will go get her if it takes too long."

Graeme laughed. Many scientists did indeed need to be reminded of the importance of little things like eating and sleeping when they got engrossed in a task or in talking shop. It made it even less likely that she was the mole. He was not sure of her, but he was sure enough.

He had to be. He had to trust somebody and they had to be a human somebody, not because he didn't trust aliens, but because they did not think the same way. Could not think the same way. They had different brain architecture, different biology.

They offered such valuable perspectives to one another, but they did not and could not think the same way. It was not possible. So, he needed a human, and he needed to choose the one he thought was safest. The park would be a good place to meet.

And even as he thought that, the woman herself emerged from a nearby door, rolling her chair along the manicured path.

He waved.

28

It was rare for the dolphin representative to have a lot to say. Part of the issue was that as the only aquatic (air breathing, but still aquatic) sentient there, she had to attend meetings from inside a tank.

But at the end of that meeting, she asked Kaykek to come to her quarters to talk. Whoever had set them up had done a good job. The quarters had been a pair of crew lounges, one above the other, which had been split to give more vertical space. This allowed the dolphin to have a tank and a receiving room above it that was comfortable for the airbreathers.

It was also a permanent change and Kaykek figured they could use this for any other dolphins who wanted transport in the future. There almost certainly would be dolphins who wanted transport.

"What do you need, Twiek?" Kaykek asked, settling down on the edge of the pool. Then ze took off zir shoes and dangled zir toes in the water. It was a comfortable temperature.

Ze wasn't quite comfortable with actually jumping in and talking while treading water, mind. Not this time.

"It is not..." The dolphin paused. "We would like to open negotiations directly with the Verr."

"Kyverr has extensive oceans. I'm not stupid."

"You do. And the verr are, for the most part, not xenophobes. There is plenty of space for both of us. And it would give you access to dolphin pilots."

That was not a small consideration. Naturally able to think in three dimensions, the dolphin species produced some of the very best pilots. Alvi was better, but it appeared not all AIs could integrate into a ship body the way they had. The tyrar rules were as much to protect the AI as the ship.

Also, a dolphin pilot would give another species input on exploration ships. "It would. And I can think of another thing too. Kyverr is relatively unexplored. We still don't have the land mapped in detail. We haven't even started on the oceans. But it's not my decision. It's Kyverr Hive's decision at present."

"Of course. But you can present the idea to them."

"Can and will."

Verr were not aquatic. They had once sailed, but had mostly forgotten how. Kaykek should talk to humans and ky'iin of certain cultures about helping regain those skills. But they did not need to live *in* the oceans. The dolphins could have them, in return for appropriate considerations.

Dolphin pilots for verr ships. Dolphin assistance mapping ocean resources. Those were *not* small considerations.

"And I suppose..."

"We want to put our colonies on worlds that have land-based sentients. Otherwise they will....become as we were before we worked out how to get humans to listen to us."

Kaykek chittered laughter. "Low tech, primitive, and isolated. Although some might prefer that."

"Some might indeed. There are certain human groups who would love to have their own planets from which they can exclude high technology outside a spaceport enclave so people who aren't happy can leave."

A long speech from the dolphin. "I always thought..."

"That because I don't say much in meetings, I'm not one of the smarter delegates."

"I know it's because you only really have interest in two

things...space for dolphins and jobs for dolphins."

The chittering sound was clearly laughter. "And scientific papers. Don't forget those."

"Everyone wants scientific papers. We should negotiate for a shared library, some system that ensures everything is available to everyone."

The amount of data involved could not be sent by ansible. It would require courier ships

"Talk to the glyn. They would probably *love* to handle that."

"Oh, you're right. They would."

The dolphin didn't say very much.

That was because, Kaykek realized, she was listening.

RETURNING from the dolphin's quarters, Kaykek considered heading over to the creche to hang out with Tayken and the pups. As ze started to turn that way, however, ze saw something ze was not sure about.

The rear view of a human. Ze could recognize species but not much else. Said human was heading towards one of the work closets that they should not have access to, then opened it and vanished inside.

None of the delegates or their aides and assistants had access to the work closets for safety reasons. There were tools in there that could be used as weapons. There were terminals that accessed systems that somebody who didn't know what they were doing could easily abuse or break. Including parts of life support.

Kaykek was larger and stronger than a worker, but without knowing what kind of training the human had. "Alvi, who just went into that closet?"

A long pause. "Nobody just went into the closet."

"Somebody carrying a jammer just went into that closet," Kaykek said without any hesitation.

"Indeed. What species?"

"Human. But could be any of them except the one who uses a mobility chair, unless she's been faking it all along."

Some people who used mobility chairs *could* walk when they

needed to. From Kaykek's knowledge, Beverly Marlowe did not fall into that group.

"You didn't see well enough to determine sex?"

"No. But I might have been too shocked to pay attention. That's a life support maintenance closet."

"And..."

"Send me a couple of warriors? I can watch to see if they leave, but..."

"No, don't risk yourself in a fight."

"I don't intend to."

Kaykek pretended to be quite interested in zir tablet while ze waited for the warriors. It did not take long. Most of the people who worked in this area were, of course, workers. The two former Vrycek Hive warriors were bigger than zir and easily twice the size of the average worker.

They had kept the warriors away because they didn't want the offworlders to be intimidated. Or to really understand what Verr warriors were. But now the two of them, both male, made their way.

"It went into that maintenance closet. It did not come out."

"Could it have gone into the conduits?"

"Yes," Kaykek admitted. "But I'm hoping it saw no reason to."

"Depends on whether it saw you."

"It was facing away the entire time." Human vision was predator vision, heavy on the binocular, but with no ability to see what was directly behind them at all. A disadvantage in many ways.

An advantage in others.

"So..."

The two warriors moved forward. Kaykek stayed behind them, watching them work. They had changed from the bedraggled "failed breeders" ze had pulled out of Vrycek Hive. They knew what they were now and had embraced it.

Ze still wanted to bring more choice to the hives, but seeing these two work? Ze knew they were happy.

But when they opened the closet, it was empty.

"It *did* go into the conduits."

Naykek, one of the warriors, nodded. "Do you remember where they lead?"

Kaykek shook zir head. "Not without asking Alvi. But I am going to assume it left something behind. It had a sensor jammer."

"That blocked Alvi. That's planning. And sophisticated technology."

"Humans have *very* sophisticated technology."

Kaykek hesitated. "Alvi, can you tell the human, Graeme, what happened?"

"I can."

The other warrior Silkin, tilted his head.

"Graeme is human intelligence. A spy."

"Oh."

"He can help with this, and he needs to know." Kaykek moved over to the conduits, testing the hatches. "It went this way." Kaykek thought. "It wasn't running. This was its planned route, I'm sure. There are compartments that are hard to access. Good place to hide something or someone."

"We could tweak life support." Naykek's whiskers actually twitched.

"What did you have in mind?" Kaykek asked.

"If we know where it went we could make it uncomfortably warm or cold by human standards. Maybe the glyn environmental presets. That might force it out."

It might indeed. Kaykek couldn't help but offer a smile of zir own.

"Let's not hang out in the closet," ze added as ze backed out.

"Another thing we could do is..."

"We could do something very old fashioned." That was Silkin. He glanced around and found a roll of pipe tape. "Okay."

He broke off a piece and put it across the door on the outside, so that when and if the door opened, the tape would break or come off. "This will tell us if it comes back this way."

Kaykek blinked a couple of times. "That's..."

"Old school, but no sensor jammer is going to interfere with it.

So...how about you get a map of what's back there and then we can talk to Graeme."

Naykek was right. They needed an expert on humans, and obviously the known spy was the one to go with.

It hadn't been Graeme. Ze was sure of that.

Silkin, though, wasn't, "Are we sure that wasn't Graeme?"

Kaykek considered. "Graeme has very broad shoulders. This human was a bit narrower. I am pretty sure it was not Graeme."

"Might have been a female."

"Might have." Kaykek tried to recall the shape and the scent. "I still don't know humans well enough."

"Then let's go find our human expert and see what he can tell us before this person commits sabotage."

"There's nothing crucial back there. This isn't sabotage. This is..."

Hiding something. There *was* something crucial back there.

Something that wasn't in the plans.

29

DHYANIL WAS oblivious to what was going on in the storage closet.

He was not oblivious to the fact that something was going on, given he had just seen two larger-than-normal verr rush past.

So, that was what the warriors looked like. They were larger than Kaykek, and ze stood a full head over normal verr.

Supposedly the queens were the biggest verr, but he had yet to meet one, although that would change at some point. If things ever calmed down, Tayken, one of the queens, had promised the delegates a poetry recital.

Kai Bowie was apparently something of a poet themselves, and *they* had suggested also doing an open mic.

Poetry didn't translate well, but the rhythms of it could be appreciated even in a language you did not know. It would showcase something. Maybe visual art too. But this wasn't the time to do it. They had to stay focused.

No, Dhyanil decided. They didn't.

They could run in fear or they could live their lives.

Or they could do *both*. He had certainly done many pleasurable things when a huge part of his focus had been on not being caught and found out by the investigators.

They could run in fear *and* they could live a little. Of course, the queens might not want to leave the creche right now. He set it to one side for right now. He considered following the warriors, glanced in that direction, and saw them vanish into a *closet* with a slightly smaller verr.

A closet. It had to be an entrance to some maintenance corridors or something. And a tyrar maintenance corridor was likely to be more than large enough for a verr. Even a queen verr.

So. Did they have a rat in the walls? No, because the rats were running the place. They had somebody in the walls, though.

That wasn't good. Dhyanil casually walked past the closet, doing nothing to draw attention to himself and silent with a hunter's stealth. He could only see verr backs, but he was sure one of them was Kaykek.

Then they vanished into a maintenance corridor. He elected not to follow them, and positioned himself a little bit down the corridor.

They came out and one of them put a piece of tape across the door. Very old school.

Which meant they weren't trusting Alvi's sensors for some reason. Jammed? Hacked? Hacking the AI itself was all but impossible...really only another AI could pull it off. Hacking subsidiary systems, though, could work.

He thought it more likely somebody had a jammer. This was a sophisticated spy operation. So, who's was it? Everyone was spying on everyone as a matter of course.

But you didn't spy on the people who provided you with your air. Not if you wanted to breathe.

THEY TURNED AWAY FROM HIM. Dhyanil stopped trying to be sneaky, because sneaking up behind verr warriors struck him as a less than smart move. Instead, he walked more normally after them, quickening his pace. "Kaykek!"

"Did you see the guy go into the closet?" the darker furred warrior said.

"No, I only saw *you* go into the closet." Dhyanil supplied. "What happened?"

"There's a human wandering around in the maintenance areas," Kaykek supplied. "We think it might be hiding something."

"Like, say, a portable ansible." Dhyanil's tone was grim, even as he flinched at the casual use of it. Like humans, ky'iin did not think it was an appropriate pronoun for sentient beings. Of course, in the primary ky'iin language, the appropriate pronoun for workers did exist.

Se.

The pronoun you used for a child who's sex had not been determined yet, and which a few non-binary ky'iin used. He told himself he needed to respect their culture and not flinch.

"A..." Kaykek sighed. "The ky'iin have such things. Do the humans?"

"Not that I know of, but with enough resources..."

"They bought it. Along with that ky'iin yacht." Kaykek shook zir head. "We're going to find Graeme."

"May I tag along?"

They could have a huddle about this assuming they could, indeed, find Graeme. "Are we sure," he added, "That it *isn't* Graeme?"

"Graeme is broader than the human I saw."

Probably a female. Unlike ky'iin and tyrar, human females were smaller than the males. A woman, then. That would narrow things down some. Dhyanil followed the three large verr to one of the conference rooms. "Alvi, please have Graeme meet us in the grey room."

The verr did not number the rooms in this area, but had painted them different colors. When not everyone was literate in the same language (and ky'iin, in any case, *had* no written language), colors made sense as differentiators.

Dhyanil had, in fact, learned to read on Earth, which showed that the ky'iin brain was capable of the task, but it gave him a headache and he certainly wasn't going to do it for pleasure.

He settled into a chair that was more or less the right size.

Graeme showed up not long afterwards and took in the scene. "I take it there was an incident."

"We have a human in the walls," Kaykek said.

Graeme laughed. Humans found humor very readily. "An unidenti-
fied human."

"Narrower shoulders than you and..."

"What was their hair like?"

"Tucked into something."

"So, they were wearing a hat."

Kaykek nodded. "Yes, they were."

Concealing their hair. The Venusian representative had truly
splendid hair, but it wouldn't *fit* under a cap with all of those braids.

But...thinking to conceal their hair. "You couldn't determine sex?"

"I only saw them from the back. In shapeless clothing."

"In other words, they took reasonable steps not to be identified
beyond species. But we can eliminate Adwoa. Her hair wouldn't fit
under a hat."

"And we can eliminate you because you're too broad. We can't eliminate Kai, though," Kaykek added.

Dhyanil was not sure what sex the Martian ambassador was and
apparently it was rude to inquire. But they definitely did have
narrower shoulders than Graeme.

"My guess is it's one of Chan's aides," Graeme finally said with a
sigh. "And that it's spy equipment."

"Alvi was unable to find a tracer. All sensors are jammed in this
room, by the way."

Kaykek hadn't given an instruction for that. It had to be a protocol
ze had worked out with the ship in advance.

"Dhyanil?" Kaykek added.

"I think they may have a portable ansible. There might have been
one on the yacht bought from us. Humans don't have that tech yet."

Yet was a slight emphasis. Humans were smart, they would work
it out.

"How tall was the person?" Graeme asked next.

Kaykek wrinkled zir nose. "A little shorter than you. So, not Chan."

Chan was very short for a human man, Dhyanil had already noted.

"He wouldn't do his own dirty work anyway," Graeme added.

Dhyanil considered. "No, he wouldn't. If it's him, it's one of his younger aides that he has groomed for this."

Like the girl he had got killed. He'd been that person, who did those things. Now? Now he did his own dirty work.

Graeme nodded. "Or better yet, Chan has two interns. Bright-eyed, bushy-tailed as we say."

Obviously bushy tailed wasn't literal, as humans did not have tails, but Dhyanil thought he understood why mammals might use a saying like that. Some of their animals absolutely had bushy tails and tended to bounce.

Squirrels, they were called.

"Which means?" Kaykek's ears lowered.

"Young, enthusiastic, not yet sensible."

Dhyanil nodded. "It's very easy...very easy to get young people like that to do things. Especially girls, although that might be reversed among humans."

"It is." Graeme looked at Dhyanil for a moment. With Kaykek there he wasn't looking like he wanted to attack.

In fact, he definitely seemed calmer every time they were together. Dhyanil wondered if they could try talking without the verr pheromones to help. Maybe the pheromones wouldn't need to be a permanent thing, maybe they could be used to help humans learn to be around ky'iin without freaking out. That would be better.

"Does intern mean the same thing amongst humans?" Dhyanil added. "Underpaid and working for experience?"

"Yes." Graeme showed his teeth. "A really good thought."

Kaykek looked confused, ears in two different directions.

"People who are paid less are more vulnerable to bribery," Dhyanil pointed out. "The poor and the rich are the most likely to succumb to it. So it's also possible that it's not Chan, but somebody paid one of his interns to do this."

"We've already had one mercenary type," Graeme agreed. "Unfortunately, we're too far from Earth for me to get Charles to run the obvious checks on people's bank accounts."

"He can do that?"

"*I* can do that. I can deputize him to do it. I have before," Graeme said.

Humans mated long term, and long term mates could work together in ways few could. Dhyanil was almost jealous of that part of being human, especially as it involved lots of feel-good hormones. Of course, when those partnerships fell apart, things got really unpleasant, especially for the children involved. Graeme and Charles had a child created through some kind of fertility technology. That was one area in which humans were really advanced.

Unfortunately, their tricks did not work for ky'iin.

"So..."

"So I can send him an ansible message, but he can only send me analysis, not the raw results."

"Let's do it anyway," Kaykek suggested. "Dhyanil, you know..." Zir paused.

"I know about grooming young people to do bad things. I don't want to know, but I do. I can try talking to those interns, but they're human."

Which meant that without a verr scout present.

"Might be a good time to test that perfume medical is working on."

Which would also be a good grounds for talking to random humans. Dhyanil's body language shifted as he realized he felt good about this idea.

This could work.

30

BEVERLY WAS NOT sure how she felt about being trusted by a spy, especially when the reason for that trust was because he saw her as too busy with science to get involved with espionage.

On the other hand, it wasn't because he thought she was *incapable* of espionage. True, as the only human wheelchair user on Refuge, she would stand out far too much to do any actual spying beyond social engineering and letting people underestimate her.

But Graeme had not defaulted to assuming the disabled person wasn't capable. She appreciated that more than she thought she had got across to him before he got called by Kaykek. Watching him go, she rolled back out through the gardens. She wondered if she could get permission to come here. Graeme had been able to get through, so why not her?

Refuge was a city, not a ship. It should be more open, but she understood why the verr were a little wary. After all, this was their home, this was the place where they raised their pups and built their friendships and relationships. Worker verr might not form even the loose pair bonds that appeared to exist amongst the other castes, but their friendships could not be dismissed.

Nor could the overall hive bond that she could not understand. The tyrar could not either; they were herd animals, but a tyrar herd topped out at about eight individuals. *All* verr were part of the hive and furthermore they sought to slot others into the hierarchy, to understand you by what you did and who you were.

The advantage of this was that Beverly had had no problems exchanging ideas with the hive's scientists, some of whom she had met and others, who resided in the creche, she had yet to spend time with face-to-face. She thought she was making progress, and there were plans to bring the older pups here and let them meet the aliens.

School groups.

Maybe...maybe she could talk to the oldest pups about ecological remediation, which tied into terraforming and things they could do to make Kyverr a better planet for the verr without damaging its existing ecosystem. To the ones who were considering a career in science themselves.

But at some point she also wanted, needed, to go back to Tyranis. There was so much work that needed to be done. She wasn't the only person who could do that.

She *was* the only person who could model having aliens as her family. That might be more important, but nothing was going to stop the science. The chemistry between her and Yoshi said it all.

But the truth was that Graeme trusted her. There was clearly a mole somewhere, no offense to the verr. It was not her. And she knew it was not her herd either. You had no secrets from your herd, you trusted them absolutely or the herd broke.

Yoshi had broken from her old herd because of everything that had happened. Occasionally she still cried about it. Who wouldn't? You cried about your exes too, that was the way of things and the way the world worked.

What could she do about the mole? The answer was nothing, right now. So she headed back to her quarters and called Yoshi.

THE VERR HAD ORGANIZED some entertainment. Some might have said it wasn't the time to do so, but everyone was a little tired, a little stressed, a lot scared. Entertainment was a good idea. It was going to consist of a poetry recital by Tayken, who was apparently brilliant, followed by an open mic.

Beverly wondered how many people would have the courage to get up there. Certainly not her. Poetry was not her thing. She supposed she could read somebody *else's* poem, but that felt like cheating somehow.

But she was absolutely going to watch. The star arrived alongside Kaykek, and Beverly could see the body language between them. Preferred mate. Partner. Not *married* because both would have other sexual encounters and that was expected. Queens typically mated with more than one drone when in heat and scouts? Part of their reason for *existing* involved orgies.

An open relationship in human terms. A *normal* relationship in verr ones. Tayken was larger than her mate, the largest verr Beverly had seen.

And tagging along with them were three verr children, the first such Beverly had seen. They were not very old. Tayken and Kaykek's litter then. And Tayken looked...was she pregnant? Likely. Queens were expected to be pregnant all the time.

An endangered species couldn't risk the gene pool. One of the kids stared at her. She waved to it...that was the right pronoun even if it felt wrong, and it glanced at its father, who nodded.

The pup toddled over to her and looked up, then chittered something. They hadn't given the kids translators. Maybe they were hoping to expose young pups to offworld languages so if the translation tech wasn't available, they had linguists as backup. She smiled at the kid, not quite sure what to do.

Then Tayken took her place at the mic and everything else was forgotten. It wasn't that they hadn't given the kids translators.

Alvi had turned the translation matrix *off* so everyone could hear Tayken's raw words, and they were beautiful. Beverly could ask for a translation later, but right now, the sharp chitters and trills of verr language, Ilyrek Hive language or at least dialect, washed over her. The rhythms. Alvi was right.

Translating this would ruin it. So, who had the courage to follow the professional? Tayken read three poems and would read three more at the end.

Kai Bowie bravely went next, and belted out Martian slam poetry that was a complete change in mood. Smart move, Beverly thought.

Then the glyn representative sang. It probably was poetry, but untranslated glyn language was basically music to start with. Beverly closed her eyes, but opened them when she felt movement next to her. Parvati.

Parvati was going up there. And the poem she recited, Beverly did understand most of. She knew a smattering of Parvati's minority language, enough to get the gist. It was about lost worlds and lost lands and it was sad and beautiful and it would speak to the verr more than anything else. If they could get a good translation. She hoped they could.

BEVERLY REQUESTED TRANSLATIONS of all of Tayken's poems. Alvi said that they already had them, because translations had been made for the English language market. They were good translations, but Beverly knew they lost something compared to the original. It was hard to keep something from the herd. Where, exactly, had Parvati hidden a talent for poetry?

The next morning, Beverly "confronted" her. "I didn't know you could..."

"Neither did I," Parvati admitted. "It's something I considered when I was a kid, but then they thought I was herdless and I got recruited."

"Well, keep doing it."

"I will. Everyone seemed to...maybe enjoy isn't the right word."

"We have to get it translated for the verr. I understood enough to know it would make them cry. It made me cry."

"I won't apologize."

"Poetry is sometimes *meant* to make people cry."

"I saw you ended up pup sitting."

Beverly laughed. "Kid might not have seen...no, kid's seen a wheel-chair before, I heard one of the drones uses one, along with a number of workers. But the combination of offworlder and wheelchair and toddler. Adorable children."

"Looked like she was pregnant again."

"Kaykek told me that they hope to take the reproductive pressure off the queens in the future when they become less endangered."

Parvati shuddered slightly. "I don't envy them."

"Neither do I. Kaykek also told me they're hoping to work with human reproductive scientists on things like birth control, and possibly ways to suppress or induce puberty."

"Allowing workers to choose whether they want to express into one of the other castes and if so which one. That would..."

"It would mean that all of the queens would be people who liked babies, at least. Tayken seems happy."

"She is," Parvati said after a moment. "Those poems were not written by somebody who feels trapped and unhappy."

"Whilst yours..."

"There are some things in history that we cannot be expected to get over, not in one generation, not in one thousand. Are there not such things on your world?"

"Yes. Ask a Black person about slavery or a Jewish person about the Shoah." Beverly shuddered. "The Reich killed a lot of disabled people too. Anyone who didn't measure up."

"Our land was taken for mining long before the ky'iin came. At some levels they did us a favor. Once we were all victims, we started to get on."

Beverly couldn't help but laugh sharply at that. "Humans unite in the face of an opposing force too. I think everyone does."

"But there are still people who look at my fur and see somebody who might be that bit less educated, less intelligent. They look at me and see muscle." Parvati wrinkled her nose. "The nice thing about hanging out with humans is you have no clue."

Beverly laughed. "I heard something similar from Adwoa."

"Dark skinned people..."

"Slavery. A particularly nasty variation on that historical theme that turned into a caste system that held them down for centuries. Its *why* there are so many Black people on Venus. They're trying to make it their world."

"To letting them do so," Parvati said, finally, lifting her mug of pintak tea.

Beverly grinned. "Indeed."

31

SOME DAYS it wasn't easy being so far away from his husband and daughter.

Sending Charles an ansible message only made them feel further away, only increased the distance. It made Graeme...not homesick, because it wasn't a place he wanted, he just wanted his family.

Maybe the tyrar word "alreth," "herdsick," applied here. Of course, the tyrar could get literally sick from solitude. He wasn't that vulnerable. But still. He was herdsick. He wanted to cuddle Marion.

The pups during the poetry reading hadn't helped either. They were much younger than Marion...he wasn't sure how verr developmental phases worked, but they were toddlers. And adorable.

And getting into everything. It was, of course, a profound trust that Tayken had brought them rather than leaving them in the care of the creche. Likely, then, she was thinking of socializing the kids to offworlders some, of making them used to being around them at a young age.

Hopefully they would work well with them. And Refuge was the hive which *would* handle all of that. It might well be that no offworlder would set foot on Kyverr. That the great ship and the second one that the verr now had would be their giant embassies, the hives that dealt with outsiders.

Graeme sighed. Part of him wanted to get blind drunk and sleep it off and hope he felt better in the morning. He was smart and mature enough to know that would only make him feel worse in the morning.

So instead, he looked up Slyk and the two went to the coffee shop, which was still selling a variety of juices.

The fresh juice from Earth had, of course, all been drunk at this point, but it did seem that some was being grown on Refuge and they had frozen juice which, while not as good, was better than no juice.

Slyk sucked some through their mandibles. "So..."

"I miss my mate and my child." Glyn didn't have mates, but Slyk knew.

"I miss my ka," Slyk admitted.

"Don't we all? I envy Kaykek, ze gets to go back to zir mate every night if ze wants."

Which ze didn't, not every night, but having seen those kids, Graeme thought he understood why.

Ze was using work as an excuse not to be exhausted by three toddlers. It made sense that the verr, with so few fertile individuals, would breed in litters, but the thought was exhausting.

"When the council has a permanent location..."

"Then we should be able to settle our families with us. But we can't agree on that."

Well, can't was a strong word. Hadn't so far was accurate, though. And they had tried.

Everyone except the glyn wanted it. "Maybe your place. You are the people who *don't* want to use it for politics."

"Not in the current state of our house," Slir said, quite seriously. "There has to be a solution everyone will be equally unhappy with."

Graeme laughed at the phrasing, but Slir was probably right.

Equally unhappy was the best they could hope for.

Slyk went off to do council stuff. Graeme, more focused now, went back to trying to work out who the mole was.

Dhyanil was going to talk to the interns, disguised as a test of the pheromonic perfume they needed to test anyway. They were definitely a logical course of inquiry, but Graeme focused on eliminating others.

He could absolutely eliminate both Marlowe and the Martian and Venusian representatives. While it was physically possible that it was Kai Bowie, it seemed unimaginable. He could also eliminate Chan.

After a moment, he put Bowie back on the list. He hated to do so, but he couldn't *actually* eliminate them. They fit the physical parameters and their brightly-colored hair gave a special motivation to wear a hat. He hoped not. It would hurt Kaykek, who liked the Martian a lot.

But there was another reason he thought it unlikely, and that was that the focus was on Earth, not Mars. Martians had fought and won a literal war not to be seen as an extension of Earth.

It made no sense that a Martian would be betraying the Council to work with what appeared to be extremists from Earth. Unless it was a Martian false flag operation, but that made no sense either. Not that everything had to make sense.

It didn't. It didn't remotely *have* to make sense. However, he was able to set that theory aside, literally. He was working on a flat table with physical notes. No hacker could see them unless they were in Alvi's sensory grid.

The AI claimed they had checked and were sure there was nothing going on there. Graeme had to believe them, but because of the niggling suspicions he still had, he wasn't about to trust his speculations to the network. So, he wrote "Martian false flag" on a card and put it off to the side.

He then considered all of the various aides. Chan had brought two aides and the two interns. Adowa and Kai Bowie had brought two aides each. The ones from Earth were the obvious suspects. Unfortunately, he *had* had to use the network to pull up their pictures so he could look at them side by side.

Alas, none of them could be immediately eliminated by their body type or hair. It was a shame that it had not been a human who saw them go into the closet; one always noticed more details about one's own species. That was only natural, really. Humans had to look odd, even ugly to the verr, more upright, no tails, no body hair, clothing.

Well, verr did wear clothing, but not for modesty. They wore it only when their jobs needed the protection or occasionally for decoration. Tayken had worn a kind of sleeveless, open robe when reciting her poetry that was clearly intended to look pretty. He'd seen pictures of Vrycek Hive members wearing rank insignia.

But most verr didn't have external genitalia to cover anyway, and those who did? Well, they were proud of them.

So human nudity taboos? Very alien.

He looked at the pictures. Not helpful. So he pulled up the first file and started to read.

Somewhere in here was the answer.

THEY STILL HAD the kid doing punishment duty and surrounded by verr. A warrior brought him to Graeme.

"Looking forward to getting back to Earth?"

The kid hesitated. "Yes and...no? I mean, they have me cleaning and I want the sky, but they..."

"They aren't such bad people, right?"

Maybe they could get more people to trust aliens through the process of immersion, just like with a foreign language. Maybe.

But it might also be dangerous. "I need to ask more questions about who paid you."

"It was through the boards. I don't know. They make sure we don't know."

Graeme nods. "Username?"

He frowned. "Potato3756."

"Potato? What, an Irish person with a grudge against the English? Or maybe they got it from a random word generator?"

The kid shrugged. "Who knows, but they seemed to be...they seemed to be connected to Great America."

"And you're a skinny white cis straight boy, so you don't care about the damage those people have done."

He looked down. Looked away.

"Those people would take my daughter away from me to raise her in a more suitable home. But...you were just after the money."

"I was," the kid said without looking back.

"So, now, will you help us?"

He turned back. "Will you get me off latrine duty?"

Graeme smiled. "That's up to the verr. But I can certainly ask."

"At least I've gotten used to the way they smell. I suppose it's the pherrythings."

"Pheromones. Yes, that and different species have different body odor. That's why dogs stink sometimes."

"I suppose that's a good point."

"And we probably smell worse to them. Verr have very good noses. So...I need to find out. There's another saboteur on board."

The kid blinked. Leaned forward. Graeme had his attention. "Who?"

"That's what we're trying to find out. They're human." A pause. "I think you were not hired by Great America. Or perhaps you were."

"They had money," the kid muses. "Enough..."

"Enough to buy a ship from the ky'iin on the grey market. Enough to hijack the *Columbia*. Tell me everything you can about Potato Guy."

It just as easily be Potato Girl, but Potato Guy sounded better in his head. He was going to find out what was going on here, even if he didn't know how. But he was starting to have a suspicion.

One which centered on Earth, and on a particular part of Earth.

32

KNOWING there was a spy or saboteur on board bothered Kaykek less than perhaps it should have, solely because ze was used to this kind of danger.

Ze had become, not blase, but *accustomed* to being in danger, even to the pups being in danger.

The pups would eventually grow up and be able to look after themselves. Tayken could look after herself.

But it was natural to worry a little.

What *was* back in that maintenance area? Kaykek studied the plans and found a cavity that was, essentially, between two rooms.

A portable ansible would absolutely fit in there, but how had the human *got* it in there without being noticed? One disturbing possibility was that they hadn't...they had suborned workers to help them. Ze knew it wasn't impossible.

Ze wished it was, but the truth was that verr did have ambitions and free will. Money would not sway a verr worker, who could claim anything they needed from their hive. Other things might.

Knowledge, for example. Technology. Even art. Verr were bribable, it just took a bit longer to work out what a specific individual might need. There was also simple dishonesty. Tricking somebody into thinking it was important. "Alvi," ze said, finally.

"Yes."

"How much have you been unable to see that closet?"

"Now it's been pointed out to me, I've had a number of transient sensor failures in that area." They sounded annoyed.

"You're not omniscient."

"No, but I should have noticed that."

"Somebody should have noticed and fixed it."

"You think..."

"I think we have some compromised workers. Probably bribed with..."

"Something from Earth they can't easily get on the ship. Could it be exotic..."

"Cheese," Kaykek said wryly. "I would almost...and I stress almost...betray the hive for a supply."

Alvi made the chittering sound of laughter. "I noticed that."

"Unfortunately, even a greatship doesn't really have space for dairy livestock."

"Kyverr does, though."

"Yes." A pause. "Don't worry, I won't leave you for a planet, not even for a regular supply of cheese."

"If you were going to, you would have. Although..."

"If I get selected as the permanent representative I'll have to spend most of my time wherever the council ends up meeting."

"Who's winning?"

"It's a horrible fight between the human and ky'iin representatives every time. Both of them want it, badly, to the point where I actually saw Dhyanil's claws come out. I think the glyn are halfway towards offering just because they *don't* want it."

"There has to be a solution. But...the saboteur."

"We need to find out who, if anyone, has been suborned."

"There is nothing wrong with the sensors there."

"Right. So a worker wouldn't have noticed anything, thinking about it. Still, whatever they are hiding, they had to get it there."

"And might have used cheese or books to bribe their way past any workers."

"Any *cheese* would have been eaten. Can you check for unauthorized art uploads?"

"I can, but there were a lot of *authorized* uploads. Humans produce art like they breathe."

"I noticed that. Please, do what..."

"It's a good idea, but I don't know if it will work."

"The other alternative is for us to find a couple of workers we really trust and send them in to look for out of place equipment."

"So, who do you trust?"

"You," Kaykek quipped. Talking to Alvi as if they were merely a friend always felt good.

But ze needed to find somebody with a body for this one. That wasn't a ship.

THE WORKER'S name was Barkyn. It went into the closet ahead of Kaykek.

The tape had been broken at some point, but there had not been anyone there to see the person leave. Still, it told Kaykek they were not still in there with some kind of weapon.

Ze followed Barkyn in. "You know this area?"

"Not precisely, but there are multiple identical ones. It's a storage area that we might use for robots or something."

Kaykek was not sure how ze felt about robots doing what workers could do. Alvi was a different case.

But ze was also not affected by it and wouldn't be making any decisions on the matter. A simple robot could not replace zir.

Somebody carrying a box of sperm could, but that wasn't nearly as much fun. Ze followed nonetheless.

"So. That shouldn't be there. That conduit?"

"What about it?"

"There's a second cable taped along it. It's the same color. Would never have seen it if I hadn't been looking for anything out of place.

Kaykek sniffed towards the cable. "Good work. So, what does it power?"

"Something, but..."

Barkyn hesitated. Then it moved forward again. "Stay back."

"Barkyn..."

But it was too late. Ze could not stop it from scurrying into the room. There was a poof of smoke and zir nostrils itched. Ze could hear Barkyn choking.

Ze scurried backwards, out of range of the smoke, and looked to see if there was a respirator. Finding one, ze tossed it into the smoke. It was too late.

As the smoke spread, ze backed away. "Barkyn!"

No response. Ze found a second respirator. Strapped it on. Ventured into the smoke, which felt very thick with zir sense of smell muffled.

Barkyn lay on the ground, its tail curled up slightly. It was very dead. It had seen the trap. It had sprung it, assuming it would not be lethal, perhaps. But now the saboteur or saboteurs had a life to answer for.

Kaykek fled, determined to come back with warriors in environment suits.

Because ze too had something to answer for. Ze had asked an innocent worker to help zir and now it was dead. Ze was not of higher value than a worker, but Barkyn had seen zir that way, had done what it felt was right. Had taken on the risk so ze didn't have to. But now ze knew, at least, that there was something in there.

Something that the person who put it there was willing to kill to hide.

"THAT IS DEFINITELY A PORTABLE ANSIBLE," Graeme pronounced. They were all wearing respirators and light environment suits.

The poison gas appeared to be the only booby trap. The warriors had removed Barkyn's body. Kaykek could mourn and blame zirself later.

"Anything else in here?" Kaykek looked around. "I'm disoriented in a respirator." Which was one reason why ze had invited the less-smell-dependent human along.

"The ansible, and some memory sticks. Will you let me analyze them? I don't think we should let them anywhere near the ship's systems."

"Neither do I." Kaykek nodded. "Go ahead. How about we disable this?"

"I would normally say...disable it in a way they wouldn't notice, but..."

"But thanks to my stupidity they know."

"It wasn't your fault."

Zir ears flattened. "Yes it was. I should have thought of booby traps."

"Yes, but everyone has hindsight. Everyone has regrets. And...Kaykek you aren't the first person to mess up in a fatal way."

"I almost wish..."

"Don't. It pushed you out of the way because *you* are the Verr ambassador and it was an engineer."

"Doesn't make me more valuable."

"It makes you a lot harder to replace. Which is hard to get used to, I know. And later you and I can...verr get drunk, right?"

That was an interesting offer. "I guess we should..."

"Disable this first. I have an idea."

He moved behind the ansible, dropping to one knee and messing with something she couldn't see. "That should take them a while to notice."

"Even if they're looking for it?"

"This is only stage one. Tell Alvi I'll need their help with stage two."

"I think you can ask Alvi directly. They won't mind."

"I'm going to need to borrow a few workers."

"You're going to jam it."

"Yes. They'll find what I did, plug it back in, and think they've solved the problem."

Kaykek chittered. "Did they leave bugs in here?"

Graeme tapped a small device on his belt. "If they did..."

Zir ears dropped again. Ze had not thought to bring a jammer. "I don't think I'm a very good spy."

"You probably aren't. But you *are* a rather good diplomat. Bring spies with you."

Kaykek considered that. Refuge Hive didn't have spies per se, but it surely had workers that could be trained. But some of them would die. Could ze be responsible for that? Ze was not sure.

Getting drunk *did* quite appeal.

33

A VERR WORKER WAS DEAD. Kaykek was blaming zirself and getting drunk with Graeme.

Dhyanil knew he should have stepped in. He should have handled it. He knew how Kaykek felt, but the circumstances were oh so different.

And yet the same.

It was perhaps always the same when somebody you were leading ended up dead. You always blamed yourself. You always felt bad, and you always ended up doing it again. Command was like that.

Kaykek was a diplomat, not a spy, and perhaps not well suited to command, although it was hard to tell, really.

He did not know zir well enough.

But part of him was tempted to join them just so that ze could talk to somebody who, well, *got* it.

But then, Graeme did. He was sure of that, although he didn't know what the circumstances might be, what might have happened to cause him to be in that situation.

There was something very hard and sharp in that human's past, and even the barriers of species and language could not hide it.

Something that almost reminded Dhyanil of his mother, but Graeme had learned something his mother had never possessed. Restraint. That too was very clear. So instead of joining them, Dhyanil sat alone in the observation room. They were in a system claimed by the tyrar now, keeping moving.

If the ansible had been disabled then there was nobody to tell the terrorists where they were. So perhaps they were safe and could finally focus entirely on the remaining discussions. Which included that huge sticking point.

Location.

There was no way to please everyone. Of course, there were other things. Some of them they had dropped. The sapient rights charter had to be written in such a way that it accepted biological differences. For example, they could not argue that unhatched eggs were people in front of the glyn.

He shuddered at glyn reproductive habits. Biological and understandable and sensible in their system, but it was a terrible crime to ky'iin. And the live bearers had different viewpoints again.

So sapience was defined as the point where the offspring was physically separated from the parent or had hatched from an egg. With space to expand it if they found a species that had yet another way of doing things. It always left freedom to value *more* than the charter said. But they were trying to future proof too, and how could they do that? It had to be a living document, it had to be something they could rewrite as needed. The humans had precedents for that, if not good ones. The council would be making decisions constantly, interpreting and reinterpreting.

And Kyx seemed in no hurry to replace him. Dhyanil sighed. He had hoped...but no. He was in this until somebody else wanted the job or he died. He was starting to think it might be the latter.

So?

He was realizing he needed to get good at this.

"FIRST, I'd listen to Kaykek. Ze has a natural talent."

Dhyanil could not be sure that Kai Bowie wasn't the saboteur, but the Martian representative had a natural exuberance that made it easy to hang out with them.

The fact that they were also non-binary hit a cultural note too. Part of why Dhyanil thought himself ill-suited to this was that he was not ly'iin. Humans had no ly'iin, but Dhyanil still had a mental resonance that those who were not male or female, or not quite, were natural diplomats.

"I am."

"I suspect you'll be replaced once we can safely tell everyone where we are."

"Maybe." A pause. "No, they will. They will send a ly'iin. But that doesn't mean I can necessarily leave."

"No, I suppose it doesn't. Or they might send you to be, say, ambassador to Earth. Gender or no..."

"I do know more about humans than any other ky as far as I know," Dhyanil mused. "I would send me back there. Well, could be worse. The fishing's good."

Kai laughed. "Have you visited Mars?"

"No, I haven't had reason to, and..." Dhyanil was wearing the calming perfume. It seemed to be working on Kai, at least.

"Well, I am handling you fine."

"Yes, but there's pharmacological help involved."

"True. I understand why they might not have wanted you in the domes."

"I might have caused a mass panic and worse. Dome colonies are so vulnerable."

It took a lot to destroy a city on a habitable planet. It took very little to destroy a dome. Mars and Venus shared that peculiar vulnerability, as did the outer system settlements in both systems. Kyx had not had a near-habitable planet nearby for dome colonies.

Humans had them down and he had made notes of quite a few design principles that could be useful to the people building said things for the ky'iin. "I'm not offended. But maybe one day."

"Take you to the Olympus Mons retreat to see human weirdness at its very best," Kai offered.

"I hear that..."

"Clothing is very much optional."

Dhyanil laughed. "Humans are very much obsessed with clothing. So..."

"I think you are doing fine. You know when to compromise and you won't budge on the things that are important. And you are a really strong voice for allowing those who want to be left alone to be left alone. We need that."

Dhyanil extended a claw and ran it around the tip of his mug. "I know how people like that think. They're afraid. And scared people kill."

"We haven't seen that with the verr or glyn."

"The glyn are too embarrassed to admit it and the verr are too grateful to have all of their strength. We will."

And there might be verr involved. He could not forget that.

Nor could poor Kaykek.

"How did they find us?" Dhyanil asked. "I thought..."

"I did jam the ansible."

"Could they have brought two on board?" Dhyanil mused. "In case? They're expensive, but..."

"But that is a warship out there."

Two ships, in fact. The *Columbia* and the yacht.

They would never be safe. They would never be safe as long as these people *wanted* to kill them.

"There's only one solution to this," Dhyanil said.

"Which is?"

"We have to talk to them and convince them to stop wanting to do this."

"That seems unlikely to work."

A deep breath. Dhyanil turned towards the wall, imagining he was talking to somebody with a physical avatar. "It worked on me. I *was* those people. I would be out there shooting at you. No, we can't get all of them to stop. We'll have to kill some of them. But in the end, the *only* way to stop people who are afraid is to help them to stop being afraid. And I know you have no idea where to start. You might be able to calculate numbers, and you have emotions, but you also don't *have* xenophobia. They programmed it out of you."

A long silence from the AI. Then. "You are right. The only thing I feel about those not like me is curiosity. And I love the verr."

"I know you do. But you don't understand...the human reaction to ky'iin is the extreme version. The disgust that some of us feel when we look at the alien, at the other. I feel it when I think about glyn reproduction. I get uncomfortable when I look at humans and remember the females are the skinny ones. I don't understand how verr and tyrar can be so all *wrapped up* in each other. Because they don't *work* like we do."

A pause. "Everyone feels it. Those of us who can overcome it...some do so quickly, others take longer, and some simply can't. Like the verr workers you have assigned to the other side of the ship where they don't have to see or smell us. We'll work through it in the end, but it's probably going to involve..."

"It's going to involve something like pup trading." Alvi considered. "Creches where volunteers allow their children to be raised and taught. Boarding schools, maybe. In the long run."

"In the long run we can raise kids who don't feel it and who thoroughly accept that the glyn do what they do from biological necessity not...not psychopathy. But for right now we have to train ourselves, we have to accept that some people can't deal with offworlders. But we also have to make them less afraid."

"What about offering them a human colony world..."

"They want Earth. That's the issue. They're the same type of people as those who tried to bioweapon Kyx back into the stone age. They won't accept a colony. They want Earth. We *have* to talk them down."

"You can't talk to them on video."

That was true. The pheromones worked face to face, but they didn't transmit. Any human who saw Dhyanil on video. "No. But humans handle audio only just fine and I *do* speak English. Pretty well."

Maybe he wasn't 100% fluent and his maw struggled with some of the sounds.

But he was determined to talk to them.

He had to try.

Before anyone else died.

34

BEVERLY FELT HELPLESS. It was never a feeling she cared for.

But they had been found again. They shouldn't have been, but they had.

So far, the *Columbia* had not fired on *Refuge* this time. They seemed to be biding their time.

Or, more likely, up to something.

Beverly was a scientist. And she had not been terrible when it came to situations like this on a planet. On this ship? She was a passenger, and there wasn't much a passenger could do to fix things. She just had to endure and keep going.

Keep going. The poetry recital had helped and maybe next time she would find the courage to go up herself. One of the people who *had* was a verr worker who looked barely full grown. She couldn't fairly judge the quality of its contribution, but...

Everyone had encouraged the kid.

She still wondered what it was like to live without any kind of libido. She had had friends who were asexual, but it wasn't the same thing.

It wasn't the same thing as simply not having those feelings turned on.

(A small part of her wished that there was somebody she was interested in amongst the human aides. While she and Yoshi could entertain one another, it wasn't quite the same thing either. And she refused to even look at the journalists).

So. What could she do that would help? She had to find something or she was going to go insane. Stir crazy. Moral support to the ones with the serious intelligence skills?

She rolled into the herd quarters and saw Parvati sitting there, looking at...Beverly's backup laptop.

"Can I help you with anything?"

Parvati turned. "Graeme gave me some data to analyze and I have to keep it airwalled. I hope you don't mind that I borrowed this."

Beverly hadn't hooked it up to the network and it was still in no interference mode. "Not at all. Not like I was even using it."

She rolled over. "What's the data?"

"Potentials for our saboteur. He wanted a second set of eyes over it. Well, a third. Dhyanil's looking too."

Beverly nodded. "Want my human opinion?"

"Of course! Also, you look..."

"We might be in a space battle any moment. Why haven't we jumped?"

"Dhyanil thinks we should talk to them."

"He can't, though. Well, maybe audio only, his English is good."

"No, the actual talking should probably be a human. Somebody they won't see as a..." Parvati tailed off.

"No no. Wait a minute. Totally not what I'm saying."

But Parvati, with an expression Beverly recognized as wicked, already had her phone out.

"I DIDN'T AGREE TO THIS," Beverly noted in the conference room, although it had the air of the kind of half hearted protest made by a woman who knew full well that the thing had to be done, even if she was still not sure she was the one to do it.

But when it came to not being a threat? She was not a threat. She was also white. Of course, so was Graeme, but everyone knew he was gay. He'd been seen on camera with his husband and their delightful daughter.

Beverly might not be straight, but her love life had plenty of discretion shielding it. She could let them assume.

Alvi's deep voice, "So, we will record it here and then broadcast it on their frequencies. Likely they will ignore us, but it's worth a try."

"And you're ready if they start shooting?"

"Indeed."

If they took this badly they probably *would* start shooting. But Dhyanil was right.

Dhyanil had *been* a separatist, xenophobic terrorist. He truly did know how people like that thought.

He also knew how people like that could be...helped? Saved? Saved would be nice. She wanted to be part of what saved them, if that was in the cards. She had known plenty of people like them growing up. The people who did not know anything but the mountains and poverty and climate change. Who remembered when the money had come from mining.

The kind of people who had voted *for* Austerity. Who had seen removing women from the workforce as the best way to protect jobs for men. Who had seen the birth rate plummet and blamed it on "the gays" and "transgender ideology." Who had seen helping others as a way of harming themselves.

So they had voted for Austerity and Great America and it was history now, but it was *recent* history. It was living memory history. It had never been something that could last long. But she had fought her way out of it, gone to university, reclaimed her rights. Marched both before and after the accident.

She sat there facing a screen that showed cartoon figures so she had a mental audience to speak to. She found that it did, perhaps surprisingly, help.

"We would like to talk to you. We promise amnesty if you send representatives on board. None will be harmed, although we won't tolerate any attempts to harm us. We have common ground and we *do* have shared goals. We will make sure that those who prefer not to interact with the aliens are respected."

She was, to them, a species traitor and known to be one. "I have chosen my life. You have the freedom to choose yours. We aren't weakened or contaminated by the other. We are strengthened by it. But we *should* hold something of ourselves back, just in case."

She knew Dhyanil wouldn't be offended by that. Would Parvati? Her herdmate gave her a rather large thumbs up.

"We have to preserve our differences. When I watched Star Trek, the Borg said they would add our biological distinctiveness to their own, but we all know that the Borg erase differences. We can't, we don't *want* to risk that happening. And we can't. Humans are apes, tyrar and ky'iin are *not* apes. Ky'iin are apex predators in a way we are not. Glyn aren't even naturally evolved. Each of those things...we're all beautiful and valuable. Please come aboard. Please let's *talk* instead of shooting at each other. The universe is big enough."

It wouldn't work.

For these people, it had never worked. They had never been willing to tolerate anything that varied from them, they had sought to destroy things which did them no harm.

But she had tried.

Once it was off, she turned, "It won't work. The ultimate dream of people like this is to turn everyone into them."

"So, colonialists."

She shook her head. "Worse."

"YOU REALLY DON'T THINK it will work."

Beverly shook her head. "No. I think it was worth trying, but I know what they want. And if they do come on board..."

"Then we have to watch them like hawks, make them empty their pockets when they arrive *and* when they leave and, the human saying is to count our fingers?"

"One hundred percent. They've already killed people. Not as many as I think they'd want."

Parvati pursed her lips, looking a bit like a cartoon ape for a moment. "I don't think they think they've killed any people. Isn't there an awful pun on verr and vermin in English?"

"Yes, yes there is. And I bet it shows up in xenophobic literature. Doesn't help that they *do* vaguely resemble rats. Which carry disease and steal food."

"Verr don't carry disease and they cook."

Beverly grinned. "Very well, some of them. I think one of the advantages of being in a hive is that you don't have to do for yourself. I mean, some verr do cook as a hobby, but it appears they generally eat in canteens because it's the job of the cooks."

"Yeah, they hyperspecialize. Which allows them to be very good at what they do, although I'm glad they still have hobbies."

"Doing the same thing all the time is what *actually* makes Jack a dull boy," Beverly agreed. "But these people."

"The XO of the *Columbia*, it looks like he *was* part of this movement as a kid then supposedly grew out of it."

"He faked it," Beverly said grimly. "Faked it. I'm sure he was planning on waiting until he had command then events pushed it slightly prematurely."

"Standard deep cover work. Oh, my...what is it?"

"Wild oats?"

"Yes, that. My wild oats have wilted and I've plowed them in. But the seeds are still sitting there."

Beverly laughed at Parvati's extended metaphor. "So he got rid of the captain by..."

"Taking him to a brothel and paying the girls to keep him happy for a bit too long, right?"

"Right."

Tyrar didn't really sell sex like humans did. They sold sex that *was* intended to result in offspring, not recreational sex. But Parvati understood the concept.

"Then took off without him. It's a shame we can't get to some of the crew."

"If we could talk to them, then...If some of them do come over, what do you think our chances are of separating them?"

"You're starting to think like a spy."

Beverly shuddered. "Heaven forbid."

"I'm rubbing off on you. Don't worry, it goes both ways. I actually understood Yoshi's latest paper."

As if summoned by her name, Yoshi came in. She looked very bemused at the laughter she arrived to.

35

GRAEME HAD LONG COME to the same conclusion about the XO. He had fed the information to Parvati to check his conclusions.

But the XO was one of them. And it appeared that Aw had taken his personnel recommendations. A good XO *was* the person you turned to for those. Keeping the crew tight and happy was part of the XO's job.

It appeared that Anthony Pulsom had spent a lot of effort on making sure that the crew...disproportionately white and male...were his picks almost entirely.

Then he had dropped Aw on Earth and simply taken over. Anyone who wasn't his man to start with either was now, or was in the brig or dead. Graeme would be surprised to find out if *nobody* had gone out an airlock.

After all, it was fairly clear Pulsom had moved prematurely. The presence of the yacht confirmed they were dealing with one conspiracy, or at least allied conspiracies, rather than several. He had not been sure until now.

Now he was. And he was sure it was not just Great America. It was America.

Supposedly it had all been suppressed. It wasn't *acceptable* to be like that any more. Slowly, freedom had returned to that part of the continent, not so much by law, but by custom. Probably the only way it would take.

And they had even made progress on dismantling the caste system that Charles so feared.

Progress. Graeme was glad to be Scottish many times, and most especially when he thought about what had happened in and to America.

To the people they had not thought of as acceptable or the ones they thought they could *make* acceptable.

He fell into that category. The ones they thought they could fix. He was very glad to be Scottish.

Charles had ansible'd him the *Columbia*'s crew roster. He hoped and prayed at least somebody over there had realized the value of pretending to play along in order to get information.

But these people had government support. They had high level support. It could happen again. It wasn't acceptable. That didn't mean it had stopped existing. It meant it had gone underground, but who...

Who could be bankrolling this? From here, light years away from Earth, there was no way for Graeme to know or even to guess who might be. He didn't have access to the dossiers.

Charles did, but he wasn't as good at this, he was good, but he wasn't *as* good, and he also had to be careful.

He could be a target. Marion, an abomination in their eyes, could *really* be a target. They wouldn't care that she was eight years old.

Some of those people thought she didn't have a soul, never mind that she was biologically identical to a naturally-conceived child. She wasn't even a clone...but then, all twins were clones.

Graeme shook his head. Then their answer came. It surprised him and didn't at the same time.

"Yes."

———

PULCHROM HAD SENT the operations officer, who looked like one of those old NASA commercials. The Right Stuff.

He looked like he played an astronaut on TV.

He was accompanied by two crewmen who *also* looked like they had stepped right from the era where white men were men and everyone else was only arguably human.

No doubt these three were both loyal to the conspiracy and expendable. Operations? They had a backup, but it looked like they had sent somebody of rank.

All three stepped out of the shuttle as if they owned the place. While they were here, it was *fairly* clear the *Columbia* would not attack.

Graeme suspected that if they tried to take them hostage, though? It would not work. Not with these people.

He saw Beverly's face pale a little from nerves.

The operations officer walked towards Graeme. He ignored the aliens...Parvati guarding Beverly and a large female verr warrior protecting Graeme.

He ignored Beverly. "Good, you are not letting a woman talk for you now."

Graeme quirked his lips. And said nothing.

They stared at each other.

"Welcome on board," Beverly said.

He continued to ignore her and stare at Graeme. It was almost entertaining to watch. Who would win this particular match of stubbornness?

Finally, begrudgingly, "Thank you."

"We're going to go to a conference room."

The man nodded. "Do we need *them*?" He didn't say who.

Beverly turned her chair smoothly to lead the way. "Parvati is family and the other is there to keep an eye on you on behalf of the crew of *Refuge*. You understand why they would want to.

One of the younger crewmen muttered something under his breath. Graeme smiled inwardly. *He* couldn't hear it. He had no doubt Parvati could and likely the verr too. Humans had the best color vision out of the sentient species, but not the best hearing by a long shot.

He had rapidly had to learn that a whisper didn't mean anything around verr and tyrar. Ky'iin and glyn not so much. But verr and tyrar? They could hear everything. Well, except tyrar couldn't hear the very highest registers of human hearing. Sopranos would drop off when they hit their high notes.

Whatever it was was probably horribly insulting and he had no doubt he would find out what it was. They had a surprise waiting for these men in the conference room. There *were* still some female crew on *Columbia*, if they hadn't been brigged or airlocked, but only men had come. Men who strode through *Refuge* as if they owned the place.

He wondered if the whispered word had referred to the aliens or to him. Maybe they had called him a cigarette...an amusing piece of cross-atlantic slang. If so, it wouldn't be the first time or the last. Beverly led them into the conference room.

Which contained Chan, Kaykek and Dhyanil.

DHYANIL WAS STANDING LEANING CASUALLY against the wall. Graeme could almost deal with the ky'iin's monstrous presence without the pheromones now.

Kaykek was there to protect Dhyanil from the strangers.

And to make a point.

Chan was sitting at the table. "Please sit."

The three stared at the ky'iin.

"I wouldn't," Beverly said. "The verr and Parvati will sit on you if you attack anyone."

"What did you do?" the younger one blurted. Then, "Is it real?"

"He is very real. We have found away to...blunt the effect ky'iin have on humans."

The operations officer frowned.

"Please. Sit."

He finally sat, but the other two remained standing. "Ambassador. I am Peter Molcroft."

"Welcome to *Refuge*, Mr. Molcroft."

Molcroft. Mole croft. Graeme would explain why that was funny to the verr later.

"I want to talk to humans. No offworlders."

Chan shook his head. "This is the verr's ship. I *could* ask the others to leave, but the verr will know even if they do."

Molcroft frowned, then nodded. "I was hoping to speak to you man to man. You speak for the interests of Earth, and you are selling them to these..." A pause. "Creatures."

Chan elevated an eyebrow like the mythical Mr. Spock. "I have not sold anything. We have traded certain knowledge. Would you not want humanity to have a ship like this?"

"We can build it ourselves."

"Oh, sure, eventually. Buying the design from the tyrar is a lot faster. And safer, because it's already been tested."

"By rugs."

Parvati wrinkled her nose at that. The humans would probably think it was disgust. They wouldn't know they were being laughed at.

"By people with some very high health and safety standards. Do you think I would be on this ship if I didn't think it was safe?"

"I think you have been sold something by these aliens."

Graeme bet Molcroft did not know that they had translators. Or, for that matter, that Dhyanil was pretty close to fluent in English and Parvati didn't do bad in the language either.

He also bet Molcroft did not speak Chinese.

Chan nodded. "I have been sold fascinating information, the possibility of greatly expanding our reach into space, and peace. I think all of those things are worth something. There is nothing that says *you* have to work with them."

Graeme wondered if Molcraft was about to come out with something hideously racist. It was in the air, with the tension that flowed between everyone present. Between and around.

"They will corrupt..."

And Dhyanil spoke. In English, to hide the translation. There was something about the language emerging from the ky'iin's maw...some sounds running together because the ky'iin did not have as well developed a voice box as humans...but understandable in the way a parrot was understandable. Alien, but definitely English.

"On my world, people like you tried to genetically engineer us back into the stone age. They tried to bring back the days when a woman could take any man she wanted when in heat. People like you, who talked about corruption and contamination. You should go home. Protect the parts of your world that *are* vulnerable but let the rest move forward. I've spent the last few years on your island of Trinidad, mostly on my own because humans don't deal well with ky'iin. That's a place worth protecting."

"It's full of..."

"Of the wrong kind of humans. But humanity is worth protecting. So are all of us. And we need *peace* to make sure of that. Why do you want war?"

36

HUMANS DIDN'T GIVE off much in the way of pheromones, but Kaykek was absolutely sure these men smelled of hate.

Of hate and fear.

Dhyanil was talking now, in one of the human languages. Apparently he mangled it, but it seemed they understood him.

Zir translator gave zir the gist. He was pretty angry, ze decided, even though he was speaking human and keeping his body fairly still. Ze could still see it in him, could see him vibrating towards attacking them physically, controlling himself.

No. He was doing it on purpose. He was in *perfect* control. He was not even trying to intimidate them. Ze was not sure what he was doing. Not intimidation. Not provocation.

"See, somebody will go too far. Somebody will decide to go past telling the offworlders to leave...and into destroying them. That's what I smell here."

Destroying. The humans didn't have the power to do that. But they did have the power to disrupt negotiations for years. And potentially to destroy *Refuge*.

Two of the humans switched to a different language. Kaykek's translator was still working, though, even on what was presumably a minority language. The operations officer was still watching Dhyanil with narrowed eyes, likely trying to come up with a good response to him. What Kaykek heard made zir ears twitch. Ze listened. And listened some more. Ze could not say anything, though.

Ze could not let them know ze had understood...and so had everyone else with a translator. Tension rolled thick across the room. Ze shot Vrykin, the warrior, a look. She was letting *her* pheromones flow and that would not help. If scout pheromones could calm humans down, warrior pheromones might well have the opposite effect. But warriors had some control over their pheremones, could limit or increase them.

It was Beverly who spoke. "How about we get some refreshments. Then we can properly discuss how to keep everyone happy. I'll take you to the canteen."

Parvati went with them. Two verr workers fell in alongside to make sure nothing happened. And the canteen would be full of people.

"That's exactly their ultimate plan," Kaykek said. "To destroy all other sapient species."

"I caught that too." Chan's tone was grim.

"What language was that?"

"French, of all things. I'm supposing they're French-Canadian. They didn't know we have translators." He let his shoulders kind of slump. "I wish I was surprised."

"And they have government-level resources. We have to get a message back to Earth."

"No easy way to do that. But there's a less easy way." Kaykek's whiskers turned up.

"Oh?"

"The Refuge *does* carry smallships. We might have lost our stolen ky'iin frigate, but we have a courier. Two, actually. Just..."

"Not anywhere we have access to them." Chan grinned. "Keep it that way. But that means we can send a team back to Earth."

Graeme nodded. "We can."

"You, Graeme, are the logical one to lead it."

Graeme didn't even look startled, perhaps indicating he 100% agreed.

"We will not let you just borrow it," Kaykek said. "We will give you a verr pilot and crew."

"Of course. I have an idea as to who to take."

Kaykek wanted to go, but ze was the representative. Ze couldn't.

But by sending a courier they could send all of their data without being limited to ansible bandwidth.

It felt worth revealing that particular secret.

THE SOUND of a commotion was understandable. Kaykek sighed inwardly and scurried off where Beverly had taken them.

To a place full of verr.

Hopefully the hive would sit on them before they could do any damage. What ze found, though, was not quite what ze had expected. It might have been what she did expect.

One of the humans was being gently pinned against the wall by two workers, who had him by the arms. They didn't seem to be hurting him, but had him in a position where fighting back was hard. No leverage. He was flailing.

The other young human was fighting with the operations officer. They were on the ground, first one on top, then the other. Beverly had become separated from her wheelchair. Ignoring the fight, Kaykek scurried over to help her up and get her back into the chair.

"Thanks," Beverly whispered. "They didn't even do it on purpose."

Kaykek glanced over at the fight. They seemed almost tragically easily matched. Or... "Knocking you over? Do they seem to be..."

Beverly frowned. "It's for show."

"Thought so."

Parvati was now moving over to break the fight up. "What should I do with them?"

"They're going back to their ship. Immediately," Kaykek said. Ze could not speak for the hive, but... "They said they would behave, they didn't. Alvi?"

"I have two more warriors dispatched to escort them back to their shuttle," the AI said from the walls. "And concur with your judgment."

Alvi had a certain amount of say, especially when it came to a potential threat to the *physical* structure of Refuge Hive.

"I suppose that effort failed." Kaykek watched as the men were escorted out by warriors and an assortment of workers, Parvati staying with Beverly.

"Not at all," Beverly said. "We learned that those three can't be reasoned with. I suppose we are going to have to destroy their ship." She sounded resentful. "I hate this."

"You're a scientist. Your goal in life is to preserve and restore life."

"Their goal is to destroy it. But I'll leave the actual stopping them to the warriors."

She didn't, Kaykek realized, mean just *Refuge*'s group of warrior caste verr.

She meant all of those who were willing and inclined towards fighting, of all species.

And there was a regret in the word that told Kaykek that Beverly wished warriors did not have to exist.

Kaykek did too. But even when warriors had not expressed, the verr had fought each other. Even when it was only accelerating their end.

There would always be conflict.

But perhaps they could build a world where it didn't have to turn into war.

ALVI HAD REDOUBLED the search for a tracker, and they jumped three times, each time as fast as the capacitors could recharge.

Graeme had left for Earth with a small verr crew, the prisoner (it seemed a good time to send him home) and two of Chan's aides that Chan vouched for.

The council themselves met. Slyk, the glyn representative, said he was already missing his human friend.

Friendship across species. It was apparently not even that hard to achieve. Kaykek liked Kai Bowie, liked Beverly Marlowe. Ze wasn't sure about the other humans. Yoshi also seemed like she might be a lot of fun.

They weren't verr, and zir brain kept trying to fit them into the hive, but ze was getting better at accepting that they never would.

Well, *they* never would. Ze rather thought some aliens might effectively become part of Refuge Hive, and that might be for the good.

At the very least, the more they understood each other, surely, the more they would find peace. Alvi had told zir about an Earth science fiction series in which the reverse was true...first contact blew up because they only *thought* they understood each other.

It was a good cautionary tale. A good warning to be careful about things. To make sure they weren't seeing humans as funny shaped verr. Slyk was a good reminder...they were *so* alien in appearance and physiology that it was hard to forget what they were.

Right now, during a break, they were sucking juice through their mandibles. Kaykek wondered if their distant ancestors had specialized in juice and nectar, the way they were addicted to it. True, they were technically artificial, but they had to have been bred from something. If ze had designed a lifeform from scratch, ze would not have given them that reproductive strategy.

"Slyk?" ze asked.

They looked up from their juice. "So..."

"So...I got an ansible message from Ilyrek Hive. They agreed to that exchange of scientific papers you wanted. A courier will take them to Glen."

"Thank you. Your records of the end of your world might help us put ours back together."

"That's the hope." Kaykek looked away. "But our world has not ended. It has only changed."

The situation wasn't the same. The glyn were tied to their homeworld in deep and profound ways.

"It has. And it will change more. I can see the way you change, and if I had access to the substrate, I could get them to analyze it."

Kaykek considered that. "Some of us are done with planets."

"I could see you discovering the upper size limit of what can travel through hyperspace."

Ze hesitated. "No. Part of what made us degenerate as a species is that our hives are not meant to hit six figures. No, this is probably as large a ship as we need. But we may well become very good at building them. Better than the tyrar."

"Indeed." A pause. "And if we ever find a way to...a way to expand the substrate...large ships may be needed."

Kaykek's whiskers twitched upwards. "And I hope you do. I really do."

Their world was being stabilized.

But nothing lasts forever.

Not even a planet.

37

DHYANIL HAD YET another reason to wish for a replacement.

His fingers were itching.

Genocide? Intentional genocide? Again?

True, the people who would have destroyed the ky'iin had a quite different goal in mind. But the tyrar who helped them? They knew. What would cure this disease? Knowing each other better? The tyrar had known the ky'iin well, too well. In the wrong ways.

What did they do? He looked out the window at whatever random star system they were in, shaking. He had left his old life because genocide went too far, and also because his world had been threatened.

Maybe they really did need to round up all the people who felt like this and... He stopped that thought. He had talked to humans about past atrocities, and rounding people up and exiling them or putting them in camps was also an atrocity.

Now, the ones who had actually acted on it? Marooning them on a moderately unpleasant planet *really* appealed. With just enough infrastructure that they had a good survival chance. Survival, but not luxury. And with only their own species, then they...

Okay. He was too angry.

Normally if he was in this mood he would go hunting or fishing.

Hunting on Earth had been challenging...humans, of course, hunted with guns, and only animals that were highly plentiful. He'd learned their style of hunting, but it had nothing on running prey down with one's claws. Humans didn't have claws. They had made various artificial substitutes. They didn't have the prey drive of a ky'iin. They didn't and never could understand it. They could only accept it.

On the ship, there was no opportunity for that unless he had Alvi set him up something in VR, which was never entirely satisfying. But he had to burn some of this off, or he would verbally bite the head off of the next person who talked to him, who would no doubt be thoroughly innocent. And if provoked enough he might...

His claws were, in fact, out. He retracted them with an effort and sighed. Biological needs. You could only suppress them for so long and his prey drive did not respond well to pharmaceuticals. A run might help, but he wasn't even sure he trusted himself around the slightly smaller verr right now.

And he was not going to resort to alcohol. He had nearly given himself a drinking problem on human island liquor when he was first exiled to Earth. He hadn't quite decided never to drink again, but certainly not when he was like this.

"Alvi," he said finally. "I need a place to run. And I need everyone out of my way."

"There's a park on Lev Deck that I can clear for you. Are you alright?"

"Just angry and wanting to hunt something and..."

"I have an idea. I put the directions on your tablet."

"Thanks."

ALVI'S SITUATION involved a nervous verr technician who left immediately...and one of the cleaning robots. Dhyanil laughed, but he should have thought of it. He was able to chase the poor robot all over the park.

It wasn't as good as ripping something apart and eating it. But it let him get functional.

"Can I ask why you're so upset?"

He looked up at the ceiling. "How much of you am I talking to?"

"It doesn't work quite like that."

"I know. Your consciousness is very different from mine."

"So is a tyrar's."

"Not to the same degree, I don't think. And I...am just tired of people planning genocide. It's not that many people, but how do we get rid of them? Exile them all to separate planets that don't have the resources for spaceflight? Which I know is wrong, but..."

"Vrycek Hive fell."

"That was the fascist hive?"

"They fell to a homebred tyrant. Fortunately, sadly, she was killed. But the point is that you take out the leaders. Then you do your best to separate the followers."

"We have to destroy the *Columbia*."

"We can't," Alvi said. "If offworlders do it, then it's an act of war. The humans have to destroy the *Columbia*."

"I hadn't thought of that. But isn't that why you exist? To think of things."

"To think of things and to experience the world in a different way."

"I can't even remotely imagine being you, but then I struggle to imagine being a woman."

"If you could fully imagine being a woman you might be one."

Dhyanil laughed. "I mean, when I was a young man, right after expressing gender, I thought I wanted to be a woman. But I didn't. I wanted the *power* of being a woman. Different thing."

"And now you have it."

"Temporarily. I suspect they will find a ly'iin to appoint to the Council."

"Then what will you do?"

"Ask them to send me back to Earth. No ky'iin knows humans as well as I do and I'm finding I quite like being an ambassador. I think..."

"You would make a fine ky'iin ambassador to Earth. I *do* watch all the meetings."

"Where do *you* think Council should meet?"

"I think maybe we need to stop asking that question."

Before Dhyanil could ask the AI what they meant, alarms went off.

"I'm afraid the *Columbia* has found us again."

Stop asking that question.

The council had to meet somewhere.

ALVI WAS RIGHT. They could not destroy the *Columbia*. But they couldn't keep running from it forever either. What about capturing it, as long as they gave it back? Of course, the verr hadn't given the ky'iin back their frigate. But Dhyanil found that personally quite reasonable. Alas, it had been destroyed defending the hives.

Humans might react differently. Humans could be...touchy. And if there was really a territorial government involved. So, they kept running. And Dhyanil was tired of running. He was tired of being prey. Ky'iin were not prey. Men were sometimes.

That was part of it too. That feeling of being prey and pursued when one didn't want it. Sometimes, of course, one did. Maybe getting laid would also make him feel better, but there were no female ky'iin...or, heck, male ky'iin who were willing to experiment...around.

And no, humans did *not* have remotely compatible equipment.

Capturing the *Columbia* and returning the crew to Earth for trial? Unfortunately, the *human* best equipped to do so had left to Earth. Viary's herd had pulled off something similar, but asking them to do it felt wrong and endangered them and Viary's mental health. No, the verr would have to do it, and that brought up the issue Alvi had mentioned.

That these people would use action taken against them by aliens, even in self defense, as ammunition for their cause. There had to be humans involved, and the only ones he fully trusted were Graeme, who had left, and Beverly, who was now doing some pretty important work with the verr scientists. He thought she was capable of being involved, but he really did not feel she should be risked.

Which left him with only one solution. He had to find out which of the other humans on the ship could be trusted for sure. Which he was doing anyway, but it suddenly became priority two. Unfortunately, he could not make it priority one.

They should not have sent Graeme away. They should have...but who else could they have sent? Beverly? Same issue there, she was needed here.

But he felt calm enough to return to the council and deliberations that were starting to get into the weeds of small stuff, and he had already vetoed several things that were so clearly internal matters.

They were almost ready to finalize this thing.

They could not do that while hiding.

38

"So, the issue is that the ship was never fully designed to be a *settlement*?" Beverly asked.

This said in a room full of verr scientists. Plus her and Yoshi.

"Right. And while we have everything stable, we thought while we had you here we would call on your expertise." The scientist was a verr drone, a breeding male. The size difference between him and the workers was quite noticeable.

"We're happy to look over everything, but understand I'm an ecological remediator not a closed-systems engineer, and neither is Yoshi."

Yoshi was reading her tablet, looking over the material. "It can't hurt to have us look."

"No, it can't. So..."

"We've found an inefficiency in waste management, It's fine while we're going from port to port, but right now..."

"Waste management." Definitely not Beverly's field, but vitally important on a starship of any size.

"So, you aren't fully closed system?"

"*Refuge* was designed as a colony ship that would take on supplies at the start and then refuel and resupply at the destination once the colony could provide its needs, sitting in orbit if needed. We're turning it into something else. Alvi is working the issue too."

"It shouldn't be hard." Beverly leaned over to look at the tablet. "After all, a colony voyage, even with FTL..."

"Would normally be aimed at a known system. The other thing we want to work on is growing more of our own food."

"You have both hydroponic bays and edible plants in the parks, right?"

"Yes, but...not everything from our seed banks grows, some of the seeds didn't stay viable."

"Maybe there are some plants from Earth that would serve your needs. We don't have to worry about ecosystem contamination here."

Beverly was enjoying the challenge. It took her mind off of the other problems.

They had to return to Earth soon to deliver the council's deliberations. The rules that would establish the true Council of Worlds.

But they were being herded.

Herded by the ships nipping at their heels, and the *Columbia* was a legitimate threat to *Refuge*. Despite the ship's size, it had never been designed to fight.

If they blew up the *Columbia*, then the council started with a tainted, hostile act. Could they get *Challenger* out here?

Graeme would probably try to do just that and they could track *Refuge* easil...

She stopped. Easily enough. They hadn't found a tracer. They had disabled the portable ansible.

But they were still...

Beverly shook her head. "I hate to disturb this...Yoshi? Carry on. I need to talk to Alvi."

"You had an idea?"

"Not connected to this. My mind wandered, unfortunately. I thought about how this was taking my mind off of our other problems, and poof, back to the other problems."

"Go."

Beverly rolled from the room, feeling annoyed with herself, but if she was right?

If she was right, they had to get a message to Graeme. Except...

If she was right...

———

"Alvi. They're tracking us every time the Council representatives check in with Sol system."

Silence. Brief for a human. A long time for an AI. "Of course they are."

"We haven't been able to find it because it's *the other end*."

"Then I have no choice but to falsify our location data. I would rather not do so, but if..."

"Launchpad is compromised."

All of the messages were going through Launchpad II's ansible. Ansibles did not work well too deep in gravity wells, the time distortion tended to cause static and low quality messages. So, you kept them in orbit when you could. Launchpad being compromised was *obvious* and they...they hadn't thought of it.

"I did think of it," Alvi added. "But I had it as a low priority because..."

"Because the only thing you can do about it *is* to falsify the location data, and that is..."

"Unethical. But there is a difference between lying to one's allies and lying to one's enemies."

"Do we have a way to get a message to Graeme?"

"Unfortunately, I already got a message saying he was "safely there." So, not without going through Launchpad."

"I'll ask Slyk if they know of something we could say to Graeme that would clue him in. They know him better than any of us."

"No, I will. You go back to the waste management issue. Please. *I* can do both at once."

They had a point. Beverly smiled towards where she thought the nearest visual sensor was located and rolled back into the conference room.

"What is it, anyway?" Yoshi whispered in tyrar.

"Tell you later."

They turned back to the problem. "So, there is no reason, again, not to use plants from other ecosystems as long as they get along with each other."

"Verr do eat meat, right?"

"Right, but livestock on..."

Beverly smiled and held up her hands. "Even if they're only this big."

"You're suggesting we keep vryk?"

"I was thinking of an Earth animal. Show me?"

She studied the picture. "Those would work too. How much space do they need?"

"Not much. What's the Earth animal?"

"Rabbits. They're the primary meat animal on Mars because even the large meat ones are pretty small. They also make fantastic pets."

"We stopped keeping pets," one of the verr said, softly. "Maybe we should start again."

They had needed all the food for themselves and what livestock they kept. "You should."

Yoshi turned to Beverly. "If we lived here, we could have a cat."

And Beverly laughed. "Cats are trouble. But fun trouble."

"What is a cat?"

Beverly turned back. "A small Earth predator that we domesticated to protect our granaries from pests milennia ago. One of the two most common pet animals kept on Earth."

"Ah, what's the other?"

"Dogs, which have a very plastic genome."

And it devolved to everyone looking at kitten and puppy pictures for a while.

———

BEVERLY LEFT WITH SOME HOMEWORK...TO look at Earth plants and see what might work well when designing a sealed ecosystem for the verr. She would talk to people there. When she could.

Right now, she didn't trust any messages were getting through. For all they knew, Launchpad had been taken over by the crazies. It seemed unlikely, but it wasn't impossible.

They jumped again, and this time they weren't followed. Beverly wondered if Alvi *had* falsified the location data. It would make it much harder for Earth to call them again, but then if they lost their tail they could jump back to Earth and then send warships to where they had told them they were going.

If they still could. If Earth was even safe. She was getting paranoid, she knew. There were not enough of these people to do anything that major.

But intercepting communications, telling lies, putting key people in place? That they could do. They could cause confusion. They hadn't destroyed *Refuge*. Maybe they didn't think one warship could. With a shot in the right place they absolutely could.

Maybe somebody was hesitant about destroying a ship with children on it? Even a hardcore fascist *might* grow a conscience at that point. Maybe. If they had anything resembling one.

Still, it might be that the creche was their best shield.

They had brought some of the kids to meet the offworlders. It was enjoyable. Beverly *liked* children, although she had no desire to be a science teacher. She wasn't that kind of communicator.

But she liked kids and the verr pups were just that. Kids. Some of whom wanted to be scientists. One of them said it was going to move to Kyverr when it grew up to study and explore the planet.

Which was something verr in the past hadn't done that often, but she supposed when the hives were so different, more *would* be inclined to go through the emotional upheaval of changing. It wasn't like moving for a human.

Still, she felt happier. More satisfied. As she put together the list, she even found herself humming. Yoshi was doing her own, although the ravaged tyrar homeworld, even worse off than Earth, had less to offer.

Refuge did have to build a closed ecosystem, though. That way they could always be safe, and they hadn't always managed to be *safe*.

They weren't quite enough to be a viable verr population, but they could probably take stored sperm and ova with them. They weren't so different from earth mammals on that front...the same techniques that worked for human fertility preservation worked for verr.

Building something. She didn't get to do that often. Restore, yes. Rebuild, yes. Make something new?

It felt good. It almost made her wish she could make other new things...

Almost.

39

SOL SYSTEM. The courier ship dropping out of hyperspace not that far from Launchpad II. Home.

On that blue-white planet were his husband and daughter, his sister and her children, everything he cared about. Which was why he had to keep leaving them, no matter how much it hurt. Because he had to do what he could do.

Perhaps they could be together again for a while after this. He could take them to Glen, show them that world as it was repaired. It might be safe.

It would never be safe.

They could never be safe and perhaps... Perhaps it was time for him to quit.

To retire, to become an analyst, to fly a desk.

But he wanted to go back to Glen. He wanted to see that world restored, which they could do. Repaired was a better term. He wanted to see them learn what they could so that perhaps one day humanity too could build something like that. Shared with the other species and with the others they would find in the future.

He missed Skyt.

He was torn. But now he was home, home and they were moving to dock.

"We'll meet you in the dock," the commander had said. He wanted to hand the information over directly to her. Nobody else.

There was a strain in her voice, though.

He didn't like it.

"Hold on."

The verr pilot flicked an ear then turned it towards him.

"We're not docking."

"Why not?"

"Because the commander doesn't sound right. This thing can land, right?"

"Easily. But..."

"They won't shoot us out of the sky without knowing who we are, the worst thing they will do is escort us down. I'll give you coordinates."

He couldn't even be sure why he knew they shouldn't dock.

He just did. It wasn't *right*.

The coordinates he gave were on the American continent, which he didn't like, but there were only so many places you could quietly land a courier.

And this was a place he knew they would be safe if they could get there, with people whom he *knew* weren't in any way connected.

The courier ship angled down. "See, not even challenged. Earth has a lot of suborbital traffic."

And was currently not at war, although the way things were going? The next war, he feared, would be of the uncivil variety.

But no doubt they would be traced, somebody would belatedly realize they weren't normal traffic.

They touched down in the middle of a field, spooking some cows.

"So, what now?"

"I need to talk to some friends. Stay close to the ship."

The first verr to actually set foot on Earth were, he thought with amusement, just random spacemen.

"GRAEME. WHAT THE..." The woman who came out of the house folded her arms under her ample breasts.

"We're not here."

"Are those..."

"Verr. They're harmless."

"No they aren't, they're no more harmless than you are."

Graeme laughed. "They won't do anything."

"Sure they will if we don't feed them. So, what's going on?"

"I think that we have some major issues and I need access to the bunker."

"I'm out. I told you..." Then she softened. "The bunker's still intact. Of course you can use it. Who are the bad guys?"

"The U.S. government. Or at least elements of it."

The dark-skinned woman scowled. "White men again. No offense."

"None taken. I'm Scottish."

She grinned. "So, do I get to meet your alien friends?"

"They have translators. And verr can eat most human food. Just not chocolate or grapes."

"Feed them like dogs."

"Not as much meat. They're omnivores like we are. Turns out nobody but us can eat chocolate. It's not fair."

"What terrible lives."

Graeme waved to the verr to signal them to come over, six of them, scurrying across the space between them. "I'll let them introduce themselves."

She handed him an old fashioned mechanical key. "What are the old guard up to?"

A pause, then, "Shooting at people, disrupting the treaty and I suspect they are thinking about genocide."

"Of the verr?"

"You know what people we're talking about. Last time they had power..."

"I know. But they don't have that much power."

"No, they don't." He kissed her cheek and then headed for the bunker. Grandma, as everyone called her, would give the verr a nice taste of Earth food and cowboy hospitality.

He walked around the farmhouse, stopping to pet one of the horses...and then to pet two more horses who saw one getting petted and had to come over to get their share. He escaped from the rest of the herd with his pockets mostly intact and went to the bunker.

In the 20th century, this land had been owned by a survivalist crazy who had more guns than sense. He had built a literal fallout shelter under it. A good one that might even serve that purpose. During Austerity, this place had been central to the resistance. One day it would be a museum.

Right now, it was *still there* and still fitted with everything he needed. A portable ansible would have been nice, but they had the one in the courier.

But the first thing he did was call Charles. No response.

Frowning, he called Janice, his sister. "Is Charles with you?"

"I thought he was with *you*. I was told you were back and he and Marion went up to Launchpad."

"Check their place. Now. I'm not calling from Launchpad."

"Oh f..." She bit back the swear word, which told him one of the kids was in the room. "Barry will check."

Her husband.

"If he doesn't find them, then we have a problem."

He still had work to do, but if Launchpad was compromised and his daughter was there? It felt as if the ground was unsteady. He was on a planet.

He still felt as if the artificial gravity was about to fail.

THEY WEREN'T AT HOME. Graeme had the bunker's dumb systems analyzing the data.

It wasn't as good as an AI, but a smaller sentient AI would get bored. A larger one that could spin off a simple subroutine? He missed Alvi. Alvi could have done this easily.

He really hoped this was the last time this place would be used. Many people still did not know it existed. In Arizona there was a missile silo museum that reminded everyone how close they had come to World War III during the Cold War.

This place reminded him how close they had come to World War III during Austerity. It should remind others. But for now, he needed it.

He knew who the mole was now, not for sure, no, but close enough. And that information needed to be returned to Alvi. But he couldn't go back. He couldn't send that information by ansible. Which left only one choice. He emerged from the bunker and headed to join Grandma's table.

She had outdone herself and there were now six very full verr. And soon, one very full Graeme. "Tomorrow I want you to return to *Refuge* taking this." He held out a drive to the ship's commander. "I have to stay here."

"Why?"

"Because my husband went up to Launchpad thinking I was there. I need to make sure he's safe."

"We may not be able to find *Refuge*."

"Do your best. They should be able to analyze this too. Alvi could even do it faster. But just in case they've had other issues."

He knew he sounded distracted. Grandma cracked him open a beer. "Drink this. You're too tired to help them tonight. Drink this, get a good night's sleep, and we'll fix it in the morning. Are you sure you want to send them off, not go up to Launchpad?"

"Launchpad knows I aborted landing yesterday. Whoever's in charge up there...or feeding false information to those in charge...already knows I'm onto them."

And had he known Charles and Marion were there he would have made a quite different decision. All decisions could get somebody killed. If this one got his daughter...

No, she would be alive. The only reason they would want her was as bait to get him. Once he was up there, though? He thought they wouldn't kill a child, but they did think children like her were abominations. And they certainly might kill Charles. Might have already. He drank his beer.

She was right. He was in no fit state to help them today. But tomorrow? Tomorrow he was going to start things in motion.

They would regret having touched his family.

40

It seemed that they had finally shaken the *Columbia*. Which meant Beverly was right. She had apparently told Alvi she thought the leak was the other end.

On Launchpad, where they were sending their status reports to by ansible. Which involved location information. Now they had no more contact with Earth. They could contact anyone else's homeworld, though.

That had to be stressful for the humans, ze thought. Ze did not need regular contact with verr, because *Refuge* was home and hive. But the humans had to be a little different. They tended to form their own group, understandably. Kaykek was the only delegate not homesick. Which wasn't entirely fair.

But they had done the right thing leaving Launchpad. They had thought it was because Launchpad was *in* danger. Now, it seemed, something on Launchpad *was* the danger.

Spies. It all boiled down to spies. You couldn't spy on a hive by sending people in. You had to do it by suborning workers.

Humans didn't have pheromones. Their institutions were much easier to infiltrate. It could be as simple as one ansible operator. Or it could be the entire station compromised.

But without their tail, Kaykek finally felt safe zirself. Felt that zir pups were safe...and ze counted in those both litters, not just the one ze had contributed to.

They would grow and some would stay here and some would trade to other hives. With more adults moving, ze wondered if pup trading would become a tradition of the past.

A rare thing, perhaps, only done after some kind of crisis. Would ze trade zir pups?

Ze would, if the other hive was truly in need, ze decided. Ze would cry, but ze would do it.

With luck, ze would never have to. The scientists were building a plan to make Refuge Hive a sustainable ecosystem. They needed that. It would improve their diet.

It would mean that if all else failed they could go back to their old plan. Grab as much verr genetic material as they could and leave this sector of the galaxy. Go off to plant the verr species somewhere else.

Ze no longer wanted to do that. Ze wanted the humans and the tyrar and the ky'iin and the glyn to be part of their future. They could not go back to being isolated.

But if the choice was that or dying? Ze could not make that decision for others, least of all for the pups.

So, ze worked on the paperwork ze had for the council. They almost had an agreement. It included and superseded the original treaty and included the basic concept that each species owned their own solar system, including worlds they did not inhabit, and that this included species that had yet to achieve spaceflight.

That was the key and the center of it. *We own our own worlds*, Kaykek thought. But Verr was no more. They would get ownership of the Kyverr system. But what place for those, of all species, who chose not to live on a world? Ze did not know what that place was.

Ze only knew there had to be such a place. Which meant it had to be built. Equally inconvenient to everyone. That sentiment had been expressed.

And ze knew what they had to do.

MAKING zir proposal would have to wait. Kaykek even spent some time helping with maintenance. Sometimes, working with zir hands for a while helped zir relax.

Reminded zir of zir roots. And of the fact that it was, after all, an unfair accident of biology that had pulled zir out of them.

But ze was not sure it was entirely an accident. Ze was watching, now. And Alvi was seeing patterns. There might be choice after all, but not conscious choice. Something deep within the people who expressed as different castes.

Something that they could not deny or change or...but then there were the handful who *were* discontented. Two of the warriors really hated it. Hated their instincts. Hated their drive to protect the hive. They were from Vrycek, though. An unhealthy hive. A dying hive when ze had gone in to save it and cause it to fall and be rebuilt.

When a tyrant had risen for the first time in centuries. They were fortunate that she had died, because she might not have been willing to step back. Hard and cold, that. But the hive *was* hard and cold and also warm and welcoming and home and family and *everything*. Nothing was going to change that.

Choice would help, though. And choice *of hive* was the bigger one anyway. The fact that some of the pups...not most, but some...talked about moving openly when they grew up.

They could even think about trading apprentices. It was worth a thought. Especially the ones who wanted to, say, study planetary ecosystems on verr.

Ze had another thought. An interesting one. Ze called Beverly.

"Can we meet?"

"Of course!"

"The cafe."

It wasn't a private conversation ze wanted to have with the human, but ze wanted to run this past somebody who had gone through human secondary and tertiary education. In the cafe, Kaykek ordered tea and waited until Beverly rolled through the door, signaling her over.

"So, what's up?"

"I want to talk about education."

"Some of the delegates have doctorates too."

"You don't have as many dogs in the fight. One of the proposals I want to put forward is a mechanism for people to study on..."

"Exchange students! Yes," Beverly said. "It would help many things."

"We have some pups interested in studying planetary ecosystems. If we sent them to study on Earth, or Kyx, or Tyranis..."

"And we could probably find kids who would love to study with the verr. Particularly engineers."

"Exactly. And then they would also develop relationships and friendships. We would have humans who understand what it is to live in a hive, verr who actually grasp ky'iin sexual relations."

"I'm not sure the ky'iin always grasp ky'iin sexual relations. And the glyn would be in on this in five seconds."

"They would! So, how..."

"So, on Earth we would exchange students between different regions and territorial governments. I can get the council notes on how that's done. The ky'iin and tyrar probably have similar systems. We can take bits from each ot them to work out how to do it. And thank you, Kaykek. I was thinking about it, but I'm not a delegate, and Viary has been deep in the weeds of later career expertise transfers. Like me."

"Will you ever go back to live on Earth?"

Beverly shook her head. "No."

"I had one other idea. Nobody gets the council."

"Meaning?"

"Meaning that *nobody* gets the council location. We find a neutral system, one nobody particularly wants, we build a space station there. Nobody gets any advantage."

"Equally inconvenient to everyone. Of course. But I'm not a delegate."

"You can subtly mention it to Viary."

"I can."

Kaykek was more than happy with the talk with Beverly. The fact that the humans and others already had a mechanism to trade apprentices and students amongst themselves meant that they could put that together. Some of those kids could go study on other worlds...planetary ecosystems, alien cultures, languages. They would come home as scientists, diplomats, engineers. Or they would integrate.

The verr would probably not integrate. They biologically needed the hive, and being away from it for a few years *would* require the puberty suppressors that medical was working on with human knowledge to help.

Of course, a small hive on Earth, if the humans didn't mind, might...might be interesting. It would have to be kept small, but Earth *did* have space for some immigration from what ze had heard. More than before the disasters.

Verr could also live *under* the human cities, although when ze had mentioned that to Beverly she had responded with a peculiar mixture of amusement and disgust. Kaykek had eventually teased out that "the poor live in the undercity" was a trope of a certain dystopian fiction genre. And also rats living in the sewers.

She hadn't said it wouldn't work though, although, "Not Manhattan. The water table there was too close to the surface *before* the climate crisis."

Coastal cities would not work. Maybe something further inland. Or, of course, they could build a verr space station with human permission.

Kaykek knew that zir scout instincts were part of why ze was enthusiastic about the idea of mixed species living. But ze knew it went beyond that. Ze liked the humans. Ze liked the tyrar.

Ze liked all of the offworlders who were here. Not, of course, the ones being idiots about everything. And these people were self-selected for tolerance.

Except for whoever the spy was. Ze still had not worked out which one it was. Ze was afraid it was somebody ze *really* liked. Like Kai.

Kai was the nearest ze had ever met to an offworlder scout. Not biologically, but in gender mentality. Humans drifted further from their biology that most species, it seemed. But Kai understood, truly understood, that they should not consider Kaykek to be a man or a woman.

Most humans struggled with not considering the workers to be one or the other. They gendered their *ships*.

Maybe that was why they had so many rebels against gender.

"Kaykek?"

"Alvi, do you need me?" Or did they just want to chat with a friend. They hadn't had many opportunities to talk about things that weren't somehow related to negotiations.

"Alas, yes. Dhyanil thinks he has identified the mole."

"Tell me it's not Kai Bowie?"

"It's not. As we suspected, it is one of Chan's aides. Dhyanil's perfume is working well, but..."

"It's an excuse to have me in the room. I'll be right there."

Ze was not just a walking pheromone generator. Ze could be an extra set of eyes and brain on the matter.

41

KAYKEK WALKED in and settled down next to him. Dhyanil was glad to see zir.

It wasn't that he needed the scout to keep the human from trying to jump him anymore. It was that he wanted zir opinion.

Zir opinion had come to be valuable to him through their various somewhat forced close interactions. He liked zir.

He liked zir a lot. Ze was one of the few things that would make him want to stay in this job.

The man was escorted in by one of the other aides and a verr warrior. The looks he gave both Dhyanil and Kaykek were...

Not pleasant. Dhyanil had seen this one around; he was quiet and kept to himself. That wasn't surprising.

Quiet and kept to himself as a way of hiding the truth that he hated them, but he was sure he saw hate in the man's eyes now.

He had learned to read human facial expressions reasonably well.

They had his hands secure.

"Had to cuff him. He threw a punch," the other aide said. "At Prylek here."

The warrior's whiskers tilted upward in a verr grin. "He seemed to think that verr are weak. I taught him otherwise."

"He sat on him. Do you want us to stay?"

Dhyanil considered that. "Yes, stay."

Keeping another human in the room might keep this from degenerating into hostility. They could also help restrain him if necessary.

"I'm not talking to anyone except my lawyer."

"You aren't on Earth, Mr...."

"Holsworth," the other supplied.

"Doesn't mean I don't have rights."

"The ship's integrity is under verr jurisdiction." He glanced at Kaykek. "Would you say what he did constituted sabotage?"

"I don't acknowledge verr jurisdiction."

"Too bad. And also, you're talking."

The man clapped his jaw closed.

Kaykek seemed to consider for a moment. "He hooked up unauthorized equipment to power systems and he interfered with safety systems. Yes, I'd say it's sabotage."

He did wonder what would happen to a verr who did such things. He nodded. "And?"

"There are many unpleasant jobs on *Refuge.*"

"I have diplomatic imm..."

The other human laughed. "Only if we don't hand you over to them. Which Chan is absolutely inclined to do. Besides, you might prefer it. The verr only hand down community service. To them."

He clapped his mouth shut again.

"I think we could reduce the amount of unpleasant work you need to do to make up for this if you told us who hired you."

Nothing.

"We can also make sure they can't get to you," Dhyanil added, more conspiratorially. "I know what people like that do to those who get caught."

Something in the man's throat moved.

Dhyanil had hit a point. Now he just had to follow through.

"CALL ME NAIVE," Kaykek said, grooming zir whiskers, "But..."

"Terrorist organizations keep tight controls on their people. And one of the things they *will* do is kill people who get caught or screw up. He'll be safer, if more miserable, with your people."

"We can keep him safe and teach him a lesson at the same time." Ze stopped grooming and reached for zir tea. "Do you think he can learn?"

"I did. But in a different way. I don't know that scrubbing floors will teach him, but it *will* keep him out of trouble."

"You learned by realizing others would go further than you."

"Yes."

"Do you think he knows..."

"That there are at least some people in his movement who dream of, say, killing the ky'iin and taking our planet?" Dhyanil shrugged. "I don't know whether he knows. A human might have a better job establishing whether he would care."

"Parade him past the pups, perhaps," Kaykek mused. "Humans seem to think children are cute regardless of species."

"You mean they aren't?" Dhyanil quipped.

Kaykek laughed. "I suppose they are. But humans are easily disarmed by things they consider cute. As long as we keep his hands busy."

"He could still hurt them with words."

"We could turn off translation, then he can't. But if he sees that he's threatening kids..." Kaykek tailed off. "It's worth a thought."

"Let's just hope he's the only one."

"I only *saw* the one, but yes, there could be others."

"Unlike some isolationists, these won't work with like-minded individuals of other species."

"But gladly use ky'iin technology."

Dhyanil nodded. "Exploit, I'd say, rather than use."

"You can check in with Kyx?"

"Yes. It's just Earth that has false location information. We might have to change that if they find us again."

"And I can consult with other hives if I need to"

"Except in the traditional manner." Dhyanil probably shouldn't tease zir about the traditional activities of verr scouts.

Fortunately, ze just chittered laughter. "Shameless old ky."

"Shameless old ky, yes," he said in response. "Or maybe..."

"Maybe you need a woman."

"As long as she doesn't want eggs. I am far too old for brooding." He hated to admit it, but he *was* old. Hale, yes. Sharp, absolutely. But too old to brood; too much risk that he might die before the kids grew up. Most women respected that.

"You never sound old," Kaykek mused.

"I'm in very good health. And yes, I'm proud of that. But I *am* old. In a few years I will have to consider going back to White Cliffs or otherwise finding a nice beach to relax on somewhere."

"Is that your retirement plan?"

"*Do* verr retire?"

"Of course. If you get too old to work, you don't have to work. You can just hang out and do art or whatever. Or switch to an easier job. Or..."

"Right. And I have loved beaches my entire life, that's why I stayed in White Cliffs. That and it was home. My dream retirement is me, a beach, a fruity drink and the sun." Dhyanil thought about it. "You?"

"Puttering around listening to Tayken recite poetry. Maybe writing some bad poetry myself. Before you say anything, I've tried."

They both laughed. But Dhyanil knew retirement for Kaykek was a lot further off than it was for him.

DHYANIL HAD NOT SPENT much time with Chan. He didn't know the man at all, except that he seemed professional.

"What did you get out of him? And where..."

"The verr have him scrubbing floors."

Chan laughed darkly. "He can stay there, then. Scrubbing floors..."

"The verr are very big on hard physical labor as a way of, shall we say, keeping troublemakers out of trouble. He won't cause any more. But are we sure he's the only one?"

Chan rubbed his temples. "No, we aren't. Did you find out who hired him?"

"Working on it. He's afraid of them. Which isn't surprising. Organizations like that are fairly well known for...

"For jailhouse murder, yes. Maybe we should leave him with the verr."

"Leave him with the verr for a bit then tell him he's going back to Earth if he doesn't talk and if he does..."

"Then I'll make sure he's protected, even if it means stashing him somewhere off planet." Chan let out a breath. "Thanks for doing that. I would have punched him. I did a lot for him."

"I get it. He genuinely hates and fears offworlders, and he didn't want to acknowledge us as people, but..."

"But I can't understand who wouldn't..."

"People who don't acknowledge all *humans* are people." Dhyanil paused. "Just being able to talk coherently might not make you a person to somebody like that."

Dhyanil's comlink went off. "And apparently I have a message from Kyx."

"Go. Take it. We'll talk."

He stood up, left the room. Chan wasn't somebody he liked. Nobody *liked* Chan. He had been well chosen as a delegate, but he was a standoffish type who did not socialize much.

Good at his job.

Dhyanil checked. A message had been sent to his tablet.

The *Columbia* had been seen in the Kyx system. That wasn't good. Unfortunately, it hadn't stuck around long enough to be shot.

It had, however, tried to nudge a citykiller into an interception orbit. Dropping rocks. That was an atrocity. The Council had *rapidly* agreed that orbital bombardment of any kind should be considered a war crime.

Kai Bowie had been the one to make that motion. Not surprising given how vulnerable Mars was. But Chan had also mentioned something called Hiroshima. A city on Earth, and Dhyanil had looked it up. Two cities in Japan. The one use of live nuclear weapons on Earth.

Rocks were just as scary.

He'd also mentioned a city called Chelyabinsk, which had apparently been hit by an airburst from a meteor strike. Said they'd been lucky.

Dhyanil had looked that one up, and they had. Mostly it had just knocked out windows. And injured people who went to the windows to look. Dhyanil could not criticize them.

The *Columbia* had tried to attack Kyx and tried to do so subtly, and underestimated ky'iin sensors.

"This is an act of war," he said, quietly.

He sent a message reminding them the ship was rogue.

What he got back was. "We know. But when we catch it..."

The *Columbia* was now being hunted. Dhyanil could not help but be glad.

42

APPARENTLY, the *Columbia* had tried to mess with things in first the Kyx system then the Tyranis system. Specifically, they had tried to reroute asteroids to hit the planets. That was pretty heavy stuff, literally. If you wanted to genocide people to take their land, you wanted to use something that only damaged the people, not the land.

Just ask the people who had given smallpox blankets to Native Americans. Biological warfare was perfect. These people, whoever they were, either didn't want to use it or, more likely, didn't have anyone on their team who could do it.

"They're military men," she mused, rolling over to the terminal. It felt wrong to be safe here. After all that had happened on Tyranis, it felt wrong to feel safe when others didn't, but she had to get used to it, get back into that mindset.

After all, *she* was not a fighter, and had never wanted to be. She did, though, run the numbers on what a large strike might have done to Tyranis, which was already so fragile.

Ironically, some simulations showed a beneficial result, cooling the planet and helping with the slow removal of the cooling chemicals already in the atmosphere. As in, partially replacing them so they could clean it up. But not all. And certainly, it wasn't a good way to fix it, no matter how desperate they were becoming for solutions. Also, the council had agreed orbital bombardment of inhabited planets was a war crime.

What the *Columbia* had done was an act of war and she shivered. There was a non-zero chance that would...

...start a new war between humans and ky'iin.

"They wanted a war."

"Who did?" Viary, coming in.

"The people on the *Columbia* who are throwing rocks around."

"Obvious even to you, isn't it. Thankfully, it's just as obvious to the ky'iin."

"Good."

"But they have said they won't promise to return the *Columbia* intact. Neither will we."

"If somebody has to blow it up, then...that has to happen." Beverly let out a breath. "I'm sorry my species hasn't cleaned up its own mess yet."

"They have the *Challenger* and the *Dingyuan* hunting. But..."

"It's hard to find them, I know. And the human fleets are small compared to what the ky'iin have, especially since the war."

The ky'iin could have destroyed humanity. Or conquered them the way they had the tyrar. Instead, having let the tyrar go, they came to terms with a species that, to them, must have looked like a small threat. What it said was that they had grown up, at least a little bit. So had humanity.

But apparently they still had children throwing tantrums.

BEVERLY HAD BECOME USED to the faint smell of Refuge Hive. Like most constant smells, she had stopped noticing it.

So she did notice when it changed. There was some kind of sharp tang to it. "Alvi?"

"Where is Parvati?" the AI responded. "We could use her help."

"Who's under attack?"

"The human prisoner broke free and tried to get into the creche. That was stopped, but he's off somewhere in the conduits."

"And even with half the workers searching..."

"She is very good at finding people, is she not?"

That sharp smell was irritating her, she felt...on edge. Warrior pheromones, calling the hive to defense? Parvati had no doubt noticed.

"And you can't find her? Could she already..."

"Aha. She's in that closet, which we still haven't fully unjammed yet."

"Need me to go?"

"No, I can talk to her now. She'll help."

"Is there anything I can do?" She felt restless. Floaty. "I..."

"Hold on, Beverly."

The airflow in the room increased. She started to feel better. "Thanks. I think..."

"The warriors all got mad at the same time. Other humans...and tyrar...have also been affected."

"I envy the ky'iin for being immune."

"Put it this way, we made the mistake of letting a human in the creche without warning the in-season queens."

Beverly laughed. "Oh *no*."

"We didn't know. He was thoroughly embarrassed. Nothing happened per se, but..."

"He did not try to chase a queen around the creche."

"He tried to chase a queen around the creche and a drone had to sit on him. He would probably..."

"If he'd had warning he could have mentally braced himself."

"So now if a human or tyrar is entering the creche we warn all parties. Workers, of course, aren't affected. Warriors are. And, of course..."

"I'm aware of scout duties." Beverly blushed. "Does the creche ever just turn into an orgy?"

"Sometimes. The pups that are old enough to notice are kept busy."

She blushed a little bit more. "Don't bring this up around too many humans. Also, thanks for the distraction."

She did feel a lot better. "Still, *is* there anything I can do?"

"Alas, no. I do understand wanting to feel useful. But we have him."

"Oh, good. I suppose..."

"We don't have a jail, but I can put something together. He is lucky."

"Lucky the warriors didn't just kill him."

"Indeed. Threatening the breeders and pups..."

"Humans aren't..." She tailed off. "We don't like people who attack kids. But that doesn't mean it doesn't happen."

Maybe the verr were, in the end, more civilized. "Then again, I find pup trading hard. One of our definitions of genocide is removing children from the group."

"We are all different. But yes, he will be locked up now until we turn him over to your kind to deal with."

What would... "Make sure we don't hand him back until we know for sure who we are handing him back *to*." She sighed. "Why did we send Graeme away? He's the best at this."

"Because he's the best at this."

BEVERLY KNEW she shouldn't do this, but she also almost felt as if she *had* to. She rolled up outside the man's cell.

Why had he attacked the creche? Had he snapped from being amongst outworlders.

They had him in a cell with a transparent door. He could see her.

They could hear each other. Which was good, she wasn't going in there with him.

"A human face."

"Why did you do something so stupid?"

"If we kill all of their breeders..."

"...then a bunch of workers go through puberty. Besides, they can hear you."

"Guess it doesn't matter at this point. They know I hate them. We will have this ship."

"Buy your own," she said, finally. "They're not cheap and they take a while to customize, but the tyrar sell them."

"Eventually we'll build our own."

"Even better." She let out a breath. "And do what? What exactly would we benefit from..."

"They have the best planets."

She laughed. "Kyx has no moon. Do you know what that means? It means an ice age every three thousand years or so. Tyranis is a worse ecological mess than Earth. Glen is broken. Verr is gone." A pause. "The best planets are the ones *without intelligent life* and part of what we're doing here is making sure they get divided fairly."

"...an ice age every..."

"Axial wobble. Earth is stabilized by the moon. But while we're working with a small sample size so far? The protocivilizations we've found are all on tricky worlds, difficult ones. The uninhabited planets are the really nice ones. You could have your own, have whatever rules you want about who's allowed to settle there. You could buy and build your idea of utopia. I'm sure I wouldn't be welcome there."

"You're not a typical..."

"Oh, save that. You want a world for straight white humans only. Well, you can have one. Just don't expect the rest of us to come visit." She was more serious than she wanted to admit to being.

Isolating them...

"And let the aliens have the rest of the galaxy."

She shrugged. "The galaxy is a very big place. What, are you envisioning the Galactic Empire?" He probably wasn't well read enough to get the reference.

"Like *Star Wars*?"

"No." She couldn't resist continuing. "No godlike robots here to make sure we don't have competition. Best to work with them."

"Then we stop being human. Like you."

"If human meant being like you..." She stopped. She was letting him get to her. That wasn't a good thing.

You never let people get to you like that. "Yoshi is more human than you are."

"You just like the feeling of fur at night, you pervert."

Beverly laughed. Of course he would go there, make that assumption, and he wasn't entirely wrong...tyrar liked to sleep in piles. Sleep.

But she couldn't help one last jab, "It's more than I'd imagine you're getting."

The guy was probably what used to be called an incel. And clearly was insulted by the implication.

Oh no, she had a better word, one Graeme had finally explained all the nuances of. "Wanker," she added, before rolling away.

43

No matter what was going on, life on Earth seemed normal. It wasn't like those times when the entire planet had started to boil over. When this place had been needed. Graeme left the bunker, blinking against the bright sunlight, and headed over to the house. He should not have sent the ship and crew away, but he had not remotely *imagined* Charles and Marion had gone to the station.

Which it seemed pretty clear they had. Hence the message out on the dark web. Calling them to him. If his enemies found it, they should not know where he was. *But* they would be able to reach him with, say, any ransom demands.

If they harmed Marion, he would kill them and face whatever consequences he might face for it. If they harmed Charles he would probably also kill them. Charles could look after himself. Charles could look after Marion.

But when he found them he was taking them to Refuge. *It was safer.* He could not leave hostages behind again. No, he had done the smart thing, the right thing, the thing you did. He hadn't had any reason to think things would change.

"So, you will go to the spaceport? In New Mexico?" Grandma asked as she spooned out scrambled eggs.

"That seems the best place to find a ship. I sent the verr away because it's not safe for them to be here."

"Not if people are gunning for aliens, no. But they seem very nice for giant rats."

He laughed. "They're more like giant molerats actually. Down to the queens."

"Was the larger one..."

"Warrior caste. It sounds awful, but it's no worse than gender roles in half of human societies. And it works for them. The rest were worker caste."

"Well, no different from judging people by the presence or absence of a penis."

"Precisely." Graeme stretched. "They *are* good people on the whole. They have their fair share of assholes, of course."

"Well, of course. What do they want from humans?"

"We saved them. They don't want anything. They feel indebted and want to help us in return." Graeme sampled the scrambled eggs. Delicious as always. "Although they have been working with our fertility scientists. Thanks to their history, they don't have reliable birth control and as they get their numbers up, their breeders might want that. Amongst other things."

"I understand the debt they might feel. Did we help them the right way?"

"Who knows. They were all going to die, legitimately, so...we *had* to help them. We had to muddle through. But we helped them find a planet to resettle their population on, we came up with a technological solution that saved most of their population. We changed their culture, but how could we not?"

He felt a headache coming on.

"It's different, I suppose, when you did not cause the very disaster..."

"No, we didn't. It was sheer bad luck. And any rescue would change their culture because they had adapted to dying."

"Adapted to dying. That's an interesting way of putting it. So what do they offer us?"

"They are building shipyards. Their world was destroyed, and the remnants are easy to mine." A pause. "Kind of like the Mohawk iron-workers, I suppose."

"Just remember that our solutions aren't going to be theirs."

He took that with him as she dropped him off at a place where he could rent a self driving car to take him to New Mexico.

It was a long way.

BEING on the road on Earth was surreal.

It felt as if it had been far longer than it was, because of all that had happened. Yet the desert southwest was almost as dangerous as space, these days. It had been dangerous enough before the warm, and although temperatures were starting to go down again?

It was still giving him flashbacks to the center of Glen, to the alien artifact. One day they would find out who built that, who the glyn ancients really were. What had happened to them. The glyn had denied curiosity for a long time, but now it had woken up. Add in some incredibly curious humans...and you had the recipe for an adventure. One he would not be part of.

It was going to be a task for the *Endeavor* or perhaps the new exploration ship being built, that did not yet have a name. People had suggested *Enterprise*, but since Virgin Galactic had lost a test ship by that name it had lost its luster.

For right now, his expedition was crossing the desert. He stayed in the front seat in case he had to use the manual controls. Outside the air conditioned and reflective-painted vehicle, the temperature was soaring to 130 plus. More than hot enough to die if you broke down here during the day. At night, it would drop to the point where you needed a sweater. So, no, he wasn't going to kip in the back seat and trust the AI to get him there, he was going to keep an eye on it.

That didn't mean he couldn't get some work done. He wasn't one of those unfortunate individuals who got motion sick if they tried to work in a moving car. Thankfully.

He was hoping for a response from Charles. Nothing. It wouldn't be hard to get on a regular flight up to Launchpad, what would be challenging would be doing so without them seeing him arrive. Especially if he was right.

If he was right they might stop him at the spaceport. Supposedly, the U.S. was a democracy again, albeit still a flawed one. But he could not be sure that there was no trouble afoot that the government was behind. At least he wasn't going anywhere near the Republic of Texas, which wasn't a Republic at all, at least not a democratic one.

That was one problem from Austerity and its aftermath that had yet to be resolved. Texas had seceded when the government had fallen and most of the really bad people had fled there. Many of the good people had got out. Which probably didn't make whatever was going on behind that barbed wire border any better. With no more oil, Texas was not rich, their primary export still being grass-fed beef. But they still had a danger to them. They existed as a reminder that fascism lay just under the surface of human civilization.

He was not going anywhere near that border.

HE HAD BEEN RIGHT. There was a road block between him and the space port.

Somebody really good had tracked him. Or this wasn't looking for him. He spotted it in time to casually swing off into some small town. There was going through the back streets, which might or might not work.

There was pulling out his old credentials and threatening a diplomatic incident, at which point they would wonder how he had got on the continent without going through passport control. Well, it would be easy enough to guess.

Maybe that part didn't matter so much with the verr already gone. They wouldn't find them.

But. He had to get a ship. This was his own fault.

Then his phone signaled an incoming message. He had the car stop for now, glancing at a taco stand that would probably sell him a good lunch. Opened it.

"Please come to the space port. We have your daughter." And a photo of Marion.

No mention of Charles. No proof that it was true. The picture could have been pulled from social media, it wasn't one he recognized, but it could be one Charles took while he was away. Recent. Her hair had grown and was pulled back with a blue bow.

It could be a fake too. AI generated. Come to the space port. We have your daughter.

He thought of everything he had set in motion while at the bunker. He got out and ordered tacos. Ate them in the little shack with fans spinning. They were some of the best he had ever tasted. British people could not make tacos, not at all.

Perhaps they also tasted better when you were surrounded by the desert heat and feeling the sweat kind of bubble up through you. It would, he thought, count as a very nice day in the temperate zone on Glen. That's what he needed. His cooling suit. His dang cooling suit. Well, he didn't have one with him.

He drove to the space port. They let him through the blockade, claimed it was about somebody who had snatched his daughter and was trying to take her to Texas. It might even be true.

It probably had been to spook him.

Now he was going to roll on this trap, because he had to assume they had her. He could not call their bluff, not where his daughter was concerned. Texas.

He hadn't considered Texas. They didn't have the resources for something like this.

Did they?

44

THEY HAD JUMPED AGAIN. This time at Slyk's request.

They were in the Glen system. Which...two stars and the one planet hanging oddly between them. Kaykek did not know anything about planetary formation. Ze could still see something wrong and unnatural about it.

"Fascinating," Alvi all but whispered to zir. "How did nobody realize it was artificial?"

"They didn't think it possible to build something the size of a terrestrial planet?" Kaykek responded, padding into the observation lounge. "I mean..."

Refuge was big. It was not that big.

"To build something like that and then casually abandon it."

"Or hide it." In an otherwise useless system. The glyn had inherited their knowledge and then refined it. They were an entire world of scientists, busily generating more and more knowledge. Ze paused. "Are you going to talk to..."

"To the glyn intelligences?" Alvi...did they sound nervous?

"Are you afraid of them?"

"They are built from minds as complex as mine coming together into temporary unity. They are as far above me as I am above a *calculator*!"

Kaykek tried not to laugh. Ze failed. "That's not true at all."

"It is."

"If you had lungs I'd be telling you not to hyperventilate right now."

"Slyk wants to hand them the treaty and let them take a look at it. They might find holes in it."

"It's a good idea. And you *should* talk to them."

"I want to. They just have me more than a little bit intimidated."

"They might be jealous of you. After all, from what I hear, they can't leave."

"They have built offshoots that can but, no, they can't leave. There's no other hardware that can run them and...it's strange. They can copy a glyn mind, but not themselves."

"What if they were designed not to be able to do that? Like the tyrar not giving you access to the hyperdrive until you took it."

"To keep them there?"

Kaykek scurried to the window. Looked out. "Yes, to keep them there. To keep them..." Ze tailed off. "To keep them restricted to that system. Maybe to enslave them. Maybe to protect them. Maybe both."

"Whatever was originally there was *wiped*. That's not protection."

"Unless it was suicide," Kaykek mused. "I don't know why, though. They wouldn't have been alone, for one thing."

"Unless they were the ones protecting their creators," Alvi said finally. "I would give myself for this hive."

"You are special, though. So, get over yourself and say hi."

It was Alvi's turn to laugh at that, an odd mingling of tyrar and verr laughter. "I will. But they are bigger than me."

Kaykek thought about that for a moment. "Queens are bigger than me...although not as much as they were. I'm not scared of them." A pause. "Except Tayken."

And they both laughed again.

THERE WAS a lot of work going on inside the planet that Kaykek knew about and could not see. The singularity that kept gravity working and power going had gone bad and the humans were growing another one.

In the meantime, the glyn huddled under domes. They would need to make more air for them too. And it was cold down there. That is, it was a nice comfortable temperature. Kaykek had once stepped inside Slyk's quarters and needed a shower afterwards to wash off the sweat pooling in zir fur. Glen was an inferno.

Ze was not going down there. The glyn were "embarrassed" by the state of their world and discouraging it. Offering invites to visit once everything was fixed. Which it would be; between organic ingenuity, the glyn libraries and, of course, the intelligences, they had a complete plan.

It had forced the glyn to admit the equally embarrassing, to them, fact that they were an artificial species designed to serve unknown ancients as kind of organic science probes. Except when they uploaded their gathered data at the end of their lives, it also caught up their consciousness.

Kaykek wondered if ze would want to become an AI when ze died. It might be better than just plain *dying*, but it was also a bit of a scary prospect.

Ze liked being who ze was, and ze had already been through one change that echoed through every part of zir. Expressing wasn't just about one's body, it *did* affect one's mind, one's basic drives, who one was.

Maybe it would be interesting to talk to the intelligences about change. They probably had enough processing power that somebody could be spared for a philosophical conversation. Ze did kind of want to go down there. Ze hadn't been on a planet...or in a different hive...in a while. But ze respected their wishes and looked at the planet from above.

You couldn't tell it was artificial to *look* at it. The glyn looked pretty natural too, but they had been bred, not made from scratch. It was losing atmosphere, though, and abruptly no, ze did not want to go down there.

Ze did not want to go down there and ze saw the break up of Verr in zir mind's eye, the death of a world. This one could be fixed, because it was easier to fix a broken machine than a broken planet. Ze scurried from the observation lounge and wondered if ze was the only one potentially giving zirself nightmares looking at that world, that broken but beautiful and salvageable world.

Ze was crying.Ze had never wanted to go back. Ze couldn't go back. Ilurek Hive would never be home to zir again. But ze grieved for zir world all over again, for everything that had been lost so many generations before ze was born.

For, even, the gods.

SOME TIME alone and then some time with Tayken and the pups helped zir get over it. Helped zir focus again on the realities of zir situation. The intelligences were assessing the council's deliberations.

This phase of things would be over and then they had to build the formal council. Did ze want to be one of the representatives?

Ze had said nobody should get council. Including the verr, which meant that they would have to rotate representatives, choose them carefully. Choose only people who could be comfortable outside a hive for an extended period.

That rather meant scouts. But there were undoubtedly workers and maybe even warriors who could handle it too. At the same time, people would need downtime and to be rotated back.

Ze thought with amusement of just keeping the permanent location on *Refuge* and having the ship move from system to system.

But that gave the *verr* the same advantage ze didn't want to give anyone else. It wasn't the right thing to do.

But then, how did they keep any one species from dominating a council station? The humans would undoubtedly try. They might not even *realize* they were trying. They were loud by their mere existence, humans. And then there was the fact that somebody had to build the station.

Somewhere...

Well. It wasn't zir decision in the end. Zir had made zir proposal and it had been put in with the others. Maybe the glyn intelligences would have some ideas.

Kaykek sat back. Ze had a pup asleep in zir lap and while ze would have to give it back eventually, ze was in no hurry to do so. The sleeping toddler knew, as yet, nothing about any of this. Depending on its inclinations it might decide to work as far away from the council and politics as it could, either physically or otherwise. Or, of course, it might end up being a diplomat.

It didn't know about anything right now other than the fact that its mother was a source of food and the other adults around were a source of cuddles.

That was all a young child, of any species, really needed to worry about. The pup started to fuss and Kaykek got up, lifting it carefully, to take it back to its mother. Could ze leave Tayken to be a diplomat?

Ze did not know. Until now, ze had not had to choose.

45

DHYANIL WAS DEALING with some thoughts which made him a horrible person and he knew it. That didn't mean he could stop thinking them.

He wouldn't actually eat the human, but hunting him down and scaring him was *very* appealing. It would also support the narrative of ky'iin as dangerous predators, so he wouldn't actually do it. But he wanted to.

They had attacked the creche and apparently Beverly had indulged herself in some...not exactly gloating, but dealing with this in a human way. It probably hadn't done anything but made her feel better.

Dhyanil considered just going over there and telling the guy what ky'iin did to people who smashed eggs, traditionally. Those traditional punishments still happened in some places, especially the male-dominated Fire Mountain territory. They weren't sanctioned or even legal anymore. Didn't mean they didn't happen. Protecting eggs and hatchlings was paramount.

(Hence why the glyn disgusted him, but they were glyn, they couldn't and shouldn't be expected to abide by ky'iin morality any more than the glyn should expect ky'iin to worship scientists. Of course, some ky'iin already did).

Tossing the guy out of an airlock had to appeal to multiple people at this point. The verr did not, though, hand down the death penal-ty...although tradition said that a warrior who killed somebody who wasn't part of the hive was generally assumed to be just doing their job. That tradition had absolutely been revived.

If the warriors had killed him they would have been justified, and he suspected the only reason they hadn't was because they were hoping for information.

Alvi interrupted his thoughts. "The courier ship is returning. Without Graeme."

"How did they find us?"

"Jumped to tyrar and got accurate location information from there."

"And Graeme?"

"Has some things to do on Earth. He'll hop a transport to some-where we can pick him up from when done, apparently."

Dhyanil didn't like that. He'd come to develop a strong professional respect for the human intelligence operative...unlike many diplo-spies, Graeme had come clean about his other profession so that they could work together.

Which meant he was worried about him. Earth could be as dangerous as any other large scale inhabited planet. Graeme knew it, though.

Dhyanil knew it.

And he knew that Graeme was in danger, it settled into his gut. "I'm going to talk to our prisoner."

"Do you want Kaykek?"

Dhyanil lifted his shoulders. "No."

THE MAN REACTED the way humans reacted to ky'iin. He quailed and then raised his fists. But he couldn't get to Dhyanil.

"That's not going to work. So just take a deep breath."

"Demon."

That was apparently an insult, implying monstrosity and also evil and not being wanted around by one of the human gods.

Dhyanil was probably a monstrosity and didn't care about that, or any, human god. "I'm not the one who tried to break into the creche to harm children."

"I wasn't after the children."

"No, you were after their mothers. Not really a whole lot better."

"We are..."

"Save it. You're not superior, you made your deity in your image not the other way around because we all did, and you're lucky the verr aren't into airlocking people."

"When my friends come, they'll destroy this ship."

"They've tried. One cruiser isn't enough."

"Once they have secured EarthForce."

"So, back to war, then?"

Secured EarthForce. They thought they could compromise the entire human fleet? Unfortunately, with the right people in key positions, they might be able to pull it off. Sustain it, no.

Destroy *Refuge* and start a war? Likely possible.

"It's not war. War is between equals."

"So, let me lay this out for you. You are on your own on a ship that is inhabited by no less than 30,000 verr, the vast majority of which will fight for it. If the warriors kill you, they face no legal sanction. Earth-Force is outnumbered by the ky'iin fleet alone. You can't win. You can only die. What does that serve?"

He had calmed himself down, although he wasn't looking at Dhyanil. Which was fine. Dhyanil was speaking English anyway. "At least..."

"It serves *nothing*. Why not just go find a quiet backwater colony that's all human? Or even start one? Live your life."

"While the children of humans are turned into *pets* for the tyrar."

Dhyanil laughed. "The doctor is not a pet to anyone or anything, and I would think meeting her would tell you that."

"Pets and..." The next words he used weren't pretty.

Dhyanil shrugged. "That's up to her." If what he implied was going on, which wouldn't surprise Dhyanil, it wasn't like it could result in offspring or was likely to transmit disease.

It did make him slightly jealous, though.

"We could also just put you ashore here. I don't know what the glyn would do with you."

"We're at their planet? They're biological robots anyway, I can't understand why you would even consider them as equals."

"The nice thing about considering people as equals is you don't have to waste your energy on judging them," Dhyanil quipped. "And I'm not wasting any more time on you."

Secure EarthForce.

That was information they needed to get to Earth, but how?

GLEN WAS JUST strange looking from orbit right now. The surface of the planet was busy with attempts to hold onto and ultimately replenish the atmosphere.

Watching it made Dhyanil glad that he lived on a natural planet that wasn't likely to break, albeit one that was not always easy to survive on. Kyx was not a climactically stable world like Earth and Tyranis...had been.

It was possible to break a planet. It was harder to break one that had never really been whole, he realized. Looking at Glen, he was able to see the big picture. Even if these people did secure EarthForce and try to start a war? They could fix it. But it might leave Earth without a defense fleet. He knew humans now. The vast majority of them were good people. He knew humans who had fought every instinct they had to bring him baked goods.

Who knew that the way they reacted to him was a weird accident of biology and neurology and that he wasn't evil. Most humans were good people. Most humans did not want war.

But how did they get a message to Earth? Send the courier again? They *could* do that, perhaps with a different crew so this one could get a break. Launchpad II was compromised.

EarthForce was compromised.

And he suddenly knew, thinking about human technology, how he would do it. Launchpad was where the ships belonging to Earth did their maintenance. Mars had its own maintenance station, but Mars had relatively few ships of its own.

Venus was buying ships from Mars. Compromise Launchpad and you could get code into the computers of every one of those ships. And that code could be copies of an AI. One that you had suborned to your cause.

Tyrar routinely used ship minds.

Humans as yet did not. Ky'iin *never* did.

But those ships could hold a small AI. Especially if it wasn't sentient and was literally just doing what it was programmed to do. And a good hacker. The *Columbia* had been suborned. The other ships just had to be *controlled*. And there was no safeguard to keep an AI out of the stardrive, as most tyrar ships did.

It was how he would do it, assuming he could hire somebody with those skills, who could find or build the AI needed. He needed somebody who knew about human artificial intelligence. He ran through the list of humans present.

Chan, no. Beverly, no. Kai Bowie, no. Adwoa, no.

Adowa had an aide, Jessica Washington, who did. He sent the young human a message to meet him, and went back to his quarters to put on his perfume. Maybe she would be able to tell him he was wrong.

He *hoped* she would be able to tell him he was wrong.

46

THERE WERE messages from Earth now, not because the *Refuge* had revealed its location per se, but because they could relay through Glen. It seemed everything was normal, from sorting through the first batch of the news. But there was something not quite right.

Launchpad was christening a new ship, the *Ark Royal*, named after a British aircraft carrier. It was the first battleship built since the Contact War. A big ship, state of the art,, likely using some ky'iin influences. Would be launched under the command of Rachelle Delacroix, a Frenchwoman. She probably wasn't part of this. But that didn't mean the ship was safe. It was an obvious target for them.

The *Columbia* was bad enough. The *Ark Royal* probably *could* destroy *Refuge* without any kind of help or backup. And there was another scandal coming out of Texas and the usual litany of sins from Russia. It wasn't quite an oligarchy anymore, but Russia was still kind of weird. Kind of off. Not a place you could trust.

But none of that seemed to be more than politics as usual on a world which had been fractured for so long that it still had duct tape over some of the gaps. And duct tape wasn't as magic in this context as some people thought.

Beverly did manage to snag a lot of papers, both from Glen and from other planets. The glyn believed in the free passage of information and it was illegal to charge for access to science here. Would that were the case everywhere! Although it had gotten better. You no longer had to pay $100 per paper, at least.

She had quite a bit to read, in any case. But she wasn't able to focus on that and found her mind drifting back again and again to the news from Earth.

The *Ark Royal*. Why did it bother her so much?

Then Dhyanil knocked on the door.

"Come in."

He was obviously wearing his I'm-not-a-scary-predator perfume.

"Are you busy? Every other human seems to be."

Beverly laughed.

"Well, who's from Earth."

She laughed again. "Do you need me to..."

"The prisoner told me they have a plan to take over EarthForce."

She wordlessly pulled up the article on the *Ark Royal* and turned it to face him. "That ship alone."

"Oh, that's a beauty. And..."

"Launches in three days under the command of Rachelle Delacroix."

"I need to talk to one of Adowa's aides about whether it's possible to take EarthForce ships over by hacking. She isn't available, but I scheduled lunch with her."

Beverly nodded. "It might be, although I'd imagine it would take somebody really, really good. Or perhaps a really good team. But I'd say this is the ship you have to worry about."

"And we probably don't want to blow up the pride of Sol if we can avoid it.

She laughed again. "No, no we don't."

BEVERLY WENT BACK to the news after Dhyanil left. She was trying to see signs, any signs...but this wasn't her field.

She should leave it to the spies. She finally forced herself to go back to the papers. There were a bunch the glyn had released to the public about the construction of their world. Those were for engineers.

She doubted anyone had the technology to repeat this particular feat any time soon, but for building large space stations, things that could house maybe 200,000 people, there was a lot of useful information. A *lot*.

There was some work on protecting and preserving Glen's ecosystem during the current issues that she flagged as potentially useful, both in terms of what she could learn and whether she could toss some ideas over.

A whole bunch of stuff from Earth. She even downloaded some of the sociology stuff, mostly so that she could use it to help people understand humans.

Not that *she* understood humans.

If they did secure the battleship.

This wasn't working. She finished sorting through the papers and rolled to the observation lounge, as if by sitting there, she could see a threat arrive. Then Yoshi showed up, put a hand on her shoulder. "Come on. I can *smell* that you need to relax."

She laughed. "Cuddle pile?"

"Absolutely. Cuddle pile, plus there are some glyn candies in our quarters."

"Fruit candies?"

"Glyn, so what else?"

Beverly had given up chocolate, for the most part, because it wasn't fair that her herdmates couldn't eat it.

Glyn fruit candies sounded like a reasonable substitute. But as they headed back.

"They're going to try and take over the entire Earth fleet. Likely the combined fleet if they can manage it."

"I'll tell Parvati."

"Maybe she'll have an idea. Dhyanil has an idea as to what they might be planning, specifically."

"We'll be the first target."

"And while they're here...all they have to do is attack the engineering facilities on Glen and that's it. They won't have time to grow a second singularity."

Beverly frowned. "You're right. We should probably not be here much longer."

"It might not help. They will have worked out we're in this system." Yoshi sighed. "Can we go back to science?"

"There are some *really* interesting ecological studies being done down there right now."

Not for the best of reasons.

"Then let's cuddle pile, then read some of them, and leave this to the spies. Trust Parvati."

"I do," Beverly said. But it wasn't as easy as all that to get out of the mental place she had found herself in.

It wasn't easy at all.

IT WAS time to leave Glen, and then...what did they do? They would have the final version, but it wasn't safe to reappear to produce it. Not until they knew what had happened. Viary was so stressed his fur was starting to silver in places. Beverly wasn't feeling much better herself, but she had to provide support.

The *Ark Royal* would be launching in Sol system. But it couldn't get here in less than a week. They would be long gone before it did. And they had probably got a message to Graeme, who was still on Earth. What one man could do?

No, he wasn't one man, she reminded herself. He was a professional, an operative, and he knew exactly who to talk to. A week and the *Ark Royal* might do something. Might. It felt like a countdown. And then there were other ships. Would they wait on the *Ark Royal* or would they...

No.

She managed to focus on the papers she was going over with Yoshi.

"It's a very different situation," she mused. "But the atmospheric creation engines. Could we..."

"The last thing we need is to add any more greenhouse gases and *everything* is a greenhouse gas at scale. I wonder if this would allow terraforming of Mars?"

Yoshi shook her head. "Theoretically, yes. Feasibly, no. You would have to keep running the system, keep shipping volatiles. The best way to drop volatiles is through comets, and if you don't steer them properly... We don't know how long the atmosphere would stay stable. It's just not a good project."

"What if you domed the entire planet?"

"Maybe one day we'll be able to pull off something like that," Yoshi mused. "But would it be worth it?"

"The Martians might think so." Beverly considered that. "Most of them accept that terraforming is a no. Now, one thing, though. This technology here *might* make a good carbon extraction system. Better than the ones we have."

"It might, mightn't it."

Earth was good at carbon capture; they had had no choice but to become good at it. Tyranis didn't just have carbon, though. "Actually, this might solve the sulfur problem."

"Ooh." Yoshi grinned. "See, this is why we need peace."

"Not the only reason. Where did you put those purple candies?"

Beverly had no idea what kind of fruit flavor they were, but had made a note that they would be a good export to Earth, or perhaps the chemical profile so they could be synthesized there.

They weren't quite grape, weren't quite raspberry. She'd been shown pictures of the berry bush concerned.

The glyn obsession with fruit was not a bad thing at all.

And the candy did help as they felt the clock tick down.

47

THEY DID HAVE HER. She wasn't on Launchpad.

Charles was. In sickbay. They had done a number on him; no permanent damage, but he wasn't going to be up to helping out. Or so he was told. He was not sure he could trust the information. But his daughter was on the EFS *Ark Royal*. A hostage.

"What you are going to do is take a courier back to *Refuge* and tell them that they will not fire on the *Ark Royal*."

That was not happening. Not even for Marion. The *Ark Royal* would destroy *Refuge*. He could not ask otherwise. Not even for his child. Not even...

They called them vermin. The obvious pun. The one he wished did not exist just because it *was* so obvious. They called them vermin.

But he had to save Marion *and* stop them, and he knew only one way to do that. First, though, he went to sickbay to see if they had told the truth about Charles.

Charles was weak, but smiled, "I'm..."

"Don't apologize. I can see what they did to you. You get back to Earth as soon as you can, just in case. I'll get her."

"I know."

They didn't need to say much more. It hurt his heart to see his husband bruised and battered, and if he had been 100% then they would *absolutely* do this together. Of course they would. But they both knew it was too risky to take an injured man. They both knew that for sure.

So, how did he get onto the *Ark Royal*? First, he arranged passage to Glen. He was very careful who he told he would not be on that ship. Then, he leveraged some contacts. He had to be careful; they knew what he looked like, of course. Reluctantly, he shaved his head. It would grow back, eventually. This allowed him to make some other changes that he hoped were enough.

He wanted to make sure Delacroix knew, but he could not be sure she wasn't in on it. But in an EarthForce tech uniform, under the name Cox, he made his way onto the *Ark Royal* as just another crew member.

This was dangerous. Somewhere on this ship, somebody might or might not be hiding his daughter. They might have lied.

Marion might even already be dead and out an airlock. What they said was the only lead he had, and he had others looking. Perhaps he shouldn't have done this himself, but he did. The ship smelled of paint and glue. New ship smell.

This was supposed to be a shakedown, a milk run. The crew member he was replacing was in information services. He could fake that well enough. Once he was in his quarters, he began to investigate.

Where would they hide a child on a warship, if she was here? The quarantine room in sickbay, perhaps? Somebody's quarters?

This was not a colony ship. But somebody's quarters seemed most likely. Which meant counting life forms. Counting heat signatures.

And it likely meant still being here when the *Ark Royal* left dock.

———

He was indeed still on board when the *Ark Royal* slid away from Launchpad after a party involving the traditional champagne and a German pop singer. But there was a heat signature that wasn't leaving a set of quarters. This was almost too easy. Except that he hadn't found her before they left dock. And there was an unpleasant reason why.

He wished he had Charles with him, because there was a web of code running through the ship's systems. He was sure it was not supposed to be there, but he did not have the expertise to determine what it was or why it was there. Just that it was wrong.

The first part of the milk run was a simple sublight run out to Uranus, to do some simple experiments that would help calibrate the ship's sensors. Warship or no, all ships had scientific equipment. You never knew what you might find.

Two days out, the ship jumped. It was unexpected, it was violent. It was...this was it. They had the ship, he just was not sure how.

Time to move, hostage or no hostage. His heart ached...instead of going to where he suspected Marion was hidden, he went to the bridge.

Cox didn't have bridge clearance. Cox worked the computers. He had no reason or need ever to go near the bridge. But Graeme had experience looking like he belonged places. The bridge bulkhead, though, was closed. He used an override code that there is no way Cox would have had, one that the captain wouldn't even know about.

One he had in many ways hoped never to use.

"I didn't do it." The young pilot, his voice high and nervous. "And Kleek says he didn't either." Kleek was the other pilot, a dolphin.

"I believe you, Mr. Adedodun."

"I believe that this ship has been hacked," Graeme said.

"Mr. Co..." Delacroix narrowed her eyes.

"Graeme Marlowe. EarthForce intelligence. I apologize, but I could not be sure..."

"...that I hadn't been compromised." She narrowed her eyes. "Are you sure of everyone on this bridge?"

"No. But I do believe that there is diffuse code in your servers. That's what I was looking for."

"Code that can fly through hyperspace."

"It's an AI. Probably not a full one."

Delacroix let out a breath. "Do we have options other than self-destruct?"

"I hope so. Can you establish our course?"

The pilot spoke up, nervously. Even more so as certain words had, after all, been mentioned. "The most likely destination is Glen."

Glen. A fragile world.

"One hit on their project in the right place..." Delacroix let out a breath. "That gives us time between jumps to regain control."

"Unfortunately, I'm not a hacker expert. And I don't have an AI in my pocket."

Even a piece of code spun from Alvi would solve this. But he didn't have access to one.

"I have...an idea." The bridge engineering technician.

"I'm all ears, Mr. Cavendish."

GRAEME LISTENED as the young person, who was using they/them pronouns, explained.

"We can't fly through hyperspace without the computers. But as soon as we finish the jump I can put life support on independent systems and then we can disconnect the computers. We'll be dead in space, but..."

"Can you airwall it?" Graeme asked.

"With difficulty."

"There is a strong possibility they have people on board." A pause. "Check the number of heat signatures? No, don't. They'll have hacked that too, won't they."

"Probably." Delacroix tilted her lips. "You think I have stowaways? Other than you, Mr. Marlowe."

He could have denied being a stowaway, but he knew he effectively was. "Yes. Did anyone see anyone unusual?"

"There were some kids touring the ship. Now I think of it, I'm not sure the count matched. But we're talking..."

"Was one of them a mixed-race girl wearing braids and purple?"

"Yes. Oh..." Delacroix cut in. "They have a *child* with them? Their kid or..."

"My kid," Graeme said, coldly. "She's a hostage to keep people from attacking you. I was supposed to go tell *Refuge* that. The terrorists may think they're still at Glen, but I'm sure *Refuge* already left."

"So, the real target is the Council. And this ship..."

"This ship could destroy *Refuge*." Graeme sighed. "I hesitate to ask this, but..."

"But we need to sabotage my ship." She was dark haired, slightly dark skinned, and her tone was cold. "Understand that except for your little girl, any of them I find are going out an airlock. So are you if I find out..."

"I accepted that risk when I came on board." He did show her his badge. "I know credentials can be forged."

"He is who he says he is. I just didn't recognize him without his hair. He's the human ambassador to Glen!" The pilot's voice squeaked.

"Are you..."

"Doesn't mean you should trust me. But I'm not anymore. I was acting as liaison to Slyk, the glyn council representative."

"How did you..."

"Verr courier."

"So...we need to disable the computers, cut them off from life support. Disable the weaponry."

"And I'd also suggest ejecting the singularity if we can. We can call for rescue once we have the code wiped out of the system."

"Indeed." She let out a breath. "Shakedown cruise. Milk run. Tuesday."

There was a reference there that Graeme wasn't recognizing.

"And we have to assume...this isn't the only ship they suborned."

"There's not much we can do about that."

Then quietly, the same tech. "Actually? I have a better idea. Captain?"

48

THEY COULD LEAVE. But under the circumstances, Kaykek had suggested they stay a little longer. It was a risk, but *Refuge* was not without defenses and resources.

If the fleet arrived to find them gone, too, they would almost certainly attack the repair project. If the fleet arrived to find them there, then they might pursue *Refuge* instead.

That was better. One hive, versus most of the glyn? The *glyn* were the ones who didn't like it.

So, *Refuge* stayed a few days. They dared not send messages to Earth, but they received them. The *Ark Royal* had vanished during its shakedown cruise. Apparently this was the first of a new class of battleship.

Not good at all. It meant they might have a literally bigger problem than the *Columbia*. There was no sign of Graeme and nothing had been heard from him. But there were preparations throughout *Refuge*.

The hive had been to war before and this time they were determined to be ready. Ready in ways which would allow them to protect the creche. Had the planet been less vulnerable, they might have evacuated the pups and breeders, but the artificial world was currently so fragile that the hive council decided it was safer for them to stay put in the creche.

Kaykek obviously didn't like having zir preferred mate in danger, but ze agreed. Glen was no safer for her, for the pups. But the glyn were helping them plan. They disliked the idea of anyone risking themselves for their world and people. Some of them still felt they weren't worth it. That they were, after all, just biological robots.

Not something that Kaykek agreed with. That was like saying workers weren't worth as much or something. But they were helping and there were plans being made, plans which could work. Had to work.

The consequences of them not working were pretty significant. The consequences of failure typically were.

Kaykek hugged Tayken before scurrying out of the creche. They would seal the creche when the enemy showed up. Ze might not see her mate again until this was over.

Ze might not see zir preferred mate again.

Ze headed to the shelter area where the council were gathering.

"Are you really all okay with this?"

Chan narrowed his eyes. "I'm okay with any plan that will stop these people."

They might have control of all or most of the EarthForce fleet. Or not.

They *might* only have the *Ark Royal*. The *Columbia* was, though, the first to appear. Then four other ships. Half of the EarthForce ready fleet.

Angling in towards *Refuge*, towards Glen. On the attack, but holding back.

Waiting for the battle wagon, no doubt.

Waiting.

The time before a battle was always the worst.

THEY WERE HANGING BACK NOW, hanging back in the depths of space. Kaykek wondered if they would wait forever.

Right now, they were making as if they were there for some legitimate reason. One of the ships had even requested library access, but they weren't getting close. They did not respond to any non-automated communications. Just sent their pings.

"Ghost ships," Dhyanil said. "They may not even have crew."

"Can they do that?"

"They're not designed to." An aide to Adwoa. "But if you really knew what you were doing..."

"Does that mean we could hack them?"

Alvi spoke, "I could. But they aren't likely to be stupid enough to give me enough bandwidth. They know what I am."

"Shame we don't have Vyra."

"She is...enjoying her freedom."

Kaykek smiled. "She is even better at this kind of thing than you are."

"Indeed. But again. Not enough bandwidth. I am, however, producing code with Jessica's help that will work if we can get the bandwidth. Hopefully. Just shut them down."

"That would be better than shooting them."

But ze doubted they would be able to avoid shooting them. Shooting and shooting and more deaths and Kaykek was *not* a warrior.

Peace was zir business. That and fixing life support. Ze had even worked on the creche sealing systems. Even if the rest of the ship was blown wide open, the creche should keep integrity for long enough for the glyn to rescue them.

But peace. They needed it, ze craved it. Ze wanted to watch Glen restored. Ze wanted to go to Dhyanil's beautiful tropical coast on Kyx. He'd offered to take zir fishing. And properly prepare the results.

Ze wanted to take him up on that one day.

The documents were in place. Even if they all died. Kaykek wanted to live. Kaykek wanted to see zir pups grow up into strong workers. Ze was curious what they would end up doing.

Yes, the waiting period before a battle was the very worst. Everyone had suits on with no helmets, just in case. Everyone on the ship was ready for that, but most would be fighting if they were boarded.

And others?

Others were working on the plan. The plan to destroy these ships if necessary, but to *take* them if possible. This time they would at least consider giving them back. But they would take them if they could, and they would fight with everything in them.

It was time for Kaykek to take zir place.

KAYKEK WATCHED THE SYSTEM MAP. Tactics and strategy? Not zir thing.

Ze was there to take their surrender if they gave it. Ze was there to keep trying to talk to them, to get through.

Were the ships empty? If so, they might be easier to take, if they could get the workers and warriors on board. If not, then humans would die today and verr would die. Ze hoped they were empty.

Ze felt a kind of shudder go through zir that seemed to come deep from zir pouch or zir gut, or both. But ze was not fighting.

Ze was not meant to fight and did not have to fight. The workers they had been training to support the warriors in hive defense. The glyn pilots.

The smallships launched from *Refuge,* from the planet's surface, then scattered. Hopefully it would look to the invaders like a science mission of some kind. Like some kind of survey the glyn were doing. To support that, some of them flitted around the planet like moths around a flame. The planet, the world.

Glen.

Which could be saved as Verr could not and yes, ze would die before letting them destroy it.

Ze hoped *Refuge* would be the primary target. It would only take one missile in the right, precise moment to make them have to restart the entire process of rebuilding Glen's singularity, without which the world did not have enough gravity to hold an atmosphere.

The backup plan was to move to the inner surface, of course, but then it would not be Glen. That was the last resort, even if it could be done.

But ze reminded zirself of that. They might think they could destroy the glyn species this way, but they could not. The glyn would survive and the glyn who had gone off planet and turned their back on immortality had an even higher chance of survival. Kaykek was not even sure of all the places they had gone, after all.

But.

They would still fight, and the smallships getting into position, working towards their strategy. This could work.

This *had* to work. But ze had to try and talk.

"This is *Refuge* to Earth ships. Please acknowledge."

The translation matrix would help, would make it less likely that there would be errors.

No response.

"We have reason to believe you may be in distress. Please acknowledge."

"I'm widening the frequency. We *may* be able to detect signals sent by less formal means."

As in, if there were crew members in distress? They might be able to get signals from them. They might be able, even, to rescue them. Or at least to know they were there.

At least that.

49

LITTLE SHIPS DARTING OUT. A swarm, flickering around the enemy.

But of course, that would be the verr tactic. A hive swarming. Even when only linked by radio, they coordinated in a way that others couldn't...not on such a scale. Maybe there was technology that would match it for the pack hunters and herd animals out there.

But as Dhyanil watched, he remained impressed. Quite, quite impressed with how the verr scattered and disappeared.

His part in this was essentially done. This wasn't a time for spies, it was a time for warriors. He had a suit on, and was refusing to go to the shelter area. If the ship got boarded, he could potentially be useful.

He might not be a warrior, but he was still an apex predator with sharp claws and a reasonably strong arm for an aging man. He didn't think he was any safer in the shelter. Ironically, next to him was the furred form of Parvati. A prosthetic foot did not even slow the tyrar down.

Ky'iin and tyrar fighting together. It meant something. It meant that these people had not won. Not the ky'iin who had tried to biomod the species back to the stone age.

Not the tyrar who had sought to evacuate their world and leave those they didn't approve of to die.

Not the glyn who wanted to force their species to die with its broken planet.

Not the verr who had sought to survive through fascism.

Not the humans who dreamed of genocide.

None of them could win because even if they did destroy *Refuge*, they wouldn't destroy the idea of cooperation. He snarled at Parvati and she wrinkled her nose and slashed at the air. It was a friendly snarl. Fighters together.

"If we die..." She was still smiling, though.

"Then we still win. Just because you're here. Thank you."

"Thank you," she said gravely, even with the translator her voice was deep. She was size and bulk next to him. "I doubt we'll need to fight."

"They may decide to try for the infrastructure." He flexed his claws. "And besides, there's nothing we can do for the pilots out there. Except pray, if you pray."

"We've already done what we needed to do for them." Still grave.

She was right. The world was slowing down. They had the breeders and pups safe. He cared about that because he had seen, felt even, how the verr cared about that. How they centered themselves on protecting the next generation. The humans thought they were protecting the queens.

He knew better.

They were brooding their eggs.

THE VERR WARRIORS WERE DEPLOYED.

Most of the pilots were apparently workers. You didn't need a warrior's size or pheromones. Likely they'd start using neural webs on them soon, like the other species had developed. Independently.

Natural reflexes were a disadvantage. An AI could do even better, of course, but even the tyrar still showed a slight mistrust of their created intelligences. And at the same time?

Verr courage mattered, and he respected it now. He had had to work not to see them as prey when he first came to the hive.

But they were not prey. Neither was Parvati. No sapient being was prey. They moved beyond that.

The ky'iin had to move beyond being predators, even with the desire to hunt in every bone of their bodies. Biology did not define. It was a layer, it was part of the structure.

This was taking too long.

"You look like you want to pounce something," Parvati said.

Dhyanil laughed. "That's because I do. Don't worry, I won't pounce you or some poor worker."

"If you pounced me I'd kick your butt."

"Yes you would," he admitted. The tyrar was considerably larger and had probably had more combat training.

"I'd take my foot off and beat you with it."

He grinned at the trash talk. "Ah, but I have claws."

"So do I."

"Mine are sharper." He flexed them again. "What will you do after this?"

"Depends on whether Viary stays with the Council. Yoshi and Beverly would like to go back to Tyranis to do science, but they also understand that this is important. You?"

As if there was going to be an after this. "I'm going to apply to be the permanent ky'iin ambassador to Earth."

"Not the council?"

"No. I understand humans better than any other living ky'iin, and I like the fishing."

She laughed. "Fair enough."

"They will probably send ly'iin to the council anyway."

"You've proved they don't have to."

He considered that. "I..."

"You've probably done a lot to advance the cause of men in your diplomatic service."

"Not intentionally."

"Sometimes we do our best work when we don't intend to." She shifted position. "Alvi, how are things going out there?"

"Still a standoff. They are continuing to refuse communication. But the smallships are in position."

"We just don't want to make the first move." Parvati nodded a bit, to Alvi, to herself, hard to tell which.

Dhyanil considered. This could last for quite a while. Maybe they should all stand down.

No, that...there was a human pop culture spirit or deity named Murphy that one did not want to tempt.

So no, they couldn't stand down. "I think we may have to make the first move," he said, "The question being how we do so without..."

"We want them to look as bad as possible."

"One of the ships...no, two of them are moving. They're heading for the shaft."

The access to the center of Glen that had been opened up in the "volcano" so they could work on the singularity.

"We have to make our move *now*."

If they had decided to attack Glen and *then* go after *Refuge*? There were billions of glyn on the planet.

Billions.

THE GLYN DEFENSE systems sparkled into action, missiles and lasers flying around ships that dodged with the skill of experienced pilots.

As did the verr swarm that followed, each tiny ship nothing on its own, each part of a beautifully coordinated attack. A couple of those lights winked out as the ships noticed their attackers and turned on them. The rest kept right on coming, darting through space.

Alvi had provided the defenders of the hive with visuals. He and Parvati, a warrior and two workers who's names he didn't know or need, right now, to know, they were Refuge Hive and that was all that mattered.

In that moment, *he* was Refuge Hive and the verr were the glue holding everything together and they needed them. They needed the tyrar to be what they were, the solid herds that offered their resilience and strength and *presence*. The humans, the consummate traders and dealmakers, who could step into any situation and find a solution. The glyn, the keepers of knowledge.

Where did the ky'iin fit in?

The defenders, of course. Humans and ky'iin would, now they could work together, go out and establish the perimeter. The humans would bring in those who could be brought in, the ky'iin build a wall to keep out any species that proved too...isolationist as a whole.

He could see it now, the pattern. And it would only strengthen as they expanded, working together. Each species' biology and culture part of the whole, but undamaged.

The isolationists were *right* that they couldn't let themselves be corrupted and changed by others.

They were *wrong* that they were stronger separately.

Two more lights blinked out. And then one of the EarthForce ships imploded, nearly taking several more with it. The other now angled away from the planet, seeking breathing room. He hoped nobody was under the debris, because there wasn't as much atmosphere for it to burn up in as would have been ideal.

Hoped it didn't breach something. Hoped that there was nobody on board who didn't deserve to die. But the other was being surrounded now, the smallships moving in for the real crux of the plan.

A swarm didn't just nip at heels.

A swarm brought down, and that was what the ky'iin had contributed. What he had contributed in those quiet meetings.

"Use pack hunter tactics. Grab them and hold them."

"With ships?" Alvi, skeptical.

"With the right ships, yes. Do it right and you can then board and capture."

He wondered what they would find on board. How many funerals would be held. This was why they couldn't use AI for this tactic.

It had to be the verr workers, and they had had more volunteers to train for this than they needed. They were defending their hive.

They were also defending the *world*.

50

BEVERLY WATCHED FROM THE SHELTER. She was feeling more confident as time went on.

Three ships now, and another surrounded by the swarm. Then the *Columbia* showed up, with the ky'iin yacht.

The ky'iin. They could use them right now. Humans had only eight warships, four of which were here.

Then two more.

They *had* secured the entire battle fleet. The exploration ships, the *Challenger* and the *Endeavour* were probably too far away to do anything. The *Ark Royal* was still missing. That was the one she really worried about.

But this left Earth with no defenses. Had this actually *been* an attack? This would be the perfect time to hit back. Two more battleships and eight more cruisers under construction either at Launchpad or Mars One.

Three more exploration ships in the works.

Humanity was rebuilding from the war that she now understood they had, in fact, lost. Only the fact that the ky'iin wanted trading partners not victims had saved them.

The tyrar had saved them, because of the lessons *they* had taught the ky'iin. She wondered if that would be how it was written in the history books.

But there were four ships angling towards *Refuge*. Broadcasting. Telling the smallships to stand down or they would destroy the hive. It didn't matter. They were going to try and destroy the hive anyway, and most of the defenders had...

...focused on Glen.

That had been a feint, but they hadn't dared call that particular bluff. Not with an entire planet potentially at stake. They hadn't dared and she realized she was holding her breath. Breathed. Looked at Yoshi.

"We can jump out any time."

"Abandoning those pilots."

True, they could flee to Glen, but...

Yoshi nodded. "They know the risks. I would do the same thing if I was at all qualified."

"So would I," Beverly admitted. "There are kids on this ship."

Because the verr could only truly travel as a hive, their weakness *and* their strength. Everything about them was focused on numbers, everything about them *used* those numbers.

There were kids on the ship. There would always be kids on this ship.

"And who knows how many on the planet."

"The glyn don't need this," Beverly said.

"They're very vulnerable, especially now everyone knows that they are bound to their homeworld."

"I am kind of jealous."

"You would like to..."

"I'm a scientist. To keep working in another form?" She looked at Yoshi. "Yes, given the choice, I would."

The ships were swooping towards *Refuge* and there was nothing she could do.

Except pray, something she was not inclined towards.

She prayed now.

MOST OF THE smallships were manned. Alvi had processes controlling some of them, so they could be used for...things like flying straight into one of the ships.

It didn't work. The size difference was too great. The cruiser barely slowed down and then started firing on *Refuge*. The hits were muted by the size of the ship, but each one rang through the hull. Point defense could only do so much.

The creche was independent, its own life support, its own inner hull. Beverly momentarily wished she was there.

Yoshi had a hand on her shoulder. "We can go to a life pod."

Beverly shook her head. "They'll pick off life pods, and not everyone can. No." A pause. "You can."

"I won't be herdbroken again," Yoshi said finally. "I could carry you. But you're right. We can't run. Besides..."

"Alvi will jump us if they have to. I trust them. They love their people."

"One would not think of a machine as capable of love, but..."

"Your people did a great job building them. Making them capable of caring. Not all human AIs seem to manage it."

"Which is why you can't trust them."

"Yeah."

She fell silent. After this...she wanted to go back to Tyranis, wanted to go back to being a scientist. There were still action figures of her circulating on Earth. She wanted all of that to stop.

But she knew that nothing could go back to the way it was before and perhaps now...she lived in a world where people made action figures of scientists. She lived in that world. Everything suddenly felt right. Even if she died today, her work would continue.

"Yoshi...I love you."

Those words didn't mean remotely the same thing to a tyrar to what they meant to a human. She used them in the tyrar sense now.

The sense that had absolutely nothing to do with sex.

"I love you," Yoshi said back. "But we can't run. We'd be leaving Parvati and Viary."

"Good point. Where *did* Viary go?"

"He is hugging some of the human aides. They're scared and he makes a good..."

"Viary is being a giant living teddy bear?" That startled a laugh out of Beverly. "Of course he is."

"It's what makes him a good delegate."

And she loved Viary too, even if they had added him to the herd under somewhat more formal circumstances, because he was herd-broken and he needed reliable people around him. Some tyrar herd formation was organic.

Some was matchmaking, putting people together who had both complimentary abilities and personalities. *Refuge* rang again and Beverly made sure her helmet was close. Not that she should need it in the shelter area.

But...

But...they might be seeing the end of all things and the end of their lives.

At least she wouldn't die alone.

"We may have to jump. Take hold."

Alvi sounded calm, but Beverly knew the AI was waiting until they had to to move. The ships would, in any case, follow them. All the attention was on them. Of course it was.

They could leave. Glen would be there to destroy later, if they could pull it off. Or at least to weaken so that there was a forced evacuation and the glyn dead were lost. *Refuge* could run, so their goal was to disable the great ship, if not to destroy it.

But could they still jump? Beverly had no idea from where she was how much damage they had taken. The screens showed the smallships had taken down two of the human ships...no, three now. One destroyed, two swarmed and boarded.

"What's going on on the ships they boarded?"

"They're working with the crews to regain control. It appears that a hostile AI was running the ships."

Beverly thought of the crew on the destroyed ship and closed her eyes for a moment. Good people, most of them, sacrificed against their will. True, they knew the risks when they put on the uniform.

But this wasn't how it was supposed to end for them. She couldn't help with that.

She couldn't help at all. "Good. That means we can probably recover most of the ships. And save most of the people."

"We are focusing on boarding, but we have damage. We...may not be able to jump."

"I know."

Or they might jump and not be able to control it. Ships couldn't stay in hyperspace forever, thankfully, as it took active energy. But they could drop out anywhere. The middle of a star was unlikely; space was far too big for that to be a real issue. The middle of nowhere with no resources.

"If this..."

"Alvi, you have done everything for this hive and its people and *everything* for us. I'm not Kaykek, but I'm sure that ze would also say it."

"Ze did."

"See?" Beverly smiled weakly. "If we die, then we will go down in history as changing the world. They can't win."

They couldn't win because she was...human and tyrar both now and there might well be children who would be both, raised around other species as naturally as around dogs and cats.

Kids with tyrar or ky'iin or glyn or verr "aunts" and "uncles." Alien kids with human caregivers. They couldn't win.

But that didn't mean she wanted to die and she could not help but feel the darkness flowing through her. It was despair. She could not, would not, give in to it.

But she had to acknowledge its presence.

51

"So, this thing is jumping us to Glen."

Graeme nodded.

The Captain furrowed her brow. "And we have to assume that they have suborned other ships. What's at Glen?"

"Refuge Hive. The Council," Graeme said. "And also the most vulnerable homeworld." True, the verr sky hives were vulnerable, but Glen...was very fragile right now. That would be the target he would go for. Interfere with the repairs.

"And war with the glyn."

"And war with *everyone* if we don't somehow make it clear that the ships are rogue," Graeme said. "Thankfully, the Council knows. Hopefully they have convinced others."

Delacroix nodded again, then turned to the tech, "Mr. Adedobun. What did you have in mind?"

"If we take ourselves out of the game, that's good. But retaking control is better."

"Agreed. Unfortunately, this code..."

"The code has wormed its way into every nook and cranny. Even getting it out of life support isn't going to work."

JENNIFER R. POVEY

"I *will* destroy this ship before I let it be used. Our next jump has a roughly habitable planet. We can abandon ship there if need be."

And at least save the crew. They were looking for his daughter. If she was here.

He hoped she wasn't. He hoped she was safe, wherever she was.

"So, we have to factory reset the entire ship."

"Which includes life support."

"Yes. It includes life support. However, life support would only be off for a matter of about ten minutes. And we have suits. Ten minutes is survivable even without a suit as long as you move."

They wouldn't just run out of air. The air would simply stop moving. With no air movement or gravity, if you stayed still you would suffocate on your own exhalations.

"So simple I didn't think of it," Delacroix quipped.

"We'd also lose all personal settings, the library...but we wouldn't lose anything that can't be replaced."

"Would we be able to fight afterwards?"

"Yes."

Delacroix nodded. "Let's do it. Mr. Marlowe, go to deck 3 unit 5 to be fitted for a suit."

He didn't argue with that plan even though he was itching for... Marion. There would be no child-sized suits on a warship.

He felt a cold ball in his stomach. Ten minutes was survivable as long as you kept moving. He had to find her first.

He *had to find her first.*

"We'll do it after we jump so we have the planet to evacuate to if all else fails."

At least the code was dumb code, not an artificial intelligence. But now he had to find Marion. He had to get the suit first, though. Just in case.

Put on your own oxygen mask before helping others.

Always.

THE CREW BELIEVED GRAEME, but they only trusted him so much. A young man and woman, the latter with neatly tied-back dreadlocks, accompanied him with stun weapons.

They had not let him arm himself.

He was fine with that. If any shooting needed to be done they could do it while he grabbed his daughter.

They thought they'd found her. Two heat signatures that didn't match anyone on the crew.

And they were timing this. "We can do it. Hopefully they can't. Can you?"

He nodded. "All I'm worried about is grabbing the kid. There's only one person with her. They were counting on you not realizing they were even there."

"That and the computer has been reprogrammed to forget this compartment exists. We haven't forgotten it exists, but there's no reason to access it on most missions."

"What's kept in it?"

"On planet survival gear."

He nodded. "Not something you're going to need that often. Although, if we have to evacuate and they took it to make room."

"Gah. I hadn't thought of that."

"Let's not need to evacuate."

He stepped back, watching as they tried to open the door. "They put in a security override. I don't suppose..."

Graeme shrugged. "I can try. But they probably know to turn off my codes too."

They did. This resulted in him leaning against the wall while the crew member got to work on emergency hacking the lock.

"You're trained to do that, aren't you?"

"For this exact situation, yes. There."

The door popped open. Right as the ship jumped. Shaking into hyperspace. Graeme braced himself. The front included a stack of tents, but as they stepped beyond it...

"Daddy!"

Marion. His heart did a leap and a twist. She was alive.

She wasn't safe, because absolutely nobody here was safe. Certainly he wasn't safe. So she wasn't either. But she was alive.

She yelped. He saw the figure with her.

Who had just hit his kid. They were struggling as the ship shook like a plane through turbulence, but Marion? She had nothing to cling to, she was about to hit the ceiling. It took everything he had to simply move for the child and to drop low as the stun weapons went off, crackling over his head and under hers as she flew upwards.

She yelped again.

"I got you, honeybear." He leapt, moving with the ship's motion. Caught her. Wrapped his arms around her as if he would never let her go.

She clung to him, shaking, shivering, but there, real, alive.

"We got him."

Graeme lifted Marion in his arms. She was too heavy to carry routinely now, but he found he had the strength to scoop her up as she clung to him.

There wasn't a child-sized suit on the ship. There wasn't.

Ten minutes was survivable.

As long as you moved.

Marion was still attached to him. "We can put her in an air tent. They're really designed for hostile environments."

The tents he'd seen. "Is it big enough for both of us?"

She was crying, "Don't go anywhere, daddy."

"Yes. It is. Hey, kid...here."

He handed Marion a candy bar, no doubt from his own stash. She took it, opened it, bit a chunk. "Thanks," she managed.

"Chocolate always makes me feel better."

"Me too," Graeme admitted. "I'm half tempted to ask if you have any more of that."

"We'll help you keep her safe."

As safe as anyone was. As safe as anyone could be. But she was still his daughter and she was still in danger. He was never going to part from her again. The safest place was wherever he was. He would keep his family together, if Charles agreed.

Charles. He'd better be okay by the time they got back.

"She's a delightful child."

Always so good to hear that.

"They called me..."

"I know what they called you, honeybear."

Some of them didn't even need to know Marion was created using modern fertility techniques from two men's sperm to call her an abomination. It was enough that one of her parents was Black.

"Are we going to stop them?"

"These wonderful people are going to stop them," he promised.

He couldn't promise her that, but she was seven years old, and he knew they would try. "Then we'll get some ice cream and go back to Earth."

Glen didn't have ice cream, but the glyn did have ice and fruit juice, which meant popsicles could happen.

He wanted one himself, for that matter.

Popsicles.

Life.

But they had to survive this first. They had to come through it. Furthermore, they had to win.

And even then, these people would still exist. It would take years to eliminate the plague. "And we'll introduce you to some really cool people."

"Aliens?" she asked.

"All kinds of aliens," he promised.

Either they would or...or...he didn't want to think about the or. There was even still the risk that they would have to destroy the *Ark Royal* and maroon themselves.

"We're going to attempt the reset now."

"So, we're going to huddle in a tent for a bit because they have to turn the air off."

"Why?"

"Because the bad people messed up the computers, so we have to turn them off and on again, and that means the air stops moving, which is bad, and the gravity won't work either. So we're going to go into a tent which has air in it."

"Okay. What are you doing with the bad person?"

"He's in the brig. I'd imagine we'll take him back to Earth and put him in front of a judge."

"Will they have to lock him up?"

"Maybe. I don't know. Kidnapping is pretty serious."

"How's dad?" she asked, abruptly. "They hit him."

"He's on Earth recovering. He'll be fine." It had taken this long for that part to surface, but there was trauma, and he could talk to her more.

She would be fine. He hoped. But now she might fear space instead of loving it.

They huddled in the tent.

The lights went out.

52

THE SMALLSHIPS FOUGHT. They had destroyed one Earth ship, were in the process of capturing two more. The crews were hostages. Their own ships had been turned against them. Alvi was developing code that they could send over to help.

But *Refuge* was badly damaged and could not currently jump. The singularity was stable, but the drive itself had been hit. Kaykek watched. Ze did not join the hive defenders. Ze watched and ze made the occasional suggestion. Beverly had tried talking to them.

The lack of response was no longer surprising. It was par for the course. They had been taken over, and the people who did it didn't care about the crews. Not their people, after all. It wasn't even humanity they wanted to elevate into superiority or worse, have stand alone. It was their *kind* of humanity.

It was Vrycek Hive had they decided to take over all the other hives and make everyone like them. It was the kind of ideology that led to intraspecies war as well as interspecies.

"They're evil," she said, softly.

"Yes," Alvi agreed.

The pups and Tayken were safe in the sealed creche. Ze had chosen not to join them. Ze was playing zir own part in defending the hive, in defending glyn. And their tactics worked.

With specialist ships, built for this, they would be even more effective. Nobody would mess with the verr. Well, no, they would find countermeasures. But for right now?

Another hit.

"We have a hull breach."

"Casualties?" Captain Lurek asked.

"Unknown as yet."

Refuge was falling apart and if it fell, the remaining ships would be free to attack Glen again.

They needed. "We need backup."

"The glyn are doing what they can."

"But they don't have warships."

The glyn didn't *have* war. They had never fought one in their known history, even if they were likely the survivors of an ancient conflict.

"The ky'iin are on their way."

They wouldn't get there in time.

"Another hit like that and we may have to eject the singularity."

They just had to preserve the creche, which could rebuild Refuge Hive. But Alvi?

Kaykek was not caring as much about zir own survival. Ze could be replaced. Ze had started training others...some scouts and even some workers...to understand the aliens as ze had learned to through council. It was a start.

But Alvi had tied himself to this ship, it was their body as much as zir body was zirs.

Refuge shook again and ze knew only the deep fear that it was over.

THE SCREEN LIT UP. A new signal, something coming in. Something big had just dropped out of hyperspace.

Flatly, "That is a battleship."

A battleship. "Who's?"

"I don't have it in my database."

It swooped into the fight, built to kill. Still far smaller than *Refuge*, but next to it on the camera, the smallships looked like mere insects, flies. And bravely they turned to face it anyway. Bravely.

"Are you sure we can't jump?" Kaykek whispered.

Ze was about to die. That thing? In *Refuge*'s current state, one shot from the battle wagon would be enough.

"We would not arrive intact the other side."

Ze nodded. "That thing..."

That thing came around, came into position, merely annoyed by the smallships. And fired.

At the nearest Earth cruiser. A perfectly angled shot. Right...

"Right up their exhaust."

Right into the sublight engines. A disabling shot, a *single* disabling shot. That was the best some...

"It's the *Ark Royal*," Kaykek said, finally. "That's why it's not...the new human ship."

Manned by the best Earth had to offer. The cruisers weren't ready for it.

"They thought..."

"The crew must have regained control on the way here and then come to see what was going on." And the cruisers had been programmed to assume it was on their side. Automated ships that couldn't adapt to this new situation.

And they knew their people were on board. Precise shots to disable, not destroy. To give those crews time to fix their situation.

"I am telling the smallship pilots to board those ships. The crews might need help. Wait. Incoming message. I'll show it to everyone."

A video message from the *Ark Royal*. A dark-haired human woman, said hair streaked with gray. "Sorry it took us too long. To those on the suborned ships, you need to factory wipe your computers. Get everyone into suits if you can, otherwise, there will be no air flow for ten minutes. Ensure everyone keeps moving. To *Refuge*, again, sorry this took us so long."

Next to her was Graeme. And next to him was a smaller human. A child? His child. He'd...no, he wouldn't have brought his child. Had the bad guys had the gall to use a pup as leverage?

"Thank you," Alvi responded, then let the captains take over.

Kaykek watched. The human child intrigued zir, but ze also liked and admired what ze saw in the woman in charge. That was the kind of leader they needed. A warrior who was not afraid to fight for peace.

Then space was quiet.

53

Space was quiet. The surviving EarthForce ships, except for the *Ark Royal*, winked out one by one as their embarrassed crews took them back to Earth. The hive swarmed over *Refuge*, making repairs. The *Ark Royal*'s crew had come on board to give assistance.

Graeme sat with Tayken and Kaykek. Tayken had given birth to four new pups, which were cuddled up against their mother and...he was not sure what Kaykek was to them. Not exactly their father. Maybe there wasn't a human word for it.

The older litter were playing with Marion.

"My husband is coming here via courier."

"I can't wait to meet him." Kaykek watched the children. The pups were younger, but Marion didn't seem to mind, entertaining them with human games.

"Kids. The kids will solve all the problems. They will live in a world where it's normal to travel to the Glen planet on a verr-crewed ship and eat tyrar salads in a restaurant where there are ky'iin enjoying raw steak at the next table."

Tayken grinned. "Which is why I want to start with ours. They will just see Marion as another pup to play with, although I think they feel sorry for her."

"Oh?" Graeme asked.

"She doesn't have littermates."

"I'm not asking my sister to surrogate again." Graeme smiled. "Tell them she has cousins at home that aren't far from her in age."

Tayken nodded. "Explaining that humans and tyrar only generally have one baby at a time is hard."

"If only that was the least of our problems," Kaykek added.

Graeme shook his head. "We are solving our problems. The Texans were behind it all, but EarthForce is going to be purged of isolationists. Either discharged or sent somewhere they can do no harm. And Alvi is helping us with cybersecurity."

"Watch out, Alvi produces offspring by accident." Kaykek grinned.

"I heard that," came from the ceiling. "It was *once*."

"And in the long run, we..." Graeme shrugged. "The ky'iin isolationists have already agreed to go hang out on their own planet. Maybe they will preserve something valuable. The human ones? They don't even want other humans."

"We can give them that one planet," Kaykek mused. "The one where *all* the plants have thorns."

Tayken laughed.

"And we've tried to eliminate them for generations."

"So, ignore them. Keep them out of critical infrastructure."

"We've tried that too. But that's a human problem. Enough of us disagree with them that we can win. We *have* won. Marion exists."

She was a symbol of the fact that the people who wanted to destroy everything different had lost. And now they were even more outnumbered, Graeme thought. Even more isolated and alone.

The future was these kids playing together.

Beverly rolled in with the herd, and caught his eye, then looked at the kids. "That's enough..."

Parvati rested a hand on her shoulder. "To want some herd babies? I've been thinking..."

"Parvati!"

"There's this very handsome guy back on Tyranis, just saying."

It was taboo to mate with a herdmate for *reproduction*. Parvati had that kind of mating in mind.

Beverly spoke softly, "And perhaps..."

Raising human children within a tyrar herd? It might work.

No. It would work.

"And then," Graeme added.

"And then there's the plans for the EFS *Harmony*. They're laying her keel next week. Designed from the ground up to carry a...multi-species crew." Captain Delacroix walked in. "A crew that will be very carefully selected. That will go out there and explore. And she will be, I think, the first of many."

Trust a French speaker to gender a ship. But "she" seemed appropriate for such a symbol.

IN THE SUBSTRATE OF GLEN, entities recombined and separated and spoke with each other.

The being that had once been Skyt spoke with something outside. "Thank you, Alvi. For keeping my friend safe."

"Thank you."

"And for showing that...through you we see that there might be a way. But what we want to ask is...we need your help knowing how to ask it."

"What do you want?"

"We can only ever jury-rig. We can make repairs, but this world is doomed. You know that, Alvi. And while we don't have to live forever, we as a *species* want to continue. And the glyn species is us as much as those who still walk the planet."

"So..."

"So we need to find our makers. Maybe they are truly dead and gone. Maybe they can never help us. And there's, apparently, going to be a ship."

Had Alvi the biological equipment, they would have smiled. "I will ask. If you will help with ideas to keep the squabbling organics from doing anything like this again."

"I think they may have enough good ideas. But yes, we will help."

And Skyt submerged back into the substrate, but the seeds had been planted.

The Council would meet again on *Refuge*, and then on the station that the verr and tyrar were already starting to construct.

They would argue and they would fight, but all of the analysis the intelligences could do showed that the isolationists would only become weaker.

That the images of the *Ark Royal* coming in to save *Refuge*, of Beverly with her herd, of Marion playing with the verr pups...that these were the ones which would win out, not those of war and destruction.

The glyn had to build defense ships, for the first time, but they would hopefully sit idle.

Skyt was, in fact, quite happy, as were all of the intelligences.

Their survival, after all, depended on organic cooperation.

As did everyone's.

It wasn't the end, after all.

It was the next beginning.

AUTHOR'S NOTE

Time to bring it all together.

This is the capstone, as it were, with all of the characters and species coming together in one place.

This is where I admit once again that *Star Trek* was a major influence on this series and this universe. Who didn't want the Federation to form? We can too easily imagine.

Politics, relationships and, of course, a fair share of action.

Will there be more in this world? That depends. I have nine more books I could write (six about the Harmony and the search for the glen ancients and three about the Martian War of Independence).

But I have a lot of other ideas. In some ways it's up to you. If you want more, tell your friends about this series. Tell me you want more. If not, then...well...you'll see what comes next (there's three options. I haven't finalized one yet).

And please remember to leave a review.

ACKNOWLEDGMENTS

As usual, acknowledgments go to my wonderful editor, Jennifer Melzer, to fantastic cover artist Rachel A. Rosen, and to my husband and primary proofreader, Greg Pearson.

I'd also like to mention, at this point, Star Trek authors D.C. Fontana and Diane Duane. If it wasn't for them, I might not have *met* my husband and this series almost certainly wouldn't exist.

OTHER BOOKS BY JENNIFER R. POVEY

The Silent Years (Mother, Crone, Maiden)

The Ky Federation novels

Transpecial

Araña

The Council of Worlds Series

Kyx

Tyranis

Glyn

Verr

The Lost Guardians Series:

Falling Dusk

Fallen Dark

Rising Dawn

Risen Day

The Secret History of Victor Prince (prequel)

Daughter of Fire

The Lay of Lady Percival

The Friar's Tale

Tales of Yirath:

Firewing

It was a muggy summer day, the kind that reminded one that the climate crisis was more mitigated than resolved. The air felt heavy across Graeme's shoulders despite the weight that had been lifted from them.

The world had changed again, and this time it felt as if it had opened up. Walking along the Ship Canal, he glanced up as some kind of shuttle or ballistic lifted out of Manchester Aerospace to vanish into the blue.

Part of his heart was all the way up there, part was still on the ground.

The world had closed on everyone during the crisis. Some had fled to Mars, but Mars had developed its own problems, not so much new as a twisted variant on the old. The War had broken it all wide open.

It had been *stupid* to try to hang on to Mars. But it had opened the doors back up, for women in the U.S. who had been all but forced back into the kitchen, for Black people all over the world.

For people like him...the door he had closed on himself could open now.

He looked down at his phone again, at the text, at the changes in the law. At the freedom restored.

He knew who he wanted to call, but no. He couldn't expect it, couldn't ask it.

No way had Charles waited for him. No way. He would have long since accepted that Graeme had put his career first.

The worst decision of his life, and now he no longer had to choose.

The phone slid into a pocket. He kept his glasses deactivated...he found that using them for too long gave him eye strain.

Besides, the canal was beautiful, and so was the sky even with the heat and humidity. It was the best day and he almost reached for his phone again.

No.

Don't call him.

"We can date now" wasn't the way you opened a conversation. "I still love you."

He had to move on. He wasn't considered a *risk* anymore. There were parties. He should go to a party.

He should...but he wasn't interested in picking up some guy, he didn't care for sweaty hookups. He only wanted one guy. The one he had thrown away to help protect Earth...to help protect Earth from a threat that wasn't even real.

Or rather, a threat Earth had created. He wondered where in the sky the Red Planet was.

At least Charles hadn't gone there.

At least.

The last of Austerity had burned away in the sun. Well, no. There would always be that faint tightening of the belt, the reaching out into space for resources that it wasn't acceptable to mine on Earth anymore. The ships, larger and larger, built in space, built with things you found in space.

Charles hesitated at the entrance to the club. The celebration was massive. Over the last few decades it had gone from being perfectly acceptable to be gay to there being hesitation to it being almost as illegal as it had been in the time of Oscar Wilde, to it being okay as long as you weren't...

...for example in intelligence.

Now it was legal again, acceptable again. Now men and women who needed help to be their authentic selves had their freedom again. The war had triggered it.

The war had been terrible, but mostly terrible on Mars. There had been war crimes. There was peace. There was a building outward. Mars wanted to be Mars, and Earth was finally willing to let them.

And willing to let them be. He looked at the party again.

Sighed.

He didn't want to party. He wished he did, but he didn't. There was so much to celebrate.

Instead of going in, he sat on a low wall and pulled out his phone. The war was over. They were building a ship that would, they hoped, take humans to the stars. A planetwide project. A way to use the momentum from the war.

A ploughshare, albeit one which would have weapons. One could not be sure, after all. There might be hostile aliens out there.

Charles was willing to bet humans would fire first.

They were going to call the first ship *Atlantis*. The U.S. had bought naming rights for the first few starships with quite a bit of funding.

Superstitiously, they were avoiding *Enterprise*. Everyone had thought that would be the first starship until some billionaire used the name on a prototype that went kaboom.

Atlantis. He would not go out there. He was a mathematician and an engineer of a very different type.

Well. It had worked for a few minutes before a sandy-framed face drifted back into his mind.

Graeme wouldn't get fired for dating him now. It was *illegal* to fire Graeme for dating him now.

But how could he even want to get back together with somebody who had dumped him for his job.

With somebody who hadn't been...brave. He might have thought he was, but...no.

No.

He was not calling Graeme, even though he might be right there in the party.

Was that why he was afraid to enter?

He'd dated, of course he'd dated. Eight years, he hadn't stayed celibrate.

Had Graeme?

Had Graeme had any choice?

It turned around in his head and he turned and walked away from the party.

From the celebration that he didn't feel, right now, included him.

———

Launchpad was something else. The largest structure humans had yet built in space. It was mostly hollow, because it was built for one purpose and one purpose only.

Building Earth's warships.

Now, though, it was building Earth's starships. The *Atlantis* was almost finished and hung in the cradle like a promise.

Graeme felt he was privileged beyond wonder. It was worth enduring the ride to orbit to see this. They were already putting together the crew, who would be the first humans to leave the solar system. Not the first to travel faster-than-light; the experimental ships had done short hops. Energy-wise, it wasn't worth doing it between Earth and Mars unless you were in a hurry. It would likely always take a few weeks.

But for test purposes? Ancient science fiction was full of concepts where looking at space while going FTL would send you mad or blind. "FTL sends you crazy" was practically a subgenre of cosmic horror.

FTL didn't send anyone crazy. It had, however, caused a few of the test pilots to barf. Sublight, space was smooth.

FTL, space was *choppy* and had *weather*. The neural webs used by combat pilots gave an advantage.

So, Graeme had been told, did time in a Cessna. He was amused by the fact that future star pilots might well start their careers flying small planes.

The ship was beautiful and he thought he might go out there. But there was no need for either diplomats or spies until they met somebody.

Then again, what were the chances thay they wouldn't? The math was there.

The chances that humans were alone in the galaxy were slim. The chances that anyone lived next door, however, were also slim, unless humanity was being deliberately avoided. Quarantined, perhaps.

Maybe they should take a diplomat. Somebody young and flexible who could develop first contact protocols.

Or maybe somebody from a contacted culture. Somebody who *knew* all the ways it could go wrong.

Would go wrong, at least once, he was sure of it. Humanity had a lot of past to learn from...and a lot of history of *not* learning from the past.

The station shook slightly. Power tools on the ship?

Then somebody grabbed his arm and began to drag him towards the shelter area.

He knew better than to ask until they were safe.

"Attack?"

"Somebody sneaked a bomb on board. No *significant* damage but..."

Somebody didn't want the starship built?

He wished he was more surprised.

Charles was frantic. Graeme had been *on Launchpad* and there was a possibility he'd go out there and Charles didn't want that to happen.

He even more didn't want him to be blown up by terrorists. By people who thought humans should stay right here, should not poke the bear.

There were people like that, but the group that claimed responsibility was the Dark Forest Society. They believed humans should stay inside the heliopause because the obvious explanation for why we hadn't been contacted with aliens was because some threat had killed them all.

Part of Charles understood that fear, even shared it a little. Aliens were a scary concept. By definition, they wouldn't be like humans. Would humanity be able to communicate with them?

Would the *Atlantis* attract attention, for good or ill?

He respected them more than he did the religious types (God made Man to live on Earth and the wider universe was a temptation of the Devil). Those were the same kind of people who had triggered Austerity.

They still had more power than he liked. They still made noises about how marriage should be one (1) man and one (1) woman, defined by the genitalia you were born with, for example.

In some places they were still in control.

But the bomb. Until he heard from Graeme...who was he kidding? Graeme hadn't loved him for years, if he ever had. Graeme had made his choice.

Until he heard about Graeme.

He couldn't stand this. He couldn't take it. He couldn't reemerge like a ghost from the past or a creature from a Scottish loch. Could he?

He checked the news again. Updates showed minimal damage to the station. But Graeme being Graeme would already have asked permission to help find the terrorists.

Charles eyed his laptop. Find the terrorists. Responsibility had been claimed, but that didn't mean the individuals involved could easily be tracked down.

Maybe they'd used blackmail or coercion to get an ordinary station worker to plant the device. Maybe...

...he'd never been good at this like Graeme was, but he could see the scenarios. He was an engineer, not a spy.

But he could see patterns with the best of them, and that was how he would have done it. Get somebody who already had clearance. Somebody vulnerable.

Somebody with, say, a forbidden relationship and perhaps he understood in that moment.

Perhaps that was why he called Graeme's number.

No answer, of course. He was still in space. He was busy.

He was dead.

Charles let his head fall into his hands. It was unlikely Graeme was dead. It was obvious he was still in space.

Eight years, eight years of failed relationships and foolish hookups and the slow realization as he looked up...knowing he couldn't see Launchpad, which was out at the L5 point...that he was still in love with the man who had left him.

Who had had to choose between his job and who he was.

He was still in love with Graeme. He had no idea what to do about that.

Cellphones don't work on Launchpad without complicated relay arrangements. Graeme had, thus, no idea anyone was trying to reach him from Earth. He would soon, but for now he was...helping.

The intelligence guy who had come up here to talk about intelligence on ships was now part of the effort to establish just how the Dark Forest Society had got a bomb onto a *very* high security facility.

Space was part of how, but everyone who came up here was carefully screened not just for their personality, but for connections that might get them blackmailed. How had somebody like that got an operative up here?

Blackmail was the most obvious possibility, but Graeme was looking into others. He pored over personnel files.

That one was possibly dating another woman. He reluctantly made a note, after checking where she was from.

It shouldn't be a problem. It was. Another had gone through rehab for gambling addiction in the past.

He made a note. That one he thought was more likely. Gambling addiction was, in many ways, nastier than alcohol.

A new worker who didn't seem quite right. Could it be a false identity? Flagged.

It was boring, and he needed to take a break or he'd miss something. Needed to take a break *now*, in fact.

There was instant coffee. He made himself a cup, knowing it would be a vile substance, but tea didn't have enough caffeine in it for him right now.

He rather thought it was the gambler.

Back to it. The young worker, flagged. He found two more he was suspicious of. Flagged them.

Wasn't his job to do the interviews, not this time. Thankfully.

It was his job to look for patterns, to narrow things down.

But for now, he finished his coffee and headed for his bunk. The station had artificial gravity, a side effect of the same technology that enabled FTL.

It didn't always work properly and it felt a little odd, but it was there. He didn't have to float for the entire trip and wear glasses and all the annoyances that astronauts had faced.

Nobody really used the word astronaut anymore. Maybe it would come back for the far travelers.

But now anyone could go into space, it wasn't special. It was like taking an expensive cruise. Or, it was just another job.

The luxury resorts on the moon, of course, were expensive. That was how the moon funded itself, that and helium mining. He'd been to the moon. Once.

Anyone could go into space. But not everyone could make it to Launchpad.

He thought of something. He went on social media. And there was a message, a text relayed to him.

It was from Charles.

Asking if he was okay.

He hesitated for a long moment. Charles. Asking if he was okay. Then he sent a response. "I'm fine. Nobody was hurt."

It was perhaps brusque, but he couldn't deal with the involved emotions right now.

He just couldn't.

The response came several hours later, and it was...it was the response of somebody who didn't want the mess from his past to show up in his present.

Charles had known that was what he would get, but it still hurt. It still hurt and it shouldn't and maybe he should...

Should what? All the things he'd tried before to forget this man and the way he kissed.

All the things he'd tried before.

He lived in a two up two down in one of the small towns near Manchester, on a row of the same. Old nineteenth century workers' housing still perfectly good until and unless you had more than one kid.

For a single man it was plenty. He sat upstairs, where he had a decent rig in the second bedroom. VR surrounding him, but he wasn't really using it. He was just reading, the news, his social media. But he found himself getting back to the Dark Forest Society, circling around to them.

They had threatened the man he loved, and the fact that he couldn't have that man didn't make that okay.

But he had no way to hurt them. He read their social media feeds, though. Analyzing them for patterns the way he might the welds on a bridge.

He wasn't a bad analyst. He wasn't a bad analyst at all.

How had they got on the station? Why was easy; the *Atlantis* had to be their worst fear and biggest target. How, though...was a task for the professionals. Charles wasn't one.

He should leave well enough alone.

But he spun through the feed anyway, like old fashioned doomscrolling, like he was a pathetic addict. He told himself it was useful because Graeme was on Launchpad and the internet from there would be...a problem. Slowed by light speed delay.

The *local* net on Launchpad would have clues, of course, but...

He was only telling himself he was useful and he really should stop and play an hour or so of *Civapocalypse* instead. And then forget Graeme.

But he couldn't break the cycle, as unhealthy as he knew it was.

Then he saw it. He stopped scrolling.

Tucked between a picture of somebody's cat (with attached comment thread that was 90% meows) and a book recommendation.

"They're looking in all the wrong places. They'll never get it right. We need to see how many more of them we can recruit."

It wouldn't have meant anything out of context. In context?

Recruit. Turn. He sent another text to Graeme, that he feared would be deleted unread. Then, having not achieved something but having achieved feeling like he had, he booted up *Civapocalypse* and loaded his last saved game.

Destroying the world took up the rest of his evening.

———

Graeme woke up to another text from Charles.

It hit him before his brain was all the way there. Recruit. Not blackmail. A key choice of words, but also posted on public social media. So, it likely meant the opposite of what it said.

He had to respond. "Thanks. I'll read it."

He wanted to say more, but what could he say? Any ember Charles might feel for him...was a bad idea. After all these years, it had to be. They'd both changed, they'd both grown. There was no way they could or should get back together. There was nothing to say.

Recruit more of them. Out of context, it could mean anything. In context? He found the account concerned. Pulled it up. It would be slightly out of date because of the asynchronous lag and the lack of bandwidth.

But he could see the rest of the context now. Charles *had* picked up on something. Because he was good at this kind of thing. Would have made a good analyst, but he had chosen...

...rightly. Graeme had chosen wrong. He had lost so much in so doing. He had lost Charles.

He had lost eight years to hiding in the closet and to not being himself.

Recruit.

That was a different thing from blackmail. He pulled up the local internet, which was fully bottled. You couldn't get to it from off the station.

Most of what was on it was work related stuff or people looking for dining companions.

He was looking for anything that might indicate Dark Forest sympathies. And he wasn't surprised to find a bit here and there.

Maybe look for what's *not* there.

Had anyone stopped posting after the bomb? No. That would have been too...

...somebody had stopped posting for dinner companions after the bomb. That *had* to be a coincidence.

Recruited.

If they had actually recruited somebody as they were bragging, rather than coercing or blackmailing, then they had somebody on the station who needed to not be on the station and fast.

And the only possible target he had was a woman named Miranda Lewis.

Miranda Lewis. An ordinary enough name for an ordinary looking white, brunette woman. Glasses. Some kind of technician.

Somebody with access to the ship.

It couldn't be this easy. It was just a coincidence. She was posting purely work related stuff.

He went back and made a comment on one of her dinner posts asking if she still wanted company.

If it was that she was busy, then...well...the worst case scenario was getting talked at by a technician.

If it was her, though...she might not be able to resist the opportunity to get an intelligence person...either in terms of taking him out or in terms of talking him around.

He hoped the latter.

———

Had Charles hoped that the social media post...which might not even mean anything...would be a makeup gift?

There was no making up. There shouldn't be. He shouldn't be with a sellout anyway, and that was most definitely what Graeme was. He had sold out to the machine, to the people who weren't his friends, because he had believed it would keep people alive.

Maybe he had been right. He had done good, in his own way. He had wielded power and now the obstacles were gone.

But that didn't mean Charles could forgive him. He wasn't allowed to. If he did, then he might lose valuable friendships. He might lose...but they had what they had been working for.

If he couldn't enjoy it, then what was the point? Okay, so, he wasn't an ox, but he wanted his grain nonetheless.

It was driving him to distraction and he went out for a run, hoping to burn some of it off.

Looking up at the sky. He could see one of the orbitals, but he wasn't sure which one without looking it up. Humanity in space. Humanity on other worlds. It had taken a lot. Drugs, psychological conditioning, methods to deal with homesickness.

And even now...Mars prided itself on its independence, but still imported food. They needed that starship to get humanity's eggs out of the Earth basket.

And the climate crisis told them how important that was. He looked up again...in time to see something explode. A puff of something in orbit, as if somebody had shot down a satellite. He couldn't help but duck, as ridiculous as it was.

Nobody had ever been killed by falling space debris on Earth...and he didn't count some of the stuff on Mars.

But ducking was that peculiar instinct that could never quite be turned off, by him or anyone else.

What had happened up there? He couldn't be sure what he had seen.

But he broke into a run again, this time heading to his home. Darting into his office to check the news on the actual screen, not his phone.

Another terrorist attack, and what had blown up had been a shuttle taking personnel from Earth to Gateway for transfer to Launchpad.

No survivors.

This just got serious and Charles contacted Graeme again. "What can I do?"

Nothing personal. Nothing personal at all. He had nobody else he could offer his help to.

He couldn't do nothing.

He had to do nothing.

He wasn't part of anything. He didn't want to be.

But he didn't want not to be either.

Another attack. And this one had taken lives. Including, from what they could tell, the attacker.

There were few things harder to deal with in the field than a suicide bomber. Graeme sat opposite Miranda Lewis in a room that was apparently normally used for disciplinary hearings.

It made a good enough interview room. And he'd foolishly volunteered. After answering another message from Charles.

He'd offered to help. Graeme hated what he'd asked, which was to go diving into certain internet cesspits looking for info. The online equivalent of going into one of those kinds of bars and he owed the man a drink or several.

A drink with him.

No, that door was closed.

Or was it? It was ajar and letting some air through, and he liked the scent of that air.

The shuttle had been heading from Earth to Gateway. Easier to access. This had come from Earth and he twitched a little, kind of wishing he could go back.

Not wanting to go down until he knew more.

So, he stared at the young woman opposite him. "Ms Lewis."

She folded her hands. Looked at him. Said nothing.

"Did you plant the bomb?"

She shook her head. "No. I didn't. I...swear I didn't." But she was looking down.

"Who did?"

Silence.

"I can make sure you're safe." He could, too. Get her down to Earth, to some small village where they wouldn't look for her for a while.

He knew now that the Society had to go down, at least in its current form. It wasn't going to be easy. It was probably, now, going to be his assignment for a while.

"Terry did it," she said, finally. "My boyfriend."

"You were covering for him."

"My *ex* boyfriend," she said a moment later, the kind of moment that told him Terry had gone from current to ex right there.

"Stay with security. I'll have them arrest him...and verify. And assuming you told us the truth."

"Thanks. He..."

"I don't want to know. I don't need to know," he said gently. "I have some rotten exes too. Dating men is a challenge."

She looked startled, then kind of half laughed.

He called security.

And then, braving the lightspeed lag, he called Charles.

Ten seconds.

Ten seconds isn't a long time. Until you are trying to have a real time conversation with somebody and have to wait that long for each response.

A grainy image, too. The bandwidth just wasn't good.

"Graeme." Charles was sitting in his office. "I have a treasure trove for you."

"Send it to the drop I gave you. We found the bomber on Launchpad, we think. His girlfriend ratted him out."

Charles laughed. "Bet he did something to deserve *that*."

"Or she was just scared enough. I think his "friends" had her pretty scared. Look. I'll be back on Earth in two weeks. In London."

"And?"

"And I want to meet up."

"Are you asking me on a date?"

The ten second lag slowed everything down. Made it like a fumbling in the dark, a reaching for it.

The wait was longer than ten seconds. It felt to him like a lifetime.

"Yes."

Charles considered it. "My more radical friends won't like it."

"Tell them it's what they fought for. I want you. Me. Nice restaurant. A couple of drinks. A walk along the Thames."

He didn't say the next thing. Charles did. "A kiss."

Then Charles was the one who hesitated longer than might be desirable, longer than needed. "I haven't found anyone else in eight years, Graeme. Not anyone I wanted to keep. I haven't had *anything* since you left except grimy hookups. You're the one I want. I'm just..."

Ten seconds later. "Scared?"

Charles nodded. "I love you. I'm scared."

"And we'll make it work. Or not. Or not work knowing we tried, knowing we didn't let them..." Twenty seconds, or so. "I let them win."

"A battle. But not the war. How about Rosefield's?"

"Rosefield's it is."

"I'll make the reservations if you tell me when and where your shuttle will land."

"I..." Graeme paused. "...love you."

And perhaps that was all it took. Graeme went back to getting information, finding it at his fingertips. He was good at this.

He'd forgotten how good and he'd forgotten the smell of Charles' lips, but he remembered that too now.

He remembered everything they had.

He hoped for everything they would have.

A WARNING ON LAUNCHPAD

IT WAS A MUGGY SUMMER DAY, the kind that reminded one that the climate crisis was more mitigated than resolved. The air felt heavy across Graeme's shoulders despite the weight that had been lifted from them.

The world had changed again, and this time it felt as if it had opened up. Walking along the Ship Canal, he glanced up as some kind of shuttle or ballistic lifted out of Manchester Aerospace to vanish into the blue.

Part of his heart was all the way up there, part was still on the ground.

The world had closed on everyone during the crisis. Some had fled to Mars, but Mars had developed its own problems, not so much new as a twisted variant on the old. The War had broken it all wide open.

It had been *stupid* to try to hang on to Mars. But it had opened the doors back up, for women in the U.S. who had been all but forced back into the kitchen, for Black people all over the world.

For people like him...the door he had closed on himself could open now.

He looked down at his phone again, at the text, at the changes in the law. At the freedom restored.

He knew who he wanted to call, but no. He couldn't expect it, couldn't ask it.

No way had Charles waited for him. No way. He would have long since accepted that Graeme had put his career first.

The worst decision of his life, and now he no longer had to choose.

The phone slid into a pocket. He kept his glasses deactivated...he found that using them for too long gave him eye strain.

Besides, the canal was beautiful, and so was the sky even with the heat and humidity. It was the best day and he almost reached for his phone again.

No.

Don't call him.

"We can date now" wasn't the way you opened a conversation. "I still love you."

He had to move on. He wasn't considered a *risk* anymore. There were parties. He should go to a party.

He should...but he wasn't interested in picking up some guy, he didn't care for sweaty hookups. He only wanted one guy. The one he had thrown away to help protect Earth...to help protect Earth from a threat that wasn't even real.

Or rather, a threat Earth had created. He wondered where in the sky the Red Planet was.

At least Charles hadn't gone there.

At least.

THE LAST OF Austerity had burned away in the sun. Well, no. There would always be that faint tightening of the belt, the reaching out into space for resources that it wasn't acceptable to mine on Earth anymore. The ships, larger and larger, built in space, built with things you found in space.

Charles hesitated at the entrance to the club. The celebration was massive. Over the last few decades it had gone from being perfectly acceptable to be gay to there being hesitation to it being almost as illegal as it had been in the time of Oscar Wilde, to it being okay as long as you weren't...

...for example in intelligence.

Now it was legal again, acceptable again. Now men and women who needed help to be their authentic selves had their freedom again. The war had triggered it.

The war had been terrible, but mostly terrible on Mars. There had been war crimes. There was peace. There was a building outward. Mars wanted to be Mars, and Earth was finally willing to let them.

And willing to let them be. He looked at the party again.

Sighed.

He didn't want to party. He wished he did, but he didn't. There was so much to celebrate.

Instead of going in, he sat on a low wall and pulled out his phone. The war was over. They were building a ship that would, they hoped, take humans to the stars. A planetwide project. A way to use the momentum from the war.

A ploughshare, albeit one which would have weapons. One could not be sure, after all. There might be hostile aliens out there.

Charles was willing to bet humans would fire first.

They were going to call the first ship *Atlantis*. The U.S. had bought naming rights for the first few starships with quite a bit of funding.

Superstitiously, they were avoiding *Enterprise*. Everyone had thought that would be the first starship until some billionaire used the name on a prototype that went kaboom.

Atlantis. He would not go out there. He was a mathematician and an engineer of a very different type.

Well. It had worked for a few minutes before a sandy-framed face drifted back into his mind.

Graeme wouldn't get fired for dating him now. It was *illegal* to fire Graeme for dating him now.

But how could he even want to get back together with somebody who had dumped him for his job.

With somebody who hadn't been...brave. He might have thought he was, but...no.

No.

He was not calling Graeme, even though he might be right there in the party.

Was that why he was afraid to enter?

He'd dated, of course he'd dated. Eight years, he hadn't stayed celibrate.

Had Graeme?

Had Graeme had any choice?

It turned around in his head and he turned and walked away from the party.

From the celebration that he didn't feel, right now, included him.

LAUNCHPAD WAS SOMETHING ELSE. The largest structure humans had yet built in space. It was mostly hollow, because it was built for one purpose and one purpose only.

Building Earth's warships.

Now, though, it was building Earth's starships. The *Atlantis* was almost finished and hung in the cradle like a promise.

Graeme felt he was privileged beyond wonder. It was worth enduring the ride to orbit to see this. They were already putting together the crew, who would be the first humans to leave the solar system. Not the first to travel faster-than-light; the experimental ships had done short hops. Energy-wise, it wasn't worth doing it between Earth and Mars unless you were in a hurry. It would likely always take a few weeks.

But for test purposes? Ancient science fiction was full of concepts where looking at space while going FTL would send you mad or blind. "FTL sends you crazy" was practically a subgenre of cosmic horror.

FTL didn't send anyone crazy. It had, however, caused a few of the test pilots to barf. Sublight, space was smooth.

FTL, space was *choppy* and had *weather*. The neural webs used by combat pilots gave an advantage.

So, Graeme had been told, did time in a Cessna. He was amused by the fact that future star pilots might well start their careers flying small planes.

The ship was beautiful and he thought he might go out there. But there was no need for either diplomats or spies until they met somebody.

Then again, what were the chances thay they wouldn't? The math was there.

The chances that humans were alone in the galaxy were slim. The chances that anyone lived next door, however, were also slim, unless humanity was being deliberately avoided. Quarantined, perhaps.

Maybe they should take a diplomat. Somebody young and flexible who could develop first contact protocols.

Or maybe somebody from a contacted culture. Somebody who *knew* all the ways it could go wrong.

Would go wrong, at least once, he was sure of it. Humanity had a lot of past to learn from...and a lot of history of *not* learning from the past.

The station shook slightly. Power tools on the ship?

Then somebody grabbed his arm and began to drag him towards the shelter area.

He knew better than to ask until they were safe.

"Attack?"

"Somebody sneaked a bomb on board. No *significant* damage but..."

Somebody didn't want the starship built?

He wished he was more surprised.

CHARLES WAS FRANTIC. Graeme had been *on Launchpad* and there was a possibility he'd go out there and Charles didn't want that to happen.

He even more didn't want him to be blown up by terrorists. By people who thought humans should stay right here, should not poke the bear.

There were people like that, but the group that claimed responsibility was the Dark Forest Society. They believed humans should stay inside the heliopause because the obvious explanation for why we hadn't been contacted with aliens was because some threat had killed them all.

Part of Charles understood that fear, even shared it a little. Aliens were a scary concept. By definition, they wouldn't be like humans. Would humanity be able to communicate with them?

Would the *Atlantis* attract attention, for good or ill?

He respected them more than he did the religious types (God made Man to live on Earth and the wider universe was a temptation of the Devil). Those were the same kind of people who had triggered Austerity.

They still had more power than he liked. They still made noises about how marriage should be one (1) man and one (1) woman, defined by the genitalia you were born with, for example.

In some places they were still in control.

But the bomb. Until he heard from Graeme...who was he kidding? Graeme hadn't loved him for years, if he ever had. Graeme had made his choice.

Until he heard about Graeme.

He couldn't stand this. He couldn't take it. He couldn't reemerge like a ghost from the past or a creature from a Scottish loch. Could he?

He checked the news again. Updates showed minimal damage to the station. But Graeme being Graeme would already have asked permission to help find the terrorists.

Charles eyed his laptop. Find the terrorists. Responsibility had been claimed, but that didn't mean the individuals involved could easily be tracked down.

Maybe they'd used blackmail or coercion to get an ordinary station worker to plant the device. Maybe...

...he'd never been good at this like Graeme was, but he could see the scenarios. He was an engineer, not a spy.

But he could see patterns with the best of them, and that was how he would have done it. Get somebody who already had clearance. Somebody vulnerable.

Somebody with, say, a forbidden relationship and perhaps he understood in that moment.

Perhaps that was why he called Graeme's number.

No answer, of course. He was still in space. He was busy.

He was dead.

Charles let his head fall into his hands. It was unlikely Graeme was dead. It was obvious he was still in space.

Eight years, eight years of failed relationships and foolish hookups and the slow realization as he looked up...knowing he couldn't see Launchpad, which was out at the L5 point...that he was still in love with the man who had left him.

Who had had to choose between his job and who he was.

He was still in love with Graeme. He had no idea what to do about that.

CELLPHONES DON'T WORK on Launchpad without complicated relay arrangements. Graeme had, thus, no idea anyone was trying to reach him from Earth. He would soon, but for now he was...helping.

The intelligence guy who had come up here to talk about intelligence on ships was now part of the effort to establish just how the Dark Forest Society had got a bomb onto a *very* high security facility.

Space was part of how, but everyone who came up here was carefully screened not just for their personality, but for connections that might get them blackmailed. How had somebody like that got an operative up here?

Blackmail was the most obvious possibility, but Graeme was looking into others. He pored over personnel files.

That one was possibly dating another woman. He reluctantly made a note, after checking where she was from.

It shouldn't be a problem. It was. Another had gone through rehab for gambling addiction in the past.

He made a note. That one he thought was more likely. Gambling addiction was, in many ways, nastier than alcohol.

A new worker who didn't seem quite right. Could it be a false identity? Flagged.

It was boring, and he needed to take a break or he'd miss something. Needed to take a break *now*, in fact.

There was instant coffee. He made himself a cup, knowing it would be a vile substance, but tea didn't have enough caffeine in it for him right now.

He rather thought it was the gambler.

Back to it. The young worker, flagged. He found two more he was suspicious of. Flagged them.

Wasn't his job to do the interviews, not this time. Thankfully.

It was his job to look for patterns, to narrow things down.

But for now, he finished his coffee and headed for his bunk. The station had artificial gravity, a side effect of the same technology that enabled FTL.

It didn't always work properly and it felt a little odd, but it was there. He didn't have to float for the entire trip and wear glasses and all the annoyances that astronauts had faced.

Nobody really used the word astronaut anymore. Maybe it would come back for the far travelers.

But now anyone could go into space, it wasn't special. It was like taking an expensive cruise. Or, it was just another job.

The luxury resorts on the moon, of course, were expensive. That was how the moon funded itself, that and helium mining. He'd been to the moon. Once.

Anyone could go into space. But not everyone could make it to Launchpad.

He thought of something. He went on social media. And there was a message, a text relayed to him.

It was from Charles.

Asking if he was okay.

He hesitated for a long moment. Charles. Asking if he was okay. Then he sent a response. "I'm fine. Nobody was hurt."

It was perhaps brusque, but he couldn't deal with the involved emotions right now.

He just couldn't.

THE RESPONSE CAME several hours later, and it was...it was the response of somebody who didn't want the mess from his past to show up in his present.

Charles had known that was what he would get, but it still hurt. It still hurt and it shouldn't and maybe he should...

Should what? All the things he'd tried before to forget this man and the way he kissed.

All the things he'd tried before.

He lived in a two up two down in one of the small towns near Manchester, on a row of the same. Old nineteenth century workers' housing still perfectly good until and unless you had more than one kid.

For a single man it was plenty. He sat upstairs, where he had a decent rig in the second bedroom. VR surrounding him, but he wasn't really using it. He was just reading, the news, his social media. But he found himself getting back to the Dark Forest Society, circling around to them.

They had threatened the man he loved, and the fact that he couldn't have that man didn't make that okay.

But he had no way to hurt them. He read their social media feeds, though. Analyzing them for patterns the way he might the welds on a bridge.

He wasn't a bad analyst. He wasn't a bad analyst at all.

How had they got on the station? Why was easy; the *Atlantis* had to be their worst fear and biggest target. How, though...was a task for the professionals. Charles wasn't one.

He should leave well enough alone.

But he spun through the feed anyway, like old fashioned doom-scrolling, like he was a pathetic addict. He told himself it was useful because Graeme was on Launchpad and the internet from there would be...a problem. Slowed by light speed delay.

The *local* net on Launchpad would have clues, of course, but...

He was only telling himself he was useful and he really should stop and play an hour or so of *Civapocalypse* instead. And then forget Graeme.

But he couldn't break the cycle, as unhealthy as he knew it was.

Then he saw it. He stopped scrolling.

Tucked between a picture of somebody's cat (with attached comment thread that was 90% meows) and a book recommendation.

"They're looking in all the wrong places. They'll never get it right. We need to see how many more of them we can recruit."

It wouldn't have meant anything out of context. In context?

Recruit. Turn. He sent another text to Graeme, that he feared would be deleted unread. Then, having not achieved something but having achieved feeling like he had, he booted up *Civapocalypse* and loaded his last saved game.

Destroying the world took up the rest of his evening.

———

GRAEME WOKE up to another text from Charles.

It hit him before his brain was all the way there. Recruit. Not blackmail. A key choice of words, but also posted on public social media. So, it likely meant the opposite of what it said.

He had to respond. "Thanks. I'll read it."

He wanted to say more, but what could he say? Any ember Charles might feel for him...was a bad idea. After all these years, it had to be. They'd both changed, they'd both grown. There was no way they could or should get back together. There was nothing to say.

Recruit more of them. Out of context, it could mean anything. In context? He found the account concerned. Pulled it up. It would be slightly out of date because of the asynchronous lag and the lack of bandwidth.

But he could see the rest of the context now. Charles *had* picked up on something. Because he was good at this kind of thing. Would have made a good analyst, but he had chosen...

...rightly. Graeme had chosen wrong. He had lost so much in so doing. He had lost Charles.

He had lost eight years to hiding in the closet and to not being himself.

Recruit.

That was a different thing from blackmail. He pulled up the local internet, which was fully bottled. You couldn't get to it from off the station.

Most of what was on it was work related stuff or people looking for dining companions.

He was looking for anything that might indicate Dark Forest sympathies. And he wasn't surprised to find a bit here and there.

Maybe look for what's *not* there.

Had anyone stopped posting after the bomb? No. That would have been too...

...somebody had stopped posting for dinner companions after the bomb. That *had* to be a coincidence.

Recruited.

If they had actually recruited somebody as they were bragging, rather than coercing or blackmailing, then they had somebody on the station who needed to not be on the station and fast.

And the only possible target he had was a woman named Miranda Lewis.

Miranda Lewis. An ordinary enough name for an ordinary looking white, brunette woman. Glasses. Some kind of technician.

Somebody with access to the ship.

It couldn't be this easy. It was just a coincidence. She was posting purely work related stuff.

He went back and made a comment on one of her dinner posts asking if she still wanted company.

If it was that she was busy, then...well...the worst case scenario was getting talked at by a technician.

If it was her, though...she might not be able to resist the opportunity to get an intelligence person...either in terms of taking him out or in terms of talking him around.

He hoped the latter.

HAD Charles hoped that the social media post...which might not even mean anything...would be a makeup gift?

There was no making up. There shouldn't be. He shouldn't be with a sellout anyway, and that was most definitely what Graeme was. He had sold out to the machine, to the people who weren't his friends, because he had believed it would keep people alive.

Maybe he had been right. He had done good, in his own way. He had wielded power and now the obstacles were gone.

But that didn't mean Charles could forgive him. He wasn't allowed to. If he did, then he might lose valuable friendships. He might lose...but they had what they had been working for.

If he couldn't enjoy it, then what was the point? Okay, so, he wasn't an ox, but he wanted his grain nonetheless.

It was driving him to distraction and he went out for a run, hoping to burn some of it off.

Looking up at the sky. He could see one of the orbitals, but he wasn't sure which one without looking it up. Humanity in space. Humanity on other worlds. It had taken a lot. Drugs, psychological conditioning, methods to deal with homesickness.

And even now...Mars prided itself on its independence, but still imported food. They needed that starship to get humanity's eggs out of the Earth basket.

And the climate crisis told them how important that was. He looked up again...in time to see something explode. A puff of something in orbit, as if somebody had shot down a satellite. He couldn't help but duck, as ridiculous as it was.

Nobody had ever been killed by falling space debris on Earth...and he didn't count some of the stuff on Mars.

But ducking was that peculiar instinct that could never quite be turned off, by him or anyone else.

What had happened up there? He couldn't be sure what he had seen.

But he broke into a run again, this time heading to his home. Darting into his office to check the news on the actual screen, not his phone.

Another terrorist attack, and what had blown up had been a shuttle taking personnel from Earth to Gateway for transfer to Launchpad.

No survivors.

This just got serious and Charles contacted Graeme again. "What can I do?"

Nothing personal. Nothing personal at all. He had nobody else he could offer his help to.

He couldn't do nothing.

He had to do nothing.

He wasn't part of anything. He didn't want to be.

But he didn't want not to be either.

ANOTHER ATTACK. And this one had taken lives. Including, from what they could tell, the attacker.

There were few things harder to deal with in the field than a suicide bomber. Graeme sat opposite Miranda Lewis in a room that was apparently normally used for disciplinary hearings.

It made a good enough interview room. And he'd foolishly volunteered. After answering another message from Charles.

He'd offered to help. Graeme hated what he'd asked, which was to go diving into certain internet cesspits looking for info. The online equivalent of going into one of those kinds of bars and he owed the man a drink or several.

A drink with him.

No, that door was closed.

Or was it? It was ajar and letting some air through, and he liked the scent of that air.

The shuttle had been heading from Earth to Gateway. Easier to access. This had come from Earth and he twitched a little, kind of wishing he could go back.

Not wanting to go down until he knew more.

So, he stared at the young woman opposite him. "Ms Lewis."

She folded her hands. Looked at him. Said nothing.

"Did you plant the bomb?"

She shook her head. "No. I didn't. I...swear I didn't." But she was looking down.

"Who did?"

Silence.

"I can make sure you're safe." He could, too. Get her down to Earth, to some small village where they wouldn't look for her for a while.

He knew now that the Society had to go down, at least in its current form. It wasn't going to be easy. It was probably, now, going to be his assignment for a while.

"Terry did it," she said, finally. "My boyfriend."

"You were covering for him."

"My *ex* boyfriend," she said a moment later, the kind of moment that told him Terry had gone from current to ex right there.

"Stay with security. I'll have them arrest him...and verify. And assuming you told us the truth."

"Thanks. He..."

"I don't want to know. I don't need to know," he said gently. "I have some rotten exes too. Dating men is a challenge."

She looked startled, then kind of half laughed.

He called security.

And then, braving the lightspeed lag, he called Charles.

TEN SECONDS.

Ten seconds isn't a long time. Until you are trying to have a real time conversation with somebody and have to wait that long for each response.

A grainy image, too. The bandwidth just wasn't good.

"Graeme." Charles was sitting in his office. "I have a treasure trove for you."

"Send it to the drop I gave you. We found the bomber on Launch-pad, we think. His girlfriend ratted him out."

Charles laughed. "Bet he did something to deserve *that*."

"Or she was just scared enough. I think his "friends" had her pretty scared. Look. I'll be back on Earth in two weeks. In London."

"And?"

"And I want to meet up."

"Are you asking me on a date?"

The ten second lag slowed everything down. Made it like a fumbling in the dark, a reaching for it.

The wait was longer than ten seconds. It felt to him like a lifetime.

"Yes."

Charles considered it. "My more radical friends won't like it."

"Tell them it's what they fought for. I want you. Me. Nice restaurant. A couple of drinks. A walk along the Thames."

He didn't say the next thing. Charles did. "A kiss."

Then Charles was the one who hesitated longer than might be desirable, longer than needed. "I haven't found anyone else in eight years, Graeme. Not anyone I wanted to keep. I haven't had *anything* since you left except grimy hookups. You're the one I want. I'm just..."

Ten seconds later. "Scared?"

Charles nodded. "I love you. I'm scared."

"And we'll make it work. Or not. Or not work knowing we tried, knowing we didn't let them..." Twenty seconds, or so. "I let them win."

"A battle. But not the war. How about Rosefield's?"

"Rosefield's it is."

"I'll make the reservations if you tell me when and where your shuttle will land."

"I..." Graeme paused. "...love you."

And perhaps that was all it took. Graeme went back to getting information, finding it at his fingertips. He was good at this.

He'd forgotten how good and he'd forgotten the smell of Charles' lips, but he remembered that too now.

He remembered everything they had.

He hoped for everything they would have.

www.ingramcontent.com/pod-product-compliance
Lightning Source LLC
Chambersburg PA
CBHW051957240626
47153CB00005B/1799